Executive Retention

Maria E. Schneider

Bear Mountain Books

A Bear Mountain Books Production
www.BearMountainBooks.com

Maria E. Schneider

Printing History:
POD printing June 2011
Second printing September 2011
Third printing July 2012
Fourth printing May 2013
Fifth printing December 2022
E-format June 2010

ISBN 13: 978-0615483771
ISBN-10: 0615483771

Acknowledgments

A big thank you: To my first readers who were brave enough to tell me that I wasn't yet good enough--yes Mom, I mean you. April, none of my covers would succeed without your advice.

To Paula Lomas, Holly and Cousin John, Renee and Cathey for encouraging me. To Marty for advice on the proper role and manners of geeks; to the real Turbo for being a great boss and friend. To Joan and LeAnn for being my safety net. To John Levitt for being a fabulously good author, but more importantly, a generous person. Jim Chambers, you too fit in that category.

To Miss Snark - May your pail be filled with gin, and may your clients set fire to your enthusiasm--never your hair.

To all the readers who took a chance on my work, especially those of you on the Amazon Cozy Forum, Kindleboards and Mobileread. A special thanks to Leo for his help after the final draft was written. Y'all know how to keep a writer going. Old Granny--you left my first review on Amazon and it still makes my day when I think of it.

To my husband: for everything. Without you and family, why would I bother?

Executive Retention

Chapter 1

As a matter of principle, I don't like working late. The truth is, I don't really like working all that much period. I could sit on a beach somewhere for days on end if I didn't have to worry about how to pay for my next meal.

Burn-out is expected and is almost a badge of honor in the computer industry. Then again, perhaps other industries have the same endless meetings where you sit and push around spaghetti. The engineer knows how to make the noodle, but doesn't have any idea why there is a meeting or why he has no say in what kind of noodle they are discussing. Eventually, the engineer realizes that even with his intimate knowledge of noodle creation, no one is listening to him, and he heads for the hills.

I can unequivocally state that despite my recent promotion into Strandfrost management and the Mercedes Huntington left behind as a gift for my investigative help, I am still tempted to drive off into the sunset. If success is so perfect, why am I stuck in the office at eight o'clock long after others have gone home? Why am I not on a beach in a cute little bikini with a cold iced tea and multiple dating prospects to reflect upon?

Steve Huntington, quiet infiltrator for companies with internal problems, finished mopping up the mess at Strandfrost, but he neglected to tidy up *my* life, a mess he helped create. Away he went into the sunset leaving me, Sedona O'Hala, a manager of computer nothingness. Oh sure, I was doing my best, but now that the criminals had been thrown out, I was left trying to help new management understand how business at Strandfrost was done. Out of guilt, I kept trying to piece things together and was therefore stuck at Strandfrost way past closing time.

Whenever I was in this mood, I should take a vacation until things calmed down. I should not stop on my way out in a dark parking lot and talk to strange men in their cars, even if they are driving a brand new Lexus. If the man was Huntington, I should run screaming.

"Sedona, do you want your old job back?"

My heart skipped a beat, and it wasn't his deep baritone that caused it. For a moment I pictured my job in the lab, setting up computers. I could stop attending reams of meetings where everyone used impressive words like "paradigm shift and synergy." I could go back to arguing with my old boss, Turbo, over the best way to prove or disprove a concept and deal only with obedient little machines.

What were the chances? "I want to move to Hawaii. Denton, Colorado will soon be getting very cold, and snow bunny I am not."

"How about the coast of California?"

"Unless the job entails sitting on a beach counting seals, I am not interested," I replied frostily, delivering on my own prediction that Colorado was about to get very chilly.

He was not deterred by the cold front. "Most of the work would be in Denton, but the main office is in San Jose. There's a state park with elephant seals a few miles from there. I am sure we could work in some time for you to go count them."

"Elephant seals?" I had been picturing cute harbor seals, the ones with black button noses and adorable faces. "Don't those have rather large, distorted noses?"

I think he was laughing, but I couldn't recall Huntington actually doing such a normal thing, so I wasn't sure.

"I'll take you there, I promise. I just want you to consider this job at Acetel Services. It should be a breeze for you. The company opened an office in Denton to support computer customers that bought equipment from various providers."

Customers always mixed equipment from different manufacturers. When something inevitably went wrong, if the customer didn't have a tidy service contract, the original manufacturers merely pointed to the competitor product as the problem and refused to look at the mess.

"I'm not interested," I said. Working for a customer that hadn't been able to get support from his original supplier would be nothing short of a nightmare.

Huntington sighed. "How about I take you out to Anthony's Grill, and we can talk about it? You can't stay at Strandfrost forever, you know."

I couldn't? "Why not?"

He purposely misinterpreted my question and assumed I was agreeing to his invitation. Without delay, he hopped out of the pearly white car and went around to the other side to open the door for me.

I wasn't sure what kind of car Huntington really owned and which ones he kept for his various assignments, but this one was certainly nice. The beautiful cream interior beckoned. Huntington didn't look bad either in his black leather jacket and perfectly-pressed khakis. By any stretch, Huntington wore his clothes well on his six-foot frame. His dark hair made his eyes look bluer and the way he used them was...suggestive.

White teeth flashed when he smiled, but only momentarily. "I decided a bit more than Chinese takeout was needed to persuade you to give up your latest position. Anthony's should be a good start."

"The Italian place by Whispering Pines?" Next to Chinese, Italian was my favorite cuisine. Actually, a well-made meal of any kind had a place in my heart, including chocolate chip cookies, chocolate cake and anything else well-prepared. I had never been to Anthony's. It was very upscale.

I looked down at my attire. At least I hadn't yanked my mousy brown hair into a ponytail like I usually did on Fridays. "I probably won't take the job, but it never hurts to eat."

Huntington knew me pretty well. The best way to reach me was through food. Flowers would have been nice too, but we weren't in that kind of relationship. Since he was pretty casual, I wasn't completely out of place in my light jacket, jeans and sweater. Although my last job for Huntington had provided clothes so that I could look the part of an up and coming executive, it had not occurred to me to buy a leather jacket when he was footing the bill. Darn. I was very certain that a sleek black jacket would go nicely with my gray eyes.

Huntington held the door and waved me forward. "Come on. It will be fun."

"I'm still not likely to take the job." I grabbed my wallet from my backpack and tossed the pack into the backseat. I hadn't planned on returning home late and should have brought a heavier coat, but unless Huntington was going to pay me on the side again, the latest job description didn't sound like it would provide a closet full of luxuries.

I expected a hard push for the job, but he was a good deal smoother than that. "How have you been?" He managed to sound genuinely interested--as if he had thought of little else for the past month.

"Oh, just fine. You know how it is, managing a group of people, all the various social engagements and the demands." In my case social engagements equaled "none," which was the primary reason I had never been to Anthony's Grill. The "demands" were work related and felt a lot like being a highly paid short-order cook. When I was lucky enough to grab an order slip, the waitress would immediately change it, leaving me trying to break up a cooked hamburger patty and reassemble it into meatloaf.

"Things are going good for you then." He hid most of his disappointment.

"Couldn't be better. Well, unless I retire early." I hedged because I didn't want to get too caught up in my lies.

"How's Turbo?"

"Fine." Missing the sort of work that he had done to help Huntington, but I wasn't going to encourage Huntington. By this time we were only a couple of blocks from the restaurant. Denton wasn't that big, but it was a Colorado resort town. Anthony's was in the same neighborhood as the Whispering Pines Resort. The restaurant was a quiet little building surrounded by a garden with little outdoor tables nestled under the trees. In the summer it would be romantic enough to sway any woman.

In the winter it was just plain cold, but the setting still had an air of promise as we walked through a wrought-iron arch and along the well-lit sidewalk. I shivered a bit and Huntington did that guy thing, putting his warm hand on the small of my back to guide me.

Where *did* those goose bumps come from anyway?

He leaned in close and whispered in my ear, "The food is great here. You'll love it."

Shivers ran all the way to my toes. I swallowed and tried to ignore my knees. They were probably weak from the wintry air.

Before Huntington was near enough to even think of grasping the door handle, the heavy wooden entrance swung open, and we were ushered inside.

The place wasn't so expensive that I couldn't come here occasionally; it was the lack of dates that was the problem. Anthony's was not the kind of place you wasted on a lonely meal.

Huntington must have called ahead because the waiter immediately led us across the deep burgundy carpet to an intimate booth with a view. The window looked out onto the faded fall garden; an empty water fountain sat outside, decorated with fallen red and gold leaves. When it snowed, the garden would fill with a magical white carpet and the fountain would drip diamond icicles.

"What?" I asked, having missed the waiter's question, busy with my daydreaming. "Oh, just water for me. No, make it hot tea."

Fleetfoot nodded and soundlessly melted away. He had left the menu by my lifeless hands.

Huntington was bemused by my attitude. "You seem a bit distracted."

"Yeah," I sighed. It had been a long time since I had been treated to dinner and lavished with attention. I narrowed my eyes at the direction of my thoughts. It was necessary to be very careful here. Huntington was way out of my league. If the man thought seduction would get him what he wanted, he wouldn't hesitate, and I really didn't need that type of complication in my life. I didn't enjoy being roadkill, and if my friend Huntington was working a case, I had best be on my toes.

"How can I talk you into taking another job?" he asked.

"Why are you even asking me? The last one didn't go all that smoothly. As I recall, you ended up in a hole in the ground."

He looked solemn and waited with his reply while the waiter presented a boxful of teas. I went with a nice, soothing herbal. We weren't ready to order, so again, Fleetfoot floated away.

"You did come in handy during the rescue."

That might have been stretching things a bit. I was almost positive that Huntington's brother, Mark, could have handled the entire rescue without me. Almost.

"And you did learn some things for me that I couldn't have figured out on my own. That's essentially what I'm after at Acetel Services. There are rampant rumors about mismanagement, but the employees aren't going to tell me what is really going on."

"Are you on the board again?" Huntington had positioned himself on Strandfrost's board during his last investigation. It gave him the power to move players around and become familiar with the politics, but it left him in the cold when it came to the grapevine.

He nodded. "They're usually the entity that hires me."

"Usually?" I wondered who else would bother. And who else could afford to?

He grinned. "Usually."

"Why me? Why not hire your brother Mark to go on the inside?"

"Mark has other skills."

He didn't say whether or not he would be using them in this case. Mark looked a lot like Huntington, enough that they could be twins, especially if one of them wore colored contacts. Mark's eyes were a deep, solid brown, and he spent more time in the sun. Whatever his skills, they resulted in a slightly more muscular build, not that Huntington was hurting in that area. Mark was also a tad shorter and didn't have the kind of suave demeanor that would win him board seats.

"Are you still on the board at Strandfrost?" I asked.

The waiter hovered again. I could have ordered the most expensive thing on the menu, but I wasn't that kind of date. Besides, I loved chicken Marsala, and it was reasonably priced.

"And would you like soup or salad?" the waiter asked.

"Caesar salad please." I handed him the tasseled menu.

Huntington ordered the sirloin Marsala and a salad. When Fleetfoot disappeared, he said, "No, I'm not on the board anymore, why?"

"Wow, that must be nice for them. You get paid to help for as long as they need you, and then they make you disappear. But I guess now you have another board seat."

"I haven't been officially elected to this one," he cautioned. "Strandfrost is privately held so getting on their board didn't require a proxy or stockholder vote. Acetel went public during the dot-com days when stocks flew into the market a few years ago. The board would have to get me on a ballot in order to get me a seat."

The salads arrived, and I dug in. "Why can't you hire someone who is already at Acetel like when you hired me at Strandfrost? Or shoot, just pay an insider to spill the beans on what they think they know."

Huntington glanced up to make sure I was serious. "It's a thought. But not everyone can…blend as well as you do. You actually know the computer job and can do the work. You have a unique way of interacting with management." He frowned. "I don't know what it is, but they don't seem to notice you. Neither do the criminals." It was a thorny sticking point in our relationship. On the last case he had hired me to be noticed. Huntington had pulled out all the stops to advertise my position to the bad guys, to management, to anyone. Despite his efforts, I had been completely invisible.

"You're thinking I can creep into this company in the dead of night and not get noticed, and maybe I can do some noticing on the side?"

"Something like that. You'll have to blend better than you did the last time."

"I thought you just said I did a great job of blending?"

"You were ignored. But I shouldn't have said you blended. You actually stuck out like a sore thumb and weren't that good at getting people to talk to you. You'll have to spend lunches at this place, date some of the guys, play dominoes, whatever it is they do until they talk to you. It won't be as easy as the last time, hanging out with other managers."

"Hanging out…" I trailed off in disbelief. Apparently Huntington hadn't noticed that the managers, a good ol' boys club, hadn't been the least interested in hanging out with me. And if he thought standing around talking with a bunch of old farts about golf and getting groped was *easy*…what the hell was he asking for this time?

He ignored my sputtering, his attention focused behind my head. He stopped chewing suddenly and put down his fork. "Uh, excuse me."

"What?" I was just getting ready with my scathing reply.

Huntington got up and walked away.

I glanced behind me. To my dismay, two large men followed the direction Huntington had taken. Wearing jackets bulky enough to hide an entire armament, they didn't look much like potential customers. The shorter of the two sported jeans with holes in the knees and the other, a large black guy, wore sweatpants.

The bathrooms were near the front entrance, and that was not where Huntington had gone. Kitchen?

What was going on? I took another bite of my salad. Should I go after him? Riiight. I was prepared to fight off two men three times my size that were probably armed with Uzis. No problem.

The bushes outside the window moved. I looked out, but even with the bright garden lighting I couldn't tell if it was the wind or if Huntington was getting strung up in a tree. I couldn't just sit here and let him get gutted, could I?

Actually…well, no, I couldn't. I sighed, wiped my mouth and got moving. I headed for the door where Huntington and his buddies had disappeared. Fleetfoot was leaning against a counter looking a lot more casual behind the kitchen door than he did when he was serving. I waved at him as I raced by. The cooks were young. They gaped at me. One of them said something in Italian or Spanish.

Luck was with me. I spotted a large cleaver on the counter and picked it up on my way out the back door. Someone, I think it was the head cook, shouted, "Hey! You can't take that. What are you doing?"

"Don't worry," I called back. "My date went out this way." And, it occurred to me, had left me with the check. Another good reason to have the cleaver handy.

Chapter 2

It was colder out than I remembered, but when we came in I had been glowing from nerves and the prospect of a good meal. Now I was envisioning a hanging corpse and trying to figure out how to throw a cleaver so that I didn't have to get too close to an overzealous boxer type. I moved quickly. If I was going to die, I was in a hurry to get the unpleasantness over with.

I rounded the corner of the building, cleaver high and found...nothing. No Huntington, no big dudes hanging around. I sped around the next corner and was just in time to see Huntington's Lexus burn rubber on its way out of the parking lot. Another car followed close behind. I thought I had lost the whole lot of them until I realized the two large guys hadn't made it back into the parking lot yet. They were standing near the archway and must have heard my shoes crunching leaves because they both turned around.

In dismay, I stared through the wrought-iron fence at the parking spot where the Lexus had been parked. "Well, rats." Now how was I supposed to get home?

The beefier of the two guys started over my way. There I stood with my cleaver. I waved it. "He didn't happen to throw any money your way for my dinner, did he?" I was pretty sure that if I ran, like a cat, Mister Beefy would decide I was prey.

Mister Beefy paused when I asked the question. One hand was deep inside his leather jacket pocket. He looked back at his barely smaller white cousin. The white guy had doubt and confusion written across his face. From the etched wrinkles, it looked like his face spent a lot of time in that expression.

Finding no answer from his buddy, Mr. Beefy turned back my way. His nostrils flared as though scenting a mouse. "Youz knows where he might could be goin'?"

"No. Man told me he'd take me for a nice dinner." I shook the cleaver at the empty road. "If you catch him, tell him he owes me, would you?" The cold and my fear made me shiver hard.

I wasn't sure if they believed me, but I didn't wait to find out. With determination, I marched right up to the front door and peeled it apart.

Apparently if you came up to the restaurant with cleaver in hand, the doors didn't magically open.

The cook, or at least the guy with the tallest white hat, was upfront now. He didn't look too keen about letting me in. Too bad, I was in, and I locked the doors behind me. Some customers this place could do without.

From the way Cook eyeballed me, it was pretty obvious he agreed, even though he had the wrong customer in mind.

"He got away," I told Cook, handing him the cleaver.

"Your date?" Cook had an accent of some sort, probably Italian.

"Yeah. Thanks for the, uh, knife." The host didn't look like he was going to escort me back to the table.

"I presume it was not a problem with the food," Cook said stiffly. He was a lot older than a running glance had shown; bushy dark eyebrows were laced with gray and his face had more than a few worn creases.

"Goodness no! The food was wonderful. The salad was anyway."

He nodded regally. My waiter hovered nervously. He actually looked relieved to see me.

"Don't worry. I would never leave without paying. My wallet is still in the booth." I was not sure when I had been this embarrassed before. The waiter obviously thought I had run out the back door rather than pay the bill. The cook believed I had chased my date with a cleaver, either because he wouldn't pay or because I was such a loser, I couldn't attract better dates. "I'm really sorry about the confusion."

"Those other peoples." Cook hesitated. "I think they were not friends of your date?"

"I kind of doubt it. Huntington didn't seem anxious to talk to them, did he?" I guessed that next time Huntington came to this establishment, he might not have a table waiting. He had a lot more to lose than I did. After all, I didn't come to these places very often.

As I paid the bill, I decided it was good I didn't visit frequently. It wouldn't break my account to pay fifty bucks for a meal, but I wouldn't want to do it often. The good news was I not only had the untouched chicken, which, miracle of miracle Fleetfoot actually offered to package for me, I also had Huntington's steak. If I couldn't eat them both I could always give the leftovers to my brother, Sean, when he next came foraging for food.

Speaking of Sean, he might be good for a ride home. Otherwise I would be forced to call a taxi. I pondered my choices, tapping my foot and staring at the phone. No, it was too humiliating to admit to my brother that my date had left me stranded. I couldn't even call Derrick Sawyer, Sean's cop friend, because Derrick couldn't keep a secret. He'd tell Sean for sure.

Before calling the taxi, I called Suzy Daniels, my best friend, but she had just put the kids down for bed. Her husband, Robert, hadn't come home yet. "Do you think he could pick me up on his way home from work and drop me off?" I begged.

"Hang on! I'll call him at the office on the cell."

Suzy was a dear. We had known each other since college, so we had swapped rescues a time or two. The worst incident was when some creep drove her to Estes Park outside Denver and then "ran out of gas." Turned out there was a little hotel nearby at which he suggested they stay. She would have stolen his car, but the guy had been clever enough to actually run out of gas. I drove two hours to the rescue.

She came back on. "Robert's on his way. Actually he had already left, but he will swing by there. What happened anyway?" Now that the emergency was over, she moved on to the important things.

"Oh, you know how it is." I watched the host watch me. He had unlocked the door now that Beef and Buns were gone. While I was using the phone, he had seated a normal looking couple. I think he would have made the couple run to the table if possible so that he could get back to his post and guard against me, the infidel. "Thought I had a nice date, but he ran out on me. I went after him with a cleaver from the kitchen, but he was too fast. Guess I shouldn't have tried to eat that last bite before chasing him."

Suzy digested that piece of information. "Uh, you chased him? Gee, Sedona, he might not ask you out again."

Now there was a rub. "Yeah, I'm pretty concerned."

Her loyalty came through. "Of course if he didn't pay, then what do you want with that scum anyway? You can do better. Who was it?"

I really didn't want to admit I'd been out with Huntington. She had met him when I worked with him at Strandfrost, and I had promised her I wasn't interested. I wasn't. And even if I was, I *had* chased him with a cleaver, which wasn't going to endear me to him.

"It was *Steve*, wasn't it?" she squealed.

"It's not what you think."

She giggled. "You're making up the part about the cleaver, aren't you? But why did he run away? Did you get the cleaver out before he ran away? What were you fighting about?"

"Uh, I think your husband is here. How about I call you tomorrow?"

"No way! I'm coming over first thing tomorrow morning." Lucky for me first thing to her was near noon. "You are going to tell me every single detail."

"Yah, yah." I hung up, smiled my best smile for the host, and clomped outside. I had to wait another five minutes for her husband, but I preferred the freezing weather to the frosty stares inside.

Chapter 3

My little house in suburbia was a wonderful haven for me. It was only a one-story, two bedroom patio home in a small neighborhood occupied mostly by retirees, but I loved it. My next door neighbor, a gruff older man, mowed my yard occasionally. More importantly, he had a mini-plow on his SUV so he cleared my driveway when it snowed. I took him cookies and various dishes to keep up my side of the relationship.

Now, you would think that my older brother, who lives in town, might do the same sorts of things for me as the neighbor does. In fact, you would think that he might do more.

But he doesn't. What Sean does is show up on my doorstep and pester me. That was precisely where I found him Saturday morning when I got back from my weekly grocery trip.

"What took you so long?" he demanded.

"I had an appointment with an oil baron so that held me up." I tried without success to hide the grocery bags.

He helped me bring them in, set them on the kitchen table and began sorting. This was not to say he put groceries away; rather, he was looking for anything edible.

"Stop that!" I smacked his hand as he snagged an apple. "That's for the chicken salad."

"Good, are we having sandwiches?"

I withered him with a glance. "We?" He ignored me.

Hungry, I started making the sandwiches. "Where's Brenda?" Since he was acting half-starved, one of his wife's cooking attempts had probably gone awry, and he had been driven out in search of food.

"At home."

I cut up apples and pulled the leftover baked chicken out of the fridge. Since I was going to be feeding him, I decided to at least get some manual labor out of him. "Here, crack these pecans, would you?"

He wanted to eat, so he didn't argue. Within ten minutes we had our sandwiches.

"I came by to remind you that you promised to teach Brenda to cook Thanksgiving dinner this year."

"What? I don't think so."

He nodded. "Yes, you did."

"No way. Not even in my weakest moment."

He reiterated a conversation of which I had zero recollection. Then he finished his case by pleading. My brother was a lawyer. He represented battered wives, rape victims and children. Pleading was something he did particularly well, only in this case, I knew he wouldn't starve to death. "Why can't you come over here for Thanksgiving dinner?"

"Because she wants to have children." He looked extremely nervous. "I think…" He licked his lips and swallowed hard. He then swept all the crumbs off his pants, one at a time, several frantic little brushes. "I think she's pregnant."

This last came out like a cross between a prayer and a curse. I stared at my big brother in disbelief. I knew he wanted children. It was bound to happen someday. "Really?" I breathed, not quite sure how to handle a pregnant brother.

He nodded tightly. "It's not completely…verified yet. Just the home test. Those can be wrong."

Ever logical, I wrinkled my brow in thought. "What does this have to do with Thanksgiving?"

His eyes widened in disbelief. "But Sedona she has to be able to cook a turkey before the kids are born!"

I wasn't sure of his logic. In fact, I was pretty sure the two things weren't connected. What I did know was that Brenda couldn't make coffee without getting grounds in the water. I also knew my brother wasn't leaving until I promised to try and teach Brenda the finer points of turkey roasting. "You'll do all the shopping. Every single bit of it." He nodded vigorously. "And the dishes. I am not staying to do the dishes!" More agreement. "If dinner fails, you aren't going to blame me. You aren't going to invite Mom and Dad unless they invite themselves. I don't need any more pressure than necessary and Mom and Dad already said they are going to Dean's." Dean, our younger brother, was currently residing in Texas so it was unlikely my parents could fit Colorado in their Thanksgiving schedule.

"Okay." He got up and flew into the kitchen. "Can I take Brenda a sandwich?"

I glared at him, a look he somehow interpreted as a yes. He made three more sandwiches, finishing off the salad. Taking the rest of the bread, he ran off, leaving me, as always, with dirty dishes.

It wasn't until he was gone that I discovered he had also snagged Huntington's leftover steak, the pig.

* * *

Suzy didn't actually make it over to visit me until Sunday afternoon. We baked cookies. Her five-year-old, Jimmy, rolled dough into balls. Rolling them wasn't really necessary for chocolate chip cookies, but it kept him busy. Maureen, the baby, slept through the entire event in her little carrier. At two months old, she didn't know about cookies yet, and the noise didn't seem to bother her either.

Suzy nagged and harassed me about Huntington. "I think he is dead," I finally told her.

"What?"

I explained how we had parted on Friday. "Since he didn't call, I assume the bad guys caught him, and he is dead. We'll have to find someone else for me to date."

She rolled her eyes. "You don't *know* that he is dead."

Of course I didn't, but we argued about it for another hour over the milk and cookies. By the time she left, I had even convinced myself he was dead. I considered trying to locate Mark, Huntington's brother, and give him the bad news.

I decided to sleep on it. After all, if Huntington was already dead, what was one more day?

Chapter 4

Monday morning, after a fretful weekend, I made my way into Strandfrost despite Huntington's job offer. After all, the man had ignored me for months. Then when he reappeared, he wanted to take up right where we left off--with me working for him. Before I could tell him no, he up and disappeared after being chased by goons.

Huntington probably thought I should jump at his job offer, but based on past experience, he didn't hand out dream jobs. Sure, the initial packaging looked good, but the dirt underneath could kill a person.

As soon as I arrived at Strandfrost, I went in search of Turbo. "Hi." I plopped down in the office chair across the desk from him.

Turbo continued to type furiously. The door had been ajar when I arrived. If it had been completely closed, I would have had to come back later. When Turbo wrote code behind closed doors, I could barge in, turn into a bunny rabbit and be completely overlooked by my mentor and friend. Half closed meant that if I sat here for fifteen minutes, he might notice me.

I played with one of the various toys on his desk while I waited. Turbo kept an odd collection of plastic cartoon characters even though he was well into his forties and didn't actually watch cartoons anymore. Well, not that I knew of.

"Watch Minnie there. I think her hand is about to break off," he protested suddenly.

Startled, I dropped Minnie. I had been trying to get Minnie to hold Mickey's hand and "walk" across the desk. "I wonder how it got that way," I murmured, removing Minnie from the odd angle required to attach her hand to Mickey's.

"No telling," he replied smoothly, ever polite. He pushed his chair back and propped his feet on the desk. "What's up?" He didn't sound terribly interested in the answer, but then, he was obviously busy.

I played with a miniature space monster. "You ever think about quitting?"

"Other than today, you mean?"

I glanced up quickly, realizing his distraction might not be due to coding. "Did he call you too?" I couldn't believe it. Huntington wouldn't dare put Turbo back in danger, would he? Last time, Turbo had nearly been killed. He had a family to support for God's sake!

"Of course no one consulted me. Do they ever? I guess since you're a manager, they asked you, huh? No luck convincing them it was a bad idea?"

"Because I'm a manager? I don't think he cares that I'm a manager. He asked me if I wanted my old job back as a technician."

Turbo sat straight up and pulled on his bowl hair-cut. Since he didn't get it trimmed on a regular basis, the minute he stopped yanking on it, it fell over his eyes. "Argh! They are demoting you on top of hiring Gary back? That's it! We can't just sit here and let this happen. It's bad enough that those losers are getting Gary back in here as a "consultant" and paying him twice what he was making before. They can't demote you like that!"

I let the explosion fester while I tried to digest the conversation. "What?"

"I'll march right in there--"

"Uh, Turbo. Turbo!" I shouted over his ranting. "I don't think we're talking about the same thing!"

He didn't hear me. I had to hold Minnie over the trashcan as hostage to get his attention. He blinked and pulled his arms back down. "What are you doing to Minnie?"

I shook my head. "I don't think we're talking about the same event. I was talking about Huntington calling and offering me a job at Acetel as a technician." In disgust, I added, "I had no idea Strandfrost was hiring Gary Marcus back. You've gotta be kidding me."

"Huntington? Technician?" He kept a careful eye on Minnie until I set her safely on the desk.

"Why would Strandfrost bother with Gary the Slacker?" I asked.

Turbo returned to looking glum. "I don't have all the details yet. I think that maybe John Arlton, the new VP that was hired to take Gary's place, actually knew Gary. Gary helped John get the job at Strandfrost. Now John is paying him back by rehiring him."

"Didn't anyone tell the board about this?" While Gary hadn't actually done anything illegal, he certainly hadn't been paying enough attention to the fact that a manager under his command was skimming charity checks.

"I doubt it. If John tried to hire Gary into an executive position, I'm sure the board would care. But if he's just a mucky-muck consultant why would they pay any attention?"

"Maybe because it was the board that asked Gary to move along a couple of months ago?"

Turbo shook his head. "Come on, Sedona. You know how it works. For all we know, they know about him coming back."

I doubted it. The board had spent a lot of money cleaning house. I only knew about the money that had floated my way through Huntington, but I knew his services didn't come cheap. "I guess it doesn't matter if the board knows or not."

Turbo didn't look like he agreed. "Maybe there's some checking I could do to determine what is really going on."

"Uh Turbo..." Turbo's idea of checking was similar to a bulldozer gone madly out of control. His style was precisely why he had gotten into so much trouble the last time we investigated something. That and he tended to assume certain things, such as the board knowing, when in fact, reality was usually a lot more complex. If the board knew, someone on the board, in my opinion, wasn't on the up and up. That didn't bode well for Turbo "checking" anything. "Checking things probably isn't a good idea."

"I'll call you tonight. After I see what I can find out."

Now, why didn't that reassure me?

Chapter 5

When I arrived home, there was a Lexus parked in my driveway. I let out a sigh of relief. It was good to know Huntington was safe, although since the car was unoccupied, I assumed that he had broken in and made himself at home.

A bit disgruntled, I unlocked the front door and called out, "Huntington?" I always called him by his last name, but since he didn't answer, I tried his first name. "Steve?"

When that didn't work, I decided maybe his brother had left the car. "Mark?"

The place was disturbingly empty. I even checked under the bed in my room and scanned the guest room. The only place I didn't look for Huntington was the trunk of the car. I was too afraid of what I might find there. Besides, I didn't have the keys.

As I was coming down from the attic, the phone rang. Assuming it was Huntington calling to apologize or explain, I shouted into the phone, "Are you crazy?" He deserved to be torn into tiny little pieces for leading a life that drove me insane.

"Sedona?" Turbo asked politely.

"Oh." I paused to take a much needed breath. "You're not being held hostage somewhere or anything, are you?" It wasn't easy to bring my focus back to the problems at Strandfrost.

"No, I'm fine," he reassured me. Then he was silent for a while. With Turbo that could mean he was thinking, but since he had called, he probably had all his cards neatly shuffled and ready for dealing. Therefore, the pause meant something else.

"What did you find out?" I asked.

"Did you like technician work?"

Uh-oh. "Why?"

With false brightness he said, "Actually, it might be a good idea if you took the job Huntington offered."

"Turbo."

He continued as though he hadn't heard me. "It would be a nice change of pace, something new, get you back into the swing of things, you know, regain that technical edge."

"Turbo."

He continued babbling. "*Turbo*!" I yelled. "What did you find out?"

More silence. "I went in to see John, the new VP."

"And?"

"Seems that Gary is insinuating that you're likely responsible for the current set of problems. He claims that when he was working at Strandfrost, you caused all kinds of ruckus, kept the schedules up in the air, and didn't get on well with the other managers."

I closed my eyes. "They are going to fire me, aren't they? They are going to believe that slimy little weasel Gary over an innocent troop."

I could hear Turbo swallow. "I, uh…"

"Turbo," another thought occurred to me, "You didn't get yourself fired did you?"

No answer for a long moment. Finally, he replied. "I guess it wouldn't hurt if you asked Huntington if they have two openings, just in case."

"They can't get the work done at Strandfrost without you! The schedules are too tight."

He let loose a long breath. "I don't think they'll fire me. John said something about forgiving my outburst. And they won't fire you. They'll just ask you to look around like they did Gary."

That certainly didn't leave me with much to say did it? The phone made noises at me for another few minutes while Turbo babbled platitudes and nonsense. I could hear Turbo's wife, Irene, in the background asking whether he wanted corn or potatoes with his supper.

Finally breaking the daze, I said, "I gotta go Turbo. I'll see you tomorrow." Maybe. It depended on whether or not management gave me any time before they made their "suggestions." My life was going to hell in a hand basket, and the devils didn't even leave a handle on the basket for me.

Looking out the window, I laughed. No, the devil in my life left me a Lexus instead of a hand basket. The problem was that I had no idea where to drive it or what to do with it.

Without any better ideas, I left the car sitting in the driveway and went to bed.

Chapter 6

Tuesday morning my life did not improve. Not only did the Lexus remain parked in my driveway, there was still no sign of Huntington. I wasn't ready to call my brother and ask how to get the trunk open.

I drove myself to work, contemplating my other problems. There was probably no good way to get fired, but if I had my choice I would go down fighting. Unfortunately, from what Turbo had said, the decision was made, and I wouldn't be given a chance.

I slinked my way into the office at seven-thirty so that I could carry down the few personal items I kept there without being seen. At eight, reading through my emails, I found one mailed late the night before from Ross Canton, the marketing and program manager. After looking at his latest proposed schedule, my heart sank. Even without Turbo's warning I would have guessed something bad was going to happen. Ross was quite creative and liberal with commitments to our customers, but not even on his worst day would he normally have tried to sell this schedule. Management was counting on me protesting so they would have a good reason to fire me.

I saw no point in torturing the others with my presence any longer than necessary. I tried Huntington's pager. I was truly relieved when he actually called me back.

"Glad to see you are still alive," I said.

"I called Anthony's and had them reverse the charges on your card and put dinner on mine."

"Oh, how sweet of you," I chirped. "I was sooo disappointed that you couldn't stay long enough to give me a ride home, but I see you made up for it by parking your car in my driveway. I must say you have an interesting way of wooing a girl."

I could hear him sigh. "I assume you called to tell me you wouldn't accept the job if it was the last one in town?"

Hmm, now I was in a pickle. It would be nicer if he would beg, but I had a house payment to make.

Before I could reply, he grumbled, "Did you *have* to chase after me with a cleaver? What were you going to do with that thing anyway? You know Scalia has been a friend of mine for years, and now he thinks I have endangered my life by dating a woman that came after me with a kitchen ax."

I bristled. "Oh, like the gentlemen that followed you through the kitchen were your buddies and law abiding citizens! Didn't your friend Scalia ask about them?"

"He mentioned that he thought they had guns, but at least I wasn't on a date with them!"

"Yeah, getting left with the bill at a restaurant makes me look really attractive. Being seen with you is certainly a statement of how good a girl can do."

"Look, if I pay you on the side, like last time, will you take the job already? You won't be able to drive the Mercedes, because it doesn't go with the pay Acetel will be giving you, but you still have your Honda, right? And I know you have jeans, despite all the money you spent on other clothes. You can keep your new lifestyle, but you'll have to bank it for a while."

"And then what? I continue working at this place, trying to eek out a living and hope I like it?"

He paused again, not a good sign. "It's quite possible I wouldn't be able to get you your job back at Strandfrost afterwards. How about an advance to mitigate the risk? Say a couple grand. That will give you time to look for something afterwards in case this doesn't turn out to be your dream job."

There was no way I would have taken the job had I not known that I was about to get fired. "Make it five thousand. You didn't tell me I would be risking my life and limbs last time."

"You won't be this time! You're just going to work, mingle and listen to gossip."

He made it sound so simple. I didn't say anything.

"Okay, five it is."

"And you'll cover the difference between the new salary and what I'm making now," I added. "I'll send you my resume, and you can pitch it to your cohorts, assuming you've got someone on the inside."

"Uh...yeah."

"What does that mean?"

"A guy, Jacques, is going to call you later today."

I was furious. "You assumed I was going to say yes?"

Before I could blister him, he interrupted. "No, I was hoping Jacques could sell you on the job. Tell you what a great opportunity it would be. I can't exactly do that."

"Not well, anyway! You couldn't even manage dinner." A sudden, more important thought came to me. "He'll call me at home?" When one is about to be fired, one can't count on being at work later to take a call.

"Whatever works best," Huntington said, pretending to be magnanimous. "I gave him both numbers. Oh, and I picked up the Lexus a little while ago, so you don't have to keep trying to locate the keys. I'll stop by tonight so we can do a little planning."

I grunted and followed his normal habit of hanging up without saying goodbye. Rats. I had forgotten to ask why his car was in my driveway in the first place. Too late now. Ross was standing in my doorway as if he had all day to wait for me to get off the phone. Instead of shouting a quick request and moving on to the next deal, he stood there fidgeting.

I waved a copy of the new schedule. "Wow, three new projects on top of the four I already have. Good thing I hired some new people. We'll just have to squeeze all the work in, right?"

Ross opened his mouth and then shut it. He started forward and then retreated. He was the kind of guy who should have run for public office, always hanging out with the right people, saying the right things and dancing the dance. Except today. He seemed to be short a step or two.

I continued smoothly. "I wasn't quite sure what you were looking for on the last project on the list, and I know how you like to have your ducks in a row by staff." Our management staff meetings started at nine. John and company knew that I'd have plenty of time to see the "new" schedule and work myself into a fit over it.

Ross took a deep breath and then blurted out, "Patrick said he couldn't handle the Mamba project either. He's giving it back to you." He loosened his tie, and in the process accidentally undid it too far. Between that and the constant motion of running his hand through his thick brown hair, he ended up looking like a drunk in a bar.

"No problem." I smiled a last grimace and sent my resignation to the little printer on my desk. Resigning probably beat getting fired. Ross stammered a few more times as we walked to the staff meeting.

At the door to John's office, Ross looked even more desperate, his eyes bulging, but not meeting mine. "Uh Sedona, listen…"

I stopped. He stared down at his shoes, and then instead of saying anything, he bolted ahead of me into the staff room.

I walked in and there smiled Gary. He looked smug, but not as happy as Dan Thorton, Strandfrost's finance manager. Dan was a womanizer and a lecherous creature. He was still angry because I had exposed his baldness in an incident involving his toupee.

"Gary, good to see you again," I said solemnly. Like moving a favorite bookcase and finding a giant brown recluse waiting.

It wasn't possible for me to hand in my resignation with him gloating. I couldn't do it. "I hope you'll fill me in on what's new with you when I get back from vacation." I stuttered a little as I made up the lie.

John, the vice president, looked over at me. "Vacation?"

I nodded and gulped. I had almost three weeks of time off because I had been so busy helping Huntington, I hadn't used any of my vacation for the year. I sure hated to let these guys mow me over before getting the time off. "Yes, starting next Monday for the next three weeks, remember? The week before Thanksgiving, Thanksgiving week and the week after." Since it was pretty obvious I wasn't going to be around to take any time off at Christmas, may as well take all my accrued vacation now.

John blinked rapidly and glanced around the room. Everyone frowned except Ross, who was now staring at me with what might have been admiration. John would look petty if he fired me today, right before my big vacation. None of them would find it strange that they couldn't recall me asking for it in the first place, because they never listened to a word I uttered. They wouldn't remember if I had announced I was growing marijuana and delivering it to Santa Claus in time for Christmas.

We all sat down around the conference table. I felt like a bag lady from the homeless row downtown, an unwanted social problem. John straightened his tie and started babbling. When Ross presented the schedule, it got really quiet. I smiled so hard my cheeks hurt. "I went over it with Ross earlier. Should work out great." And they would have to wait three weeks while I was out before they could decide who was really going to do the work. It was evil. It was mean.

My smile got wider and a lot more sincere. John couldn't very well fire me right before earned vacation, and they couldn't put the fake schedule behind them and move on to real business with me still there.

I smiled all the way through the muddled meeting. John finally gave up trying to pretend he had anything else to say, and cut us loose. On the way down the hall, I laughed. What a terrible person I was.

Chapter 7

Huntington showed up at my place just after I got home. I let him in, set his nice leather coat on the back of the couch, and regretted again that I hadn't managed a butter-soft jacket out of the last deal. "Did you bring my bonus check?"

He smiled. "I auto-deposited it. I still have your account number from the last case. Now that I've hired you again, you're officially back on the payroll."

Since the day I met Huntington, he had been presumptuous. "Ah yes, that brings us right to the point. You are here to fill me in on what you are looking for. You might also want to explain why those thugs were after you at the restaurant the other day."

Huntington stuffed his hands into his khaki pockets and rolled back and forth on his feet. He looked frustrated enough to actually kick something. "I had no idea anyone with that kind of muscle was concerned about me working on this case, but obviously someone followed me and found us sitting in the restaurant. Mark has been...hanging around Acetel. He normally drives the Lexus. Someone must have seen him."

I folded my arms and tapped my foot. If Huntington didn't know why the men had been following him or who they were, that meant they were still in the picture. This was not good news. "You have more details, I assume."

He sat down on my well-worn tweed couch while I positioned myself behind the bar counter that separated the kitchen from the living room. I started the rice cooker while he talked.

"Ben Martinez is a freelance accountant who does a lot of contract work. He mentioned how well other companies in this business are doing-- yet Acetel recently was forced to layoff people to get expenses in line with revenues. Ben was one of the layoffs. He recommended the board hire me to make sure things were on the up and up. The books added up, mind you, it's just that Ben doesn't understand why Acetel isn't more profitable." Huntington moved his leather jacket from the back of the couch and leaned back. I thought about offering to hang it, but chances were poor that he would accidentally forget it, so I let it stay on the armrest.

"This is the company's second layoff. The first occurred before the company went public. The CEO, A.J. Chambers, agreed to the first one mainly because his advisors wanted to quietly clean house prior to the company going public. It only affected about twenty people.

"A.J. is an engineer at heart. When he started Acetel, he wanted to tie small-company designs to larger ones and service them. For a while, the company was nicely profitable."

"So what happened?" The work sounded a lot like what Strandfrost did--except we didn't service the equipment after the sale, we only certified that the equipment worked in certain environments and provided performance statistics.

"Expenses and overhead grew too fast. Bottom line was that Acetel's customer account payments weren't keeping pace with hiring and expenses. A second layoff was needed. From all appearances, the hiring that went on right after the first layoff was extreme and the biggest part of the problem. Strangely, the hiring was supposedly done because accounts existed that needed people working them."

Firing people madly and then hiring them back right away didn't sound at all unusual to me. After all, Strandfrost had just hired Gary back even though there had been very good reasons to walk him out the door. Even more common than Gary's situation, every company had a greedy manager or two that built a personal empire by hiring an echelon of troops, needed or not. "So...the company is madly out of control? They hire, they fire? And one of the casualties, this Ben guy, took offense at that?"

Huntington snorted. "He's suspicious, not offended." He got up to pace. My house wasn't big enough for a dining room. Instead there was a dining nook just off the kitchen and living room, which afforded almost enough pacing room. "We aren't sure where the problem lies. The numbers add up from the audit, but Ben mentioned that when he worked there, managers were very slow to turn over requested records. Given employees' apparent productivity on cases, A.J. believes that someone might be getting work done at Acetel--but instead of Acetel getting paid, one or more individuals are pocketing the money for the work done."

"How can that happen?"

"At this point, we suspect that the customers might even be in on it. For a reduced charge, some customers could be making payments under the table to a contact inside Acetel. It could be as simple as the service contract requiring A and B, but someone does A, B and C. The payment for C goes right into side pockets, leaving Acetel out of the loop and taking away from its bottom line."

He went back to his jacket and extracted some folded sheets of paper from the inside pocket. Since I was busy cutting broccoli, he laid the papers on the bar. "Another possibility is that certain individuals might be doing work for companies that don't have an official service contract at all. I brought you a list of all the legitimate customers. If you hear customer names that aren't on this list, that means there is no service contract and payment for the job is being diverted away from Acetel."

I fluffed rice and threw thin pieces of beef into a wok. I added some soy sauce and the broccoli. "This isn't Chinese. Don't think it is Chinese. It is beef, and it happens to have broccoli in it." I had never figured out how to make the thick, rich sauces that Happy Family served. Mine was a poor substitute if mistaken for possible Chinese.

While the meat sizzled, I got out plates and sodas. "All this info still doesn't tell me why those two guys came looking for you. It sounds to me like there's been a leak concerning your involvement, and whoever is running this scheme knows all about you."

He tapped his fingers on the table. "Mark had the Lexus for a while. We were sharing it because he needed it in order to blend inside certain neighborhoods. I needed it for mixing with the board set. Mark spotted a black Lincoln following him when he delivered the car to me at a board meeting. They were still on my tail when I left. By the time I took you out to dinner, I had lost them, but apparently they drove around long enough to spot the car at the restaurant."

I froze in the motion of dumping steak over rice. "You mean someone has been following you around for a while? And you parked that thing in my driveway?"

Huntington frowned. "No one followed me here so you're safe."

I passed him a plate while I contemplated his theory. "If Beefy and Buns found you at the restaurant, what prevents them from driving around and finding it here?" I answered my own question. "Nothing."

"This is not the type of neighborhood where they would look for a Lexus. The restaurant, on the other hand, was within a mile of where I lost them. They probably cruised upscale places until they spotted it."

I took a big bite and chewed slowly. Huntington had a special way with insults. "Since I don't live in an expensive condo, you figured it was safe to park it here?"

He blinked. He started to answer, but thought better of it.

"Never mind, Huntington. I think you're wrong though. Don't leave that car sitting in my driveway." I glowered and ate another bite of steak. At least the sirloin was excellent and very tender.

"If you wanted steak, why didn't you just grill it?" was Huntington's pronouncement.

I didn't bother to answer, but I stabbed my next bite rather savagely.

"Okay, okay, it's a meal, and I didn't have to make it myself. And it's possible that I shouldn't have left the car here." He put his hand up. "Look, we won't be using the Lexus anymore except to throw them off the trail. I had to leave it here temporarily, but no one followed me. All you have to watch for is suspicious accounts. The good news is that if everyone else is watching to see what I am up to, you should be able to infiltrate without a single problem."

"Yeah. No doubt." Wasn't that what he promised the last time? Unfortunately, with Huntington, nothing ever went quite the way he said it would.

Chapter 8

My first day at Acetel was pretty standard for starting a new job at a computer company. I sat through a half-day of orientation designed to put people in a coma. The lady drone made sure I got a badge, auto-deposit and folders full of company mission statements. Unfortunately, she was from an outsourced company so she had no idea what I was supposed to do after she was done explaining all the standard benefits and stock options. I was left in a hallway with no directions.

Since the building was only two-stories, I kept my search to the second floor where I had been abandoned. I tried to tell myself that if things didn't work out I could always go back to Strandfrost.

At the end of the hallway, I found a secretary. She was tall even sitting down. Her hair was full-sized, a Dolly Parton style arrangement with a lot of hairspray. The blond curls looked natural and somehow so did her Texas boots right after she opened her mouth in greeting. "Well, howdy! You must be Sedona." She pronounced my name with a long drawl on the "o." "You can call me Becky. Name's Rebecka, but I just cain't see being a Rebecka."

It was hard to keep from backing away as she charged around her L-shaped desk with her hand outstretched.

"Uh yeah, I'm Sedona O'Hala. Hi."

"Well, aren't you the cutest little thing." She grabbed my unresisting hand and smiled big and warm. There was a touch of lipstick on her front tooth.

"Thanks. You, uh," I wiped my finger across my front teeth.

She jumped back to her seat with a curse. "I swear I always do that." Out came a mirror from the top drawer. She scrubbed at the lipstick, checked the rest of her makeup and fluffed a piece or two of hair. She was probably ten years my senior, but it was hard to tell with all the makeup. Huge blue eyes peered from underneath extra long black lashes and lipstick adorned full lips that a man would probably love if he could find them under the bright red.

"Do you need the mirror?" She started to hand it to me, an automatic politeness from one woman to another. Critically, she realized I wasn't wearing any makeup except mascara. "Well, honey, you're pale as a mouse. You've lost every single bit of your lipstick."

"I don't wear much makeup." I tried not to sound defensive, but it was hard given her stare. Dolling myself up to work in a lab environment wasn't generally worth the time or the effort. Most of the engineers didn't care that I was female, never mind notice whether I wore makeup or not. The ones that did notice would often misinterpret anything nicer than socially acceptable as a signal that I had no brains and wasn't interested in my career.

"You already married?" she asked.

"Well, no."

"You want yerself a man, yer gonna have to priss up a bit," she advised. "I bin married for ten years, and I tell you what, that man o'mine ain't seen me yet without my makeup. I swear he'd run screaming." She stood up again and sashayed her way around me. "Let's get your supplies."

I wasn't sure if she meant makeup or a laptop, but I followed along like the little lamb I was supposed to be. She must have heard me sigh mournfully, because she looked back, calculating my attitude.

"You don't look too happy, missy." She swung back around before I could think of a good response.

"Just bored from orientation," I tried. No, bored wasn't blending and fitting in. "I mean, overwhelmed."

She looked back at me again when I corrected myself, but I nodded and kept my eyes wide. Hers narrowed and she "uh-huhed."

At the supply cabinet, she unlocked it before handing me pencils, stapler, a bin with scissors, extra tape, markers and some other stuff. It piled up high.

When she tried to hand me some sort of coat hanger, she noticed I had no room for it. "We better get you a box." She stared at me with her hands on her hips and her boot tapping. "You'll need to be keeping an eye on all this stuff because these are hard times you've arrived at. I can't put in another order until after Christmas."

I nodded dutifully. "I was surprised when they hired me what with all the layoffs."

She sniffed. "Thank God it was the folks in San Jose and not here."

I tried to be diplomatic but still get some information. "I heard it was a lot. Something like ten percent."

"Yeah." She found a box near the copy machine and helped me load it. "They let the two contractors here go. My buddy Stella was one of them. But then they changed their minds, and Stella got to come on board full-time instead of contracting. Maybe they found some money so that is why they could hire you too. The other contractor, Ben, he wasn't so lucky." She made a cutting motion across her throat.

"Oh." The thought occurred to me again that this whole investigation might be because of one disgruntled accountant who had been laid off.

"You eaten lunch yet?"

Not unless the drone had given me a lunch box at orientation and being nearly comatose I hadn't noticed. "No."

"There's a great little café near here with soup and sandwiches. They have divine dessert too." She looked critically at my waist, and then sighed wistfully. "You have a great waist. Not an inch of tummy. I swear since having my two children they might as well give me surgery."

She was probably at least six feet tall and big-boned, but she wasn't really fat. "I don't think liposuction is required in your case."

She laughed and marched back to her office. "I wasn't talking liposuction." She pulled on a couple of inches around her stomach. "I was thinking they could operate and make me a pouch like a kangaroo so that I wouldn't have to carry this purse around." She leaned under her desk and produced a red purse that was only slightly smaller than most carry-ons. "I could stash stuff right in the tummy pouch. Shoot, I'd put the kids back in there and carry them around if they'd stay quiet."

"A...kangaroo pouch."

"You betcha. Liposuction they can take straight off my ass, girl!" She laughed again, a hearty boom that may have left behind some sonic damage.

I couldn't help but smile at her enthusiasm. "It would beat working out."

She nodded her agreement and led the way back through the hallway. "You can set your stuff in your office, and then we'll get lunch."

At an office barely large enough to contain a laminated desk, we set my supplies down. I grabbed my wallet and left my backpack before following her back out to the stairwell.

On the first floor, she stopped at a windowless steel door and waved at the badge reader. "Make sure your badge has been programmed to let you in the lab. They get it wrong more often than not."

The human resource lady had taken my picture and programmed the badge from a list that determined where in the building I would be allowed to go. Gamely, I held the little card to the reader. It buzzed, releasing the door lock and allowed us entrance. Once inside there wasn't time to register more than row after row of computer racks. The computer equipment wound in and around a maze of workbenches and the occasional pile of boxes. Becky knew right where my workbench was going to be.

"This is your spot and your laptop. You can haul it back upstairs when you get back."

"Okay."

We headed out to the parking lot. The asphalt lot sported protective tin-roof car covers under which her red, full-bed Ford didn't quite fit. "I tell you what," she said as she beeped her way into the cab, "children rip your body apart. Shoot, before kids I had nice perky breasts. Oh, how the men loved them." She looked critically at me. "You might not have much, but at least they are still sitting right up where they belong."

I might have replied, but she pulled out of the parking lot just then. The tires didn't squeal, but she did hit the curb.

I grabbed the armrest. If she crashed, my seatbelt probably wasn't enough to save me. Her truck created the illusion of being bigger and badder than other vehicles. I left three-inch claw marks on the armrest trying to convince myself that I could hold on through sheer force of will. How she managed not to hit anyone on the five or six-block race was beyond me.

She pulled into a parking spot and banged into the lip of the sidewalk as she brought the truck to a stop.

After hopping down from the cab, she slammed the door with considerable enthusiasm. "Come on, girl. This place is great. It reminds me of home."

I didn't have enough air to protest. Gulping, I dragged myself after her through a glass door. A cowbell announced our arrival. The shop was crammed with mismatched tables and chairs, many of them antiques or cast offs that might have come from an old barn. The back case featured cakes, cookies, breakfast breads and a smell of heaven.

"Go for the soup and sandwich combo," Becky advised, leading the way to the counter. "Or the chicken casserole is tops."

I followed her lead and ordered the soup and sandwich. The waitress gave us a card with a number printed on it. We moved to a table near the window.

Becky nearly knocked our rickety table over when she perched her purse on top. "What was I talking about? Oh yeah, kids. You're lucky, you haven't been deformed yet. When I was growing up my mother used to tell me not to give the milk away before I got the cow hitched. Little did I know that once you have kids you lose all your shape! Cain't *get* married after that, that's what she shoulda told me!"

"I'm sure your husband wouldn't dare complain." He'd probably get his head shot off if he tried.

"Shiiit," she drawled out. "He suggested that since my boobs flop like deflated balloons, we should duct tape'm in place!" She pushed them up to demonstrate, and I nearly choked on my ice water.

Changing the subject seemed like a safe response. "So, uh, how do you like working at Acetel?"

"What?" It took her a moment to shift gears. Our food arrived and that was a further distraction. "Why did you apply to Acetel anyway?"

Now you'd think I would be prepared for that question, given that I was supposed to be working undercover. "I, uh--" I blinked rapidly, holding my chicken salad sandwich with both hands like a lifeline. "I needed the money."

She roared and slapped a hand on the table. "Ain't that just the truth? I sure as hell wouldn't be working if I didn't need the money! Hard to believe with all the business Acetel draws, management screwed things up again." She started on dessert before her meal, but after I tasted the cookie I didn't blame her.

"You're lucky you didn't end up working for Ben, that contractor I told you about who was laid off. You know accountant types. That man had more questions and pinched more pennies than my grandma with her egg money. We all thought he was going to end up running the Denton office until he got laid off. Not that your boss, Jacques, is a real treat either, but he's tolerable. Technically I work for all the managers in Denton, but mostly I support A.J. He's the CEO so he's the one I really have to keep happy." She leaned forward and confided, "Luckily, A.J. only visits the Denton office about once every quarter. When he's around I work my tail off. You sure are right about working for the money." She prattled on for the next half hour about the things she would buy if she had the money, and the things she was buying anyway even though she didn't have the cash.

When we got back to work, Becky explained that all the offices and meeting rooms were on the second floor. The lab took up the entire first floor with the exception of the cafeteria, which was housed at the end furthest from the parking lot.

She then introduced me to Jacques Cardin, my new boss, whom I had only met over the phone during a quick and dirty interview. He didn't have time to say much other than "welcome" because Becky dragged me off down the hall.

"I'll introduce you to Arnold Sternof, but don't stay long." She whispered the warning before we rounded a corner. "He's okay, but he's a total geek. The man hasn't washed his hair in like, a decade."

Arnold looked up when we arrived at his office. His hair didn't look that bad, but he probably couldn't see out of his glasses very well since there were smudges and fingerprints all over them. "I heard we were getting a new person on board," he said, as he offered me a limp handshake. "Jacques has all the luck when it comes to talking management into getting extra help. I can tell you that we'll be keeping you busy too. If you get any free time, just let me know." He smiled toothily. "I suppose I should also say that if you need any help from me, stop by. The door is always open."

"Thanks," I said as Becky pulled me out of his office.

"He always complains when Jacques gets anything. If I agree to help Jacques with a report, you better believe Arnold will demand that I do every single one of his. Don't you dare volunteer yourself for anything in his group!"

"Okay." The man sounded like a ladder-climber and a scorekeeper to boot.

"He gets on very well with upper management, I guess because he's such a brain. Hangs on Pete's coattails all the time. Pete's the CFO honcho, and let me tell you that Pete isn't anything like Arnold. We're talking yin and yang. Pete's all high class and Arnold is total brainy-nerd."

Jacques had asked me to stop back by his office after Becky was done showing me around so I did. He was balding; what hair he had left was wisping. The rest of him wasn't holding up much better. His button down hung haphazardly around his soft belly. Light khaki pants lacked any semblance of a proper crease and had been used as a landing pad for a runaway pen. Jagged blue marked most of one thigh. He reminded me of a professor at college, peering from behind small glasses, waiting for someone to ask a question.

I didn't have any. After a very long pause, he handed me a couple of folders. "These will be your first assignments. We need them done as soon as possible, but that is always the case. I do not think you can be done with them today. That is unfortunate."

Since it was bearing down on three o'clock, he was right about me not making it by quitting time. I perused the folders. It would probably take me most of this week and next to knock out both assignments. "These phone numbers..." I trailed a finger down the sheets. "Both belong to the customers? Do we have a contact person at the vendor site?"

He nodded. "Kronology Servers is the vendor--the contact would be Craig Yumen, I think. He can probably help you." He tilted his head and tapped a pen on the desk. "Most likely."

I wasn't sure if his comment meant he didn't believe the contact was legitimate or he doubted Craig would help me. I thanked him anyway and wandered back to my new office. It was smaller than my old one, but since I had been about to lose that one, it hardly mattered. With little time left in the day, I checked my customer assignments against Huntington's master list of legitimate customers.

Everything looked legit so I logged onto my laptop and got it set up.

I was not working late on my first day for a lot of reasons, but I had a good excuse ready just in case anyone asked. I had been quite neglectful of my duty to congratulate Brenda on the pending arrival of her first child. A personal visit and at least a box of See's best chocolates was in order. I called Suzy, my recently pregnant friend, to check, and she agreed the chocolates would be a great gift.

"As long as you're going, could you pick some up for me?" she asked.

"Sure, how many?"

"The in-laws are coming for Thanksgiving so I need a two-pound box of the ones with nuts in them and a couple of one-pounders with just the chocolate butter ones. Do you mind? I'll write you a check when you get here."

"Not a problem."

"Oh, thanks! I hate to go to the mall this time of year and taking the kids with me turns it into a circus!"

I called Brenda's cell to tell her I was coming. She was en route from the hospital where she worked as a nurse, so I told her I would meet her at her house with the candy.

"Isn't it great news?" she chirped.

"You've been to the doctor, and it's definitely confirmed?"

"Absolutely! I'm at thirteen weeks," she whispered into the phone.

I thought there must be static. "Did you say thirteen weeks?" Sean had told me they had just run the pregnancy test at home. Wasn't that a long time to wait before getting suspicious?

She giggled. "We weren't actually trying. Not that we weren't trying either. And I wasn't really paying attention, you know. And then one morning it kind of occurred to me that it had been awhile, and I was late."

There was late and then there was *late*. "Oh, well, *yeah*."

"Isn't it going to be exciting? To be an aunt?"

For some reason, it was the first time it occurred to me that I was involved. As a relative or anything else. My mouth formed a little "oh" but no sound came out.

Brenda giggled some more and said she was looking forward to the chocolates before she hung up.

An aunt…? It seemed impossible.

Since Brenda and Sean lived in one of the sections in my subdivision, I picked up the chocolates and scooted over to Suzy's neighborhood first.

My best friend insisted that I come in. "I have to write you a check for these. I ought to give you a bonus for the delivery. Jimmy is beyond excited about the grandparents coming. He has been such a handful. There is no way I'll have time to get everything done before they get here!"

"You can write me a check later," I offered, but she was already yanking the desk drawers open.

"Do you want some tea? We can open that box you brought me and finish it!"

It was a very tasty suggestion, but I did have my own box in the car. "That would be bad of us."

She grinned. "Just one or two."

I opened the box while she wrote out the check. I glanced at the amount when she handed it to me to make sure she hadn't paid for the box I had gotten her as a gift. The check still had her maiden name, Wilson, on it. "Didn't you get new checks after you got married? You've been married, what, six years now?"

"Five." She grinned. "I ran out of our usual ones a few months ago, and I had to do bills, so I used my old ones." She shrugged. "Turns out no one ever noticed or complained about the ones with my old name so I decided to use them up. They have the same account number as the new checks. I guess that's all they look at when processing them."

"Don't they mind that your signature is "Daniels" and the check has "Wilson" typed at the top?"

She shook her head and grabbed a candy. "I guess not. When we got married I took my marriage license into the bank. They changed my name on the account and added Robert's name. I have two old boxes of checks, and I've been using them for, oh, probably six months now. No one has said boo."

She waved the candies, tempting me. "Here, have another. I'll just get fat if I eat all these, and you know I'll finish them before Robert gets home at this rate."

I declined by putting a hand out to ward her off. I had to close my eyes to have enough will power. "No! I have a box in the car!"

"Let's have tea. Hot cocoa would be too much, don't you think?" She started for the cupboard.

"No, no, I'll just savor the taste of the chocolate." I grabbed one more, gave her a quick hug and departed.

I managed to drop off Brenda's box and get all the way home before eating two more of the things from my own box.

Chapter 9

My lab duties started early the next morning. I was used to installing software but it would take some time for me to figure out all the nuances. To top off my challenges, Acetel didn't have the exact class of servers for one of the tests, although that hadn't bothered Jacques. I wasn't sure if he intended to tell the customer, but I typed the report and made a special note of the servers I was going to use.

I hadn't been working more than fifteen minutes when someone behind another row of equipment let out a belch that the very loud machines did nothing to mask. I was a little worried that whoever had burped had blown himself up.

"Hello?" I called out.

A furry face poked out from behind a wall of computer racks. "Hey, hey." The man stroked his dark, shaggy beard while he studied me, the new specimen. "I'm Bill. You new?"

"Sedona O'Hala." I returned his frank gaze. Like most engineers, he hadn't taken any special care with his attire; his denim shirt was wrinkled and not tucked in. Unlike most engineers, his pants looked as though they had been on fire.

"What in the world happened to your pants?" They weren't smoking, but I breathed deep just to make sure the lab wasn't actively burning.

He looked down at the spot where the entire lower half of his pant leg was black. There was even a hole in the center of the burn. "Oh that!" He slapped the pant leg as though putting flames out. "Something happened one day in the dryer. Not sure what. Everything was fine until I smelled smoke and darned if these weren't smoldering when I pulled them out."

My eyes bulged in disbelief. "Your dryer caught on fire?"

He shrugged. "Don't know, must have been temporary. I've been using it since and rarely smell smoke. It might be the wiring in the house I'm in. Kind of old. Breakers flip now and again. Not sure if that sparked something or what."

"Oh." I made a mental note not to attend any house parties in his neighborhood.

"Which ones did you get?" he asked.

I assumed he meant projects, so I handed him the folders. He looked them over carefully and chuckled a couple of times. "This power supply problem. Can you imagine? They sell the customer two power supplies in case one fails, but if you unplug one, the whole machine shuts off, even with the other one still working. I can't believe Jacques is giving you this. We're not supposed to take any more cases relating to Kronology."

"We're not? How did I get so lucky?" Jacques couldn't hate me; he didn't even know me yet.

Bill shrugged. "Oh, Jacques has some sort of hero complex. He thinks he can deliver where other managers failed. He's also friends with one of the guys that works at Kronology."

"Oh...dear."

"There really isn't much hope," Bill confided. "We get lots of customers asking us to be the liaison to Kronology because the poor suckers have tried everything and can't get the Kronology junk to work. The problem is, we can't help them because Kronology equipment is so bad. We end up having trouble getting paid because we can't get Kronology to deliver fixes. Arnold, my boss, won't touch a Kronology case. It makes the bottom line look bad. Arnold is a numbers man. He doesn't believe in taking on high odds."

Having met Arnold with his smudged glasses, I could believe it. He probably carried a calculator inside his pocket protector. "If Jacques has such a good friend there, why can't he get this buddy of his to pressure Kronology to fix the stuff?"

"Those guys couldn't code "hello world" without screwing it up. Summer interns have better programming skills than most Kronology engineers." Bill shrugged. "That's why I work for Arnold. He tends to assign work that can be fixed and that makes *me* look good!" He let loose a deep laugh. It echoed worse than Becky's boom. If the two of them ever laughed at the same time, they would either cancel each other out or take down the whole building.

"So what customers are you working with?" I prepared to memorize his answer and compare it to Huntington's list.

He looked up from the file and set it down before rubbing his rather large belly. In a few years when his hair went white, he would make a nice Santa Claus--if he got rid of the burned pants. "Oh, I work with them all, the banks, the local grocery store, whats-it-called, Bag'm Up, whatever. I've been in this industry so long, I'll work on most anything. Twenty years I've been in the computer industry."

"Wow, that's a long time." Only one specific name; not good enough.

"Yeah, and I made it through yet another layoff." He shook his bushy head sorrowfully. "I was sure glad they did the bulk of them in San Jose. There aren't too many jobs in Colorado, and I don't want to move."

I understood completely. The mountains had a way of working themselves into your heart. "When I left Strandfrost, I was surprised that there was even another decent-sized company in Denton."

Before I could turn the conversation back to his customers, he snapped his fingers. "Hey, I have one of those Kronology servers you need for that power supply testing. I sure don't need it anymore." He shuffled away still talking. "Over here, I think." He disappeared behind his row of equipment. The racks of computer equipment stopped just short of the ceiling and there were rows upon rows of the stuff. He could probably disappear for days before showing back up.

I kept on working, but sure enough, a few minutes later he lugged back a tower unit on wheels. "Ought to be almost exactly what the doctor ordered. We have it on loan from the Kronology office in Colorado Springs. Most of the companies lend out a bunch of equipment as long as we email them a copy of any test results. That way they can tell their customers their stuff works, but they don't have to test every single configuration."

"How convenient. Acetel doesn't have to spend as much money on equipment then. Do you have any of these HP or Dell boxes for my other test?" Even though neither of the systems had been on the list of equipment owned by Acetel, I knew how things got buried and lost in labs.

He scratched his large belly thoughtfully and wandered away again. I started setting up the power supply test and sent an email to Kronology to let them know about the problem and introduce myself. I had most of the equipment set up before Bill reappeared lugging a storage unit from HP.

"I don't know if this will really work with the Dell unit."

Digging in and having to find out if mixed equipment would work was why most computer companies didn't offer any support for competitor products. "Thanks. I appreciate the help."

I was almost finished with the first setup when my manager, Jacques, came into the lab. He wanted to talk about my career.

What followed was probably the most ridiculous meeting of my life. The guy had no less than fourteen computer survey forms for me to fill out. He had printed a copy of the directions. The first form involved hobbies, favorite places to eat and my idea of a great reward for work well done. How was I going to explain that a Mercedes was my top item? People in my position didn't command rewards with that kind of price tag.

"Do you think you can enter the information for these surveys by the end of the day? Each employee needs a performance plan so that I have something to grade against," he explained. "It will help me determine how much you've accomplished so that I can accurately assess the raise you deserve."

"The end of the day?" There was a huge list of something called, "core competencies" and a lot of other spaghetti words that managers liked to hide behind. If I didn't guess right when filling out responses to, "culture of excellence, being a customer advocate, and performing above the curve," Jacques would probably use it as an excuse to not give me a raise. From the one short example, it appeared that core competencies meant I had to be skilled in everything from fixing the copier to managing the company during flood, tornadoes and debilitating illnesses. "I'll work on it as soon as I get the first test in the lab running."

Blend, I told myself as I left. Blend.

So much for my dreams of a nice quiet job with lab work. So much for my dreams of going home on time.

It took me the rest of the morning and part of the afternoon to get my first test going. I then made good progress on Jacques' survey, but at three o'clock, we had an "all hands on deck," meeting because the CEO, A.J. Chambers, was in town to give an update.

The meeting room had a long table at the front end with a half podium on top. The room wasn't big enough to need a microphone, but it really wasn't large enough for the forty or so employees either. Several people were standing or crowded in along the walls.

A.J. wasn't a particularly tall man, but he wore a suit and tie while the rest of us were much more casual. For a CEO, he was soft-spoken and less forceful than I would have expected. Underneath the polish, there might have been a geek hiding; a guy that couldn't wait to see the next new cool gadget.

He gave a long-winded speech about how things were looking up for the industry and for Acetel in particular. When he was done, the CFO, Pete Saget, spoke. Where A.J. was bald, Pete had a full head of thick blond hair and the brash charm of a college quarterback. He showed us the earnings report and talked about how the next few quarters were going to be terrific. With the ease of a guy used to ignoring big bad defensive linemen, he managed to leave out the words "layoff" and "earnings miss" the entire speech.

I tried hard to pay attention to every little detail because I wouldn't be working here if the board didn't have some questions about how the company was losing so much money, but as far as I could tell most of the loss seemed to be due to the layoff itself. It looked to me like Acetel was writing off several million dollars. With that large of a deduction, it didn't leave much to steal.

It didn't seem as though tons of money were being wasted on equipment orders or perks. In fact, Bill had mentioned that the computer from Kronology hadn't even required payment by Acetel; a pretty slick deal if you could get companies to agree to lend equipment in return for shared results.

Pete meandered into a pep talk. "I know that times like these can be depressing when your friends are losing their jobs." He leaned forward on the table with the eagerness of a guy that wanted to win and take his team with him. "At times like these, the only way to succeed is to drive harder, to give work your all and not think about anything else. That's what I do. It's how I succeeded."

His concern was delivered sincerely and would have been overwhelmingly persuasive had he left out the self-serving part about working harder. While silence still reigned, I slanted my eyes around the room, but didn't know anyone well enough to gauge their reactions. No one looked ready to take up a war chant and follow him over a cliff. The general reaction seemed to be eyeballs studying the carpet.

Pete closed by inviting us to his vacation home at Twin Lakes for a combined Thanksgiving and Christmas party later in the month. "We need to come together as a team, and this is my way of letting you know that you *are* the team. It's a chance for the company to say thank you."

Hmm. All in all the meeting was a bit of a disappointment, but I suppose it would be too much to hope that management would blatantly stand up publicly and tell me why money was disappearing. If they knew, they wouldn't have hired Huntington.

The crowd surged through the doors, but I hung back long enough to hear Bill and a couple of the other lab technicians grumbling. I wandered closer.

Bill introduced me to Jacob Mohan and Vi Wu, but then continued with his earlier complaint. "Did you notice that neither A.J. nor Pete bothered to mention the management retention rewards?"

"What retention rewards?" I asked, as I followed them back to the lab.

Bill pulled on his shaggy beard and waved his arms around. "After the layoffs, A.J. claimed certain individuals might leave because the company situation could be considered 'risky.' He talked the stinking board into sending them a win--management got retention packages to the tune of ten percent of their salary if they agreed to stay at least a year."

"What? These guys got extra money for having to lay people off? How did they justify giving a bonus to managers that mismanaged themselves into a layoff situation in the first place?"

"When you're in charge, you don't have to justify anything! And then Pete sits and tries to tell us we're part of the team." Bill snorted. "Not the part that got the bonus!"

Jacob muttered, "And they voted us right out of a profit sharing check too."

Bill waved his arms some more and made a kicking motion towards one of the servers. He looked like an out of control Santa Claus that was having trouble getting the elves to make toys properly. "When you lay people off, that eats up all the profits! Why can't they give all of *us* a reward for doing the exact same work we were doing before the layoffs?"

I backpedaled out of the lab. It was time to call Huntington and leave him a message with an update. He needed to know about the computers being loaned to Acetel free of charge. Maybe someone was taking money out of the coffers and pretending to pay for the free loaners. I also thought he should know about the managers getting a retention bonus. If Huntington could figure out who was desperate enough to ask for a bonus during layoffs, it might turn out that the same person was slimy enough to bilk the company in other areas.

I called from behind the closed door of my office. Huntington was at his condo, and while he listened to my theories, he wasn't all that excited.

"It isn't illegal or even unusual to give out retention bonuses," he said. "It happens all the time."

"Well, it doesn't make it right, and what if it is part of a master plan to milk the company? Granting yourself a bonus during hard times doesn't seem all that moral."

"Sedona, you are the only person on this earth that would try to connect those two things," he bellowed in my innocent ear. "We are looking for something illegal here. Ethical or moral decisions made by the company don't enter into this. Even if it turns out that the same guy stealing from the company initiated the retention bonus, the only activity that is illegal is *stealing*."

"I know that! What I'm trying to tell you is that someone unethical in a gray area might not draw the line at flat out stealing."

"We can't investigate every single greedy person in the company! We'd be working on this case for years."

He had a point. "All right. But can you check with your accounting buddy on the computer loans to find out if equipment expense reports may have been padded?"

He grunted. I took that as a yes.

It was now almost six, and I had more than half of Jacques' survey to complete. I didn't want to think about my one-year, three-year and five-year goals. And why did the man need to know what I wanted said about me at my funeral? What kind of "career goal survey" asked that?

It only made sense if Jacques knew I worked for Huntington.

Five questions in, and I was really stumped. "How would you feel if your spouse remarried after your death?"

"Dead," I said to the wall. "I'd feel dead. Whether I was married or not."

Grimly determined, I worked at the report for another hour, when, to my blessed relief, the computer connection to the main server hung. "Thank God." I never worked through computer hangs. It provided the perfect excuse for quitting. Jacques could berate me endlessly, but it was too good an excuse to pass up.

Out of habit, I did reboot the machine, but saw with great happiness that the laptop still couldn't find the server. "Too bad."

I grabbed my blue backpack without bothering to stuff any work into it. The hall lights had already been dimmed. There wasn't another soul around. So much for motivating the troops. All the pep talks in the world didn't make people want to work their butts off if the reward was going to be a short walk to the door.

I opened the stairwell door, happy to be headed home. Because the lights were off, I didn't notice the arm until it grabbed mine.

"Aaa--" Before I could do more than open my mouth to scream, I was dragged forward and enveloped, face-first, in a huge bear hug.

The door to the hallway, and freedom, clanged shut behind me.

Chapter 10

Frantic to escape, I stomped down hard with my left foot, but missed. "Mhnung!" A hand pushed the back of my head into a muscled chest to keep my scream muffled.

"Shhh," someone breathed in my ear. "I need your help."

As calming phrases go, it wasn't a bad one. I'd have felt better if whoever had me let me put my feet down, but after I tried stomping, he must have decided it was too dangerous. I settled for twisting my head so that my face wasn't stuffed into his t-shirt.

His hand let up enough for me to raise my face.

Mark was smarter than his brother Steve about some things. I only had to tackle Mark once before he learned about my impulsive no-flight-always-fight stupidity. After seeing me panic once, he knew it was better to control any reaction with brute force if necessary. "Mark!"

He eased my feet back onto the floor. I glared at him, but he was busy listening and looking around to make sure the stairwell was empty. Finally certain no one else was around, he grinned down at me, his teeth flashing white. "You're cute when you're mad," he whispered.

"Leggo!" I muttered back, threatening with the one word to get loud. "What're you doing here?" I knew Steve had attached himself to the board of directors similar to the way he had at Strandfrost. I hadn't known what part Mark might be playing in the whole scheme.

Mark smiled again, stepping back enough that I could see his white t-shirt and dark jeans more clearly. "I work here. Only there was a little mishap in the lab just now. I think I knocked the computer system down."

"So?" I should probably thank him since it appeared he was the reason I was getting to leave before nine o'clock.

"Won't it be obvious to someone when they come in that I was tampering?"

I narrowed my eyes at him. He hadn't let me go completely. His hands were resting on my arms, holding me gently in place.

I finally answered. "Yeah. But the IT guy will be on call so he'll get paged and come in and fix it." I certainly didn't want to spend a lot of time making it work again. For one, I didn't get paid that kind of money and for two, once I knew it was back up, someone might think I should finish my report.

Mark swiveled me towards the stairs leading down. I dug my feet in. He sighed. "I haven't exactly started working here on the payroll," he clarified. "I would rather the IT guy not find out that I tripped the power in the locked room with all the company computers. I switched the power back on, but it doesn't seem to have brought the computers up properly."

I swung around and gaped at him. "You. Don't…work here yet?" Was I about to be fired for consorting with a burglar?

He flashed his beautiful smile again. "You could always tell them you did it."

I wasn't sure, but I had a feeling I did not want to get caught inside this building with Mark. Something told me that he could lie himself out of the Queen of England's jewelry room, and I would be the one left looking guilty. With as much dignity as I could muster, I marched down the stairs.

We both checked the hallway before exiting the stairwell.

At the lab door, I badged us inside. He stopped, removed the cover from the back of the badge reader and disconnected a wire, disabling it. The door wouldn't open from the outside with the reader disconnected, not without a key. I closed my eyes. I did not want to witness this.

At the very back of the lab there was a series of locked doors. I hadn't asked what was back there, but apparently it was where Acetel had its own servers for company business.

Someone had moved a lab bench near the locked door. The ceiling tile above the door was missing. The open cavity contained a large crawl space with air ducts, cables, and support beams.

"Let me guess," I said dryly. "You didn't have a key."

He shrugged. "How much time do we have? No one can get past the badge reader at the moment, but there are ways around that, and I would rather no one find it out of commission if we can help it."

It was pretty obvious that he knew all about getting around readers and locks. I looked at my watch. It was almost seven-thirty, too early for anyone to be in bed. I had no idea where the IT guy lived or what his habits were. Mr. IT would know that by seven or eight o'clock no one critical was likely to be accessing the network so he wouldn't have to hurry. If he was eating dinner, we probably had another hour. If he wasn't, then it depended on how far away he lived.

Mark got tired of waiting for my answer. He put his hands around my waist and boosted me onto the bench. I grabbed his head even though he was plenty strong enough to keep me steady without my help. "Just take hold of that bar and swing over," he instructed. "Or do you need another boost up?" He had one leg up on the bench and was getting closer by the second.

I grabbed the rail. He put one hand on my butt and the other on my leg and very helpfully kept me steady and going in the right direction. He didn't abandon me either. His hand strayed down my thigh and stayed there until the last possible moment. "Stop that!" I hissed back at him. I was breathing hard. The jump up hadn't really taken all that much energy.

He laughed in a whisper. Instead of sounding diabolical, it was darkly sexy as if he knew I was struggling to keep my voice even. I crawled away fast, and lowered myself into the room using one of the computer racks to climb down. There were three separate rows of computer cabinets housing various storage and networking equipment. Company equipment was always kept separate from the lab equipment. Otherwise, someone might accidentally destroy real data by using the wrong piece of equipment.

Mark had already unlocked the doors to the server cabinets. Almost all computer racks by a single vendor used the same key--which was given to all customers--so requiring a key at all was pretty silly.

I figured out the server problem almost immediately. Whatever he had been doing with the electricity had tripped the surge protectors and shut down each cabinet. When he restored power, the trips didn't reset. Even if he had reset them manually, the external storage had to be powered up first, then the switches and last the servers. I had to hunt for the various switches to manually turn off certain equipment until I wanted it powered on.

"Can you fix it?" he asked.

"Almost through." A thought occurred to me. "I can't necessarily get the servers back up and communicating. I don't have the password. But I can make it less obvious that you were here." I glanced up at the ceiling tile.

He must have agreed about the other, more obvious signs of tampering, because he left me alone to finish my work while he went and erased signs of our entry. I was guessing the door wasn't locked on this side because he went out that way and left it propped open so that he could get back in easily.

I was just about done when he appeared at my side like a ghost with a big dog chasing him. "Eek!" He put a hand over my mouth and gently dragged me backwards. Automatically I struggled, nearly capsizing us both as he tried to shove me behind the last row of racks.

"Sedona, for God's sake." He grabbed me around the waist and squeezed all the air out of me. I finally heard the key in the outer door and stopped wiggling. That, and his hands were starting to grab at things better left alone.

We were both breathing hard, but the machines made a lot of noise. It was very warm wedged behind the last row of cabinets. The disk drives generated an incredible amount of heat.

If the IT guy came back here, I was hoping Mark had a plan other than the current one, which appeared to be smashing me through the wall.

He must have been worrying about the same thing. In order to talk without being heard, he tucked his head next to mine. He skimmed my jaw, and I could feel him breathing against my neck and ear just before he whispered, "Will he come back here?"

Hot as it was, I got goose bumps all up and down my arms.

I shook my head back and forth and eased up on my tiptoes to answer him. The only way I could keep my balance was to brace my hands against his white t-shirt and hold on. "Shouldn't. Already reset."

He stayed in that position, holding me against the wall with his body, my hands over his heart.

I could hear cursing as someone rolled the chair that was in front of the main rack of servers. The IT guy had to be wondering what caused the machines to all lose power and then come back on. Just as I had done seconds ago, the guy went around checking the power at the front of the other cabinets. I knew they were fine. I was hoping he wouldn't have to come around to the back. I panicked for a minute when I couldn't remember if all the power indicators were in the front of the cabinets or if some were in the back.

With relief, I heard the chair again and then some distant typing.

It was really very, very warm in the back with all the hot air blowing and no room for daylight between Mark and myself. I was starting to have trouble breathing. He tilted my head sideways and practically nibbled on my ear in order to ask, "Doing okay?"

The whisper of touch had the effect of an electrical current. My toes tingled. So did my fingers. I told myself it was just poor circulation due to lack of oxygen. I breathed out some kind of unintelligible answer to his question. I would have nodded, but I didn't dare move.

The typing went on for almost twenty minutes. I was about to pass out when I felt more than heard the door open and close. Mark held up a hand and cocked his ear towards the door. "Will he come back?"

I shrugged and started to wiggle. "Who cares! I'm gonna pass out in a second if I don't get some air."

He stared down at my futile attempts to move him. He squeezed my waist. "Keep wiggling like that and you won't have any need for air," he muttered, his lips bending dangerously near mine.

I stilled instantly, but he didn't move away. He held me frozen in his grip, staring down at me intently. His hand moved from my waist to my face, and he caressed my bottom lip with his thumb. It was the first time I realized I was panting. "It's probably a good thing I haven't really cleared you with Steve yet."

I had no idea what he was talking about. I was breathing hard enough, and we were close enough that he could feel my breasts struggling to expand with each breath against his chest.

"Man, are you ever going to be a problem," he swore.

Without another word, he shoved himself away and disappeared around the row of machines. Without his hold, I almost fell flat. I was dizzy enough that I considered crawling, but figured I had made enough of a fool of myself.

By the time I reached the front of the room, he had the door open and was checking the lab. "Hurry! You can be found in the lab. You belong here."

He grabbed my arm when I was close enough and pushed me through. I plopped down on the nearest chair.

I rested there, trying to regain my breath and sanity. With no warning, the IT guy came back around a row of machines. I shrieked.

The poor guy jumped high enough that he could have actually dislocated the ceiling tiles again. "Aggh!" he yelled right back at me.

"Eeee!" I shouted a second time.

He stumbled back a few steps. Wildly I looked around for Mark, but he had vanished as if he had never been there. "What...what are you doing here?" I asked stupidly.

"What are *you* doing here?" Maybe I had been wrong about the guy not being in bed this early, because unless he always walked around with his longish brown hair standing on end and dressed haphazardly, he had to have been sleeping. His jeans came complete with holes, and he wore a large jacket over a very wrinkled flannel shirt.

"Working," I guessed after a significant delay.

"Oh." He blinked. "Me too. Is the server back up?"

I shrugged. "It was down a bit ago."

"I know. That's why I'm here."

I stood up. He shoved his hands in his pockets, put his head down and went for the security door housing the company servers. If Mark had gone back in, I let him get caught. I was getting out while I could still walk.

Chapter 11

When I was in high school, my parents tried once and only once to pick my friends. I did not like the prissy, straight-A, always volunteering girl they chose for me. I was told to like her anyway, right up until she was arrested for "cruising" up and down Main Street with an open container in the car. She was sixteen.

This job Huntington had picked for me was a lot like being told how to choose friends. Normally, nothing in this world short of food rationing, gas rationing and near starvation would convince me to eat in a company cafeteria. It wasn't just that I liked good food, it was that no one with a life actually sat in a dreary cafeteria eating leftover pizza cured and mummified under a heat lamp.

There is only one reason to get food in the cafeteria and that is because you have to work during lunch. As far as I can tell, there is absolutely no good reason to *eat* the lunch in the dining area. Like being seen in a psychiatrist's office, you have to make up an excuse for being there.

But Huntington had this bizarre idea that I had to make friends in as short a time as possible and that meant trolling various parts of the building, including the cafeteria.

I wandered through the line, inspecting each selection. "I'm going to starve on this job." Eyes watched me, I could feel them. I turned around.

It was my IT buddy from the night before. He tossed an orange one-handed into the air while staring in my direction. The same ragged jeans tried not to fall off his skinny frame. They were topped with a different shirt, but the same denim jacket. As soon as he noticed me notice, he put his head down and got in the checkout line. I knew he wanted to look back, so I stared hard at the back of his head.

Following his lead, I grabbed an orange and a greenish banana. Forget Huntington's ideas. If I had to stay in for lunch, I was going to sneak in takeout. Getting in line so quickly put me right behind the IT guy.

When it was his turn at the register, he turned enough to watch me through his long, dark bangs. His eyes were mostly hidden, but they flicked in my direction more than once. He was making me nervous.

"I see you got the server back up last night," I said.

He jumped, almost as high as when I had startled him in the lab. "Uh, yeah." He scrabbled away and then stopped, just as I was finished paying a ridiculous three dollars for two pieces of fruit.

"If I bring back the peelings, can I get a partial refund?" I complained.

"No, ma'am," the checkout woman replied, giving me my two bucks worth of change.

"For three bucks, maybe I'd better eat the peelings."

I think IT smiled behind the hair. "Uh, you got a second? I wanted to ask you a question."

I stopped, holding my fruit rather awkwardly. "I guess so. But do you mind if we go by the lab? I gotta make a phone call and see if I can get some Chinese ordered in here."

He shifted his feet awkwardly. "Uh, you're not supposed to do that."

There went my meek, get along with everyone act. But I was *hungry*. Huntington said I had to be nice and not get fired, but he didn't say I had to starve! "I'll meet them in the parking lot if I have to." I marched towards the lab, wondering what IT guy could possibly want. Had he seen Mark? Did he think I had shut off his stupid machines? I knew Mark was going to leave me holding the bag--or in this case the power cord.

Getting madder by the second, I stomped to my area of the lab and pulled up the phone number for Happy Family Chinese off the internet. All the while, IT stood in the background, watching and peeling his orange.

I ordered enough stuff from Happy Family that they recognized my voice. "No, I work at Acetel now." I gave them the address and said, "I'll meet Deke in the parking lot." Their eighteen-year old son did all the deliveries. I glanced back at orange-peeler and noted again how skinny he was. "You want something?"

He kind of shrugged. "Uh..."

Social skills of a computer nerd. "Do you like chicken, beef, or shrimp?"

"Yeah."

"Throw in a combination fried rice," I said into the telephone. "Okay. Twenty minutes. Front door. I'll be there."

I hung up. "The rice is seven bucks. I throw in a three dollar tip, but I'm already tipping them so you could get by with the seven."

He shrugged again. "Ok." He was looking around now, sort of swinging his head back and forth, trying to see around his hair. For some reason he didn't just reach up and push it away from his eyes.

It took me a minute to comprehend his problem. "Oh, sticky hands." I handed him a tissue from my box.

He wiped them off, pushed his hair back and walked away without another word.

The guy reminded me of Turbo, only he was younger. He moved in fits and starts, didn't say much and went about his business in a manner that a lot of people might find strange. Most people wouldn't walk away in the middle of a conversation while waiting on Chinese with no explanation whatsoever. Because I was used to dealing with Turbo, I understood that this guy had processed the likely timing of events and re-prioritized his actions. Like Turbo, he had seen no need to explain himself.

I shrugged and peeled the banana. I was too hungry to wait for the Chinese.

When the IT guy came back he handed me a ten. I reached in my pocket and gave him the two bucks I had just gotten from the cafeteria.

"Keep the whole thing for the tip," he said generously. "Is this place any good?" He noticed me devouring my banana like a starving elephant.

"Uh-huh." I pulled a tissue free and wiped my hands. "What did you want to talk to me about?"

Instead of answering my question, he asked, "Want to walk outside and wait?"

He probably didn't want to ask me questions where the other lab technicians could overhear. Rats. I had been hoping he wasn't going to pin me on the previous night, but what else could it be?

It was cold out, so I grabbed my jacket, made sure I had a twenty to pay Deke, and started walking and thinking. IT trailed along behind me like a shadow, hugging the wall and incorrectly thinking he could somehow manage to look inconspicuous.

He certainly wasn't invisible, skinny though he was. In his hoodlum attire and ragged hair, he was not ever likely to go unnoticed. His large tennis shoes were quiet on the carpeted floor, but one of them was untied and every once in a while the lace would hit the wall with an audible snap.

Once outside, we stood near the door to stay out of the wind.

"I, uh, I was wondering if you saw anyone in the lab when you went in there last night," he asked.

I thought about it. Well, I knew the answer. I was actually trying to think of what to tell him. "I dunno. I got down there after the computer was down. I was gonna check on my tests before I went home."

He nodded and crammed his hands into his pockets. His denim jacket wasn't very heavy, and it was cold out. "You got there just after the servers went down though. I was thinking maybe you saw someone leaving or something."

I glanced over at him in surprise. How did he know exactly when I got there? He flipped his hair back, and I caught sight of eyes that were a murky green, kind of hazel. It didn't take long for me to stare him down. "How do you know that?"

He shuffled his feet. "I got paged."

"Yeah," I said slowly, "you got paged when the servers went down. But how would you know that I went in the lab after the equipment went down and not before?"

He stopped shuffling and froze in place like a statue. Deke showed up just then, but it didn't derail my train of thought. Unless there were cams in the lab, and I was pretty sure there weren't, there was only one other mechanism by which the IT guy could have known the time I entered. He would have had to break into the computer database that kept records of badge use. Every employee at Acetel had a uniquely-coded badge. Every time the badge was used, like to get into the lab, the name and time of the entry was sent to a secure database. The company could use the database to track employee movement in case of equipment thefts or other mishaps. As an employee, IT guy shouldn't even know where the records were kept, never mind who had entered or exited.

After paying Deke and scurrying back inside, I led the way to the cafeteria, stopping at the soda machine for a couple of drinks. My IT buddy followed even more reluctantly than he had on the way out. I sat down and pulled out his rice. He grabbed it and started to walk away without another word.

"Hey, wait. Um..." I had never asked his name. "What did you say your name was?"

"I didn't." He kept walking so I had to raise my voice.

"I didn't think so," I replied, taking a bite of my beef and vegetables. "But I do believe you were about to tell me how you got access to the list that shows who has gone into the lab and what time they were there."

He stopped. His shoulders didn't slump, but he hunched a bit.

Hey, it wasn't my fault. What did he think I was, an idiot? Okay, given his one encounter with me so far, I could see where his first impression might not have been completely flattering.

For a minute, I thought he might walk away, but he came back and sat down with a clunk. He opened his two boxes of rice and stared at them. I handed him a plastic fork.

"To answer your question, I didn't see anyone go in or out of the lab." I took another bite, pleased at my accuracy. I hadn't seen Mark go through any doors. He had come in behind me when we entered the lab. "Your food is getting cold. There might have been another guy in the lab." I pretended to think about it. "I'm new here so I don't know everyone, and I wasn't paying a lot of attention, you know?"

"But you're paying attention now." He stabbed the rice rather viciously.

I kept eating. "So," I said around a mouthful of food, "you thought you'd accuse me of turning your servers off because I was there?"

He shook his head. Once he got around to eating, he went at it pretty hard. "No, I said I knew you went into the lab after they were down. I didn't say you had been in the server room." He pushed the hair away and stared at me.

I had been so pleased at catching him in a no-no, I hadn't thought very carefully about my words. "Uh...yeah, I guess that's true."

"What did the guy look like?"

"Why? I told you I don't know who it was."

"Maybe I know him. And then I can ask him how he got in the lab without a badge and how he then got in the server room."

His questions gave me a reason to turn my brain back on and fast. I hadn't thought about Mark getting in the lab. He obviously didn't have a badge. When I was with him, he had followed me back in. My badge would be the only one showing up in any database. I chewed slowly.

"Well?" he prompted.

"Mhm," I replied around my food. IT man was already more than half done with the fried rice order. He showed no signs of slowing down either. Unbelievable. No way could I eat an entire order of fried rice from Happy Family. The stuff was good, but they were generous with the portions. "Wow. Were you hungry or what?"

He looked down as he emptied the last of the cartons and shrugged. "It's good. I'd eat there again."

"Yeah, but geez. I'd make myself sick if I ate like that." I knew that from real life experience, and I hadn't even eaten the whole order.

He didn't look too sick or too concerned.

I swallowed my bite and drank some of my soda. "He had dark hair. A white t-shirt." I vividly remembered the t-shirt. I had been smashed against it for several minutes. "What makes you think he did something to the computers?"

"They were shut down."

"Maybe they just went down. That happens a lot to computers."

He shook his head stubbornly. "One of them maybe, but not all of the racks, all at the same time."

I couldn't think of a good reason for the entire system to go down either. "Overheated?"

"Nah, if that happens, it sets a flag so I can always tell. Besides, they still wouldn't have all shut down at the exact same time. It looked like the things got switched off from the main power surge protector or the electricity glitched or something. But none of the test servers in the outer lab suffered from an electrical glitch." He fiddled with the leftover boxes. "What I can't figure out is why? I mean, if I hack into something, say a database with badge reader information, I have a reason. Is the guy just a loser with nothing better to do or what?"

"You mean someone screwing with you personally?"

He nodded. "To make me have to drag my ass back in here at seven or eight o'clock."

"Has it happened before?" Who knew how long Mark had been at his task. Shoot, both Huntingtons could have been working on this for a couple of months before getting me involved.

"Nah. This was the first time. Most people are glad to not have to deal with the servers, but this place is kind of weird. They hired a dude to work here on the IT stuff. I was only supposed to work in San Jose, but the troll here can barely manage to find his office each morning, if that. Half the time he can't even create new users when we get new employees. I'm always having to fix his mistakes. But who else would even care?"

"Got that right." Most sane people did not want to be involved in running a network. It was way too much work. "Maybe I can tell you if I see the guy again. The lights were already on save power so they were dimmed. I didn't turn the main lights on in the lab back when I went in, so I didn't really get a good look at him."

IT stared at me through his hair for a long time. "You walked in a half dark room at night, saw a guy standing around and didn't pay much attention at all, huh?"

I stopped chewing. Okay, only a blooming idiot would do that, and it would be especially stupid of a lone female. No wonder the guy didn't think I'd catch on to his hacking. One minute I was a genius, the next, a duck waddling into a shooting gallery. "It wasn't my best night."

"Yeah," he agreed, picking up his trash. "You didn't look so good when I saw you." He threw his stuff away on the way out.

Brilliant. I had very effectively moved myself back to suspect numero uno. Mark would be so pleased.

Chapter 12

I was very late getting to work the next morning. When the phone on my desk rang, I was hoping it wasn't Jacques. Strangely, answering it didn't help me figure out who was calling.

"What am I going to do?" a voice whispered in my ear.

"About what? Who is this?"

"Me," the voice whispered. "I have to tell work, and I'm worried that they will ask me to quit."

"Me who?" I was having trouble imagining anyone I knew that would be worried about getting fired. Someone from Strandfrost? Maybe management was going after other people besides me. "Is this Sally?"

"Sally who?" the voice forgot to whisper.

The light went on. "Brenda?"

"Shhh! Don't tell anyone." Her voice instantly went back to the quieter, more breathless quality.

"What is wrong? Who is trying to fire you?" Brenda's job at Crestwood Hospital should have been relatively secure. For one, she was a good nurse and nurses were always in short supply and two, what could she have possibly done to get herself in trouble? Cooked for a patient? Brought them her leftovers?

"The nursing supervisor is a total hag. I mean, we all have to sub for each other, and she isn't going to like it when she finds out! She won't be able to put me on call. If I'm not on call like the others, they'll hate me too. How long before you think I should tell?"

I was at a total loss. "Tell *what*?"

"You know," she whispered. "The secret."

"The secret." Maybe she had cooked a meal for a patient and killed the guy. "What secret?" I was worried that she was going to ask me to cart a body away.

There was a long pause. She had either set the phone down or even worse, she was coming up with more coded words for me to decipher.

"Sean told you, and you dropped off the chocolate."

"Oh." I hadn't known it was a secret. "Why would they fire you because you're pregnant? Good heavens. Brenda, in case you haven't noticed, your husband is a lawyer. I'm pretty sure no one--"

"They could make me do desk work."

"You mean as opposed to working with patients?"

"Exactly." Her voice squeaked and then ended with a miserable sniffling.

"But why wouldn't they let you work with the patients?"

"The chief of staff is Doctor Johnson, and he is really old. He's always talking about how things used to be. I heard him mention when Alice was expecting that pregnant women didn't work in his day."

"Didn't work or didn't have to work?"

"It doesn't matter," she wailed. "He's overly protective, and I don't think he likes me, and I'm due for a promotion too. I've been taking extra care classes. I'm very close to finishing. If I don't get promoted, I won't have as much say in picking vacation, and what if they put me on nights or something because it's quieter?"

"Brenda, I don't think it's legal to remove you from your current duties because you're pregnant. And I'm certain they have to promote you if you've earned it. Have you talked to Sean about this?"

"I thought you of all people would understand! I don't want to get the promotion because they are afraid of Sean. What if they find out I'm pregnant and promote me just because of that?"

I had thought I was following the problem pretty well, but obviously I was wrong. "Wait a minute. I thought you were worried that if you told, you wouldn't get promoted. Now you're saying if you tell, you think you'll be promoted and that worries you because you'll never know if you deserved it or not?"

"Exactly! And they moved Alice to nights because it was quieter. It was a long time ago, and she got her job back, but my God! I can't go through that!"

I still wasn't certain I understood the problem. Actually it sounded like she had more than one worry. "What exactly do you want me to do to help?"

"I need you to help me with the presentation."

"The presentation?"

"How do I tell my supervisor? I have to convince her that the pregnancy won't interfere with my job duties, and that I'm still going to finish my classes. I want her to know that I deserve the promotion, but not because of Sean!"

"Why don't you tell her like you just told me?"

"Oh, no way will she promote me then. She'll justify leaving me where I am because of the time I have to take off for the pregnancy. She'll say she has to have an extra nurse helping me because I'm pregnant. Sure, they won't phrase it that way, but they'll get another nurse. Then when it's review time, *bam*, she'll tell me she had to get extra help! I know she agrees totally with Johnson on this. I heard her call another pregnant nurse a slacker."

"Well--"

"And she was," Brenda interrupted. "I mean, Cassandra was totally milking being pregnant, but I'm not like that. I get a little more tired now, but it isn't as though anything has changed. I'm thinking of not saying anything for a few more weeks. What do you think? You're a career woman, what would you do?"

My mind almost stopped working. I didn't want to think about being pregnant, and my career such as it was, did not need any additional risk factors. "I guess I would just tell them. Maybe the sooner you tell them, the more time they'll have to schedule, and the nicer they will be."

"Or if I tell them later, the less time they'll have to plot against me. Maybe I should wait until I get promoted."

"That would work," I agreed in relief. "When is that?"

"Reviews are in about three months."

I didn't even need a calculator for that. "Brenda, aren't you on the fourteenth week? You work in a hospital. You're telling me that no one is going to notice before you're six months pregnant?"

"It won't be fourteen weeks until the end of this week so I'm really only at thirteen."

I closed my eyes and pictured her dainty frame. "You're going to have to tell them before that, Brenda. Even if you worked with engineers like I do, they would notice a six-month pregnant woman."

"Maybe they'll think I've gained weight."

"You *will* have gained weight." I pictured my friend Suzy at six months. She had been huge. Totally huge. "It will be very, very obvious by that time."

"I'll never get the promotion! This is so unfair!"

I was pretty sure bringing Sean into the mix again wasn't the right answer. "Brenda, maybe you can tell your supervisor's supervisor and explain that you're worried about the promotion."

"Are you kidding me? If I go around my supervisor, they'll fire me! Could you get away with that? Oh, you're so lucky. At least in engineering no one would try and say a pregnancy affected your job. All you have to do is think. They can't say it affects your ability to give out medications and be on your feet all day."

I was pretty sure that most engineering managers didn't like it when a woman informed them a project schedule might be affected due to maternity leave. In desperation, I suggested, "Look, why don't we get together later, and we can talk about it a bit more?"

"Oh, could we? I know you've been through this with your friend, and I don't know what to do! How about you come to the next ultrasound? You'll get to see the baby and everything! Oh no, wait. The next one isn't until nineteen weeks and we're going to find out the sex of the baby. Sean is going with me."

My eyes crossed. "We can make it some other time." I was very certain I didn't want to sit through an appointment with Brenda. Every doctor's office I'd ever been to required patients to sit half naked in a room for thirty minutes, all for the pleasure of being eyed, poked at and asked a bunch of nosy personal questions. Sitting through such an ordeal with any pregnant woman, let alone my sister-in-law, was not on my list of fun things to do in life.

"Let me check my work schedule. I'll call you tonight and we can set a time to get together!"

"Sure."

After I hung up, I thought about looking on the web for advice on how to handle pregnant women. Instead, I sent Suzy an email and asked her opinion on the whole when and how to tell one's boss.

Sheesh. It didn't seem worth getting pregnant.

Talking with Brenda almost made me late to a meeting. Every Thursday the managers met with the engineers to go over projects and various company business. I was eager to attend because all the current project names would be mentioned. I should easily be able to verify the names on Huntington's list.

On my way to the meeting, I saw my IT buddy in the hallway, but instead of going to the meeting, he went the other way. Everyone else appeared to be in the meeting; the technicians, the managers and a bunch of engineers that I hadn't met yet.

Jacques, my illustrious boss, got up and gave a rundown on his projects. He tapped his leg with a highlighter as he talked. The nervous tapping provided an obvious clue as to how his pants ended up with pen marks. Jacques introduced me and then listed my first assignments. When he mentioned the Kronology project, Arnold, the other manager, actually laughed out loud.

Not surprisingly, when it was Arnold's turn to talk, he adjusted his smarmy glasses and went on at great length about his projects and responsibilities. The man actually charted his projects against those of the other managers, including managers in San Jose. Mind you, it wasn't a chart showing his success rate, it was simply the number of projects he was handling. "If any of you have slack time, let me know. I have," he pretended to stop and consider, "at least four companies I could bring on board if I had more people."

Vi, the other female technician I had met, leaned over and whispered, "This is the same reorganization speech he gave to A.J. and Pete a few days ago. He wants to hire more people."

Since Arnold was now glaring in our direction, I raised my hand to ask a question. "Which companies are you currently working with?" Okay, maybe it was a too obvious dig for information, but his chart didn't tell me anything I needed to know.

"The names?" he asked. I heard a couple of groans, and Bill actually made a snoring noise before burying his furry face in his hands. Arnold looked so delighted, I thought he might break out in song. "I happen to have that in another presentation. Let me see..." he worked at his laptop for a moment and then pulled up some more slides. Within seconds, the company names were displayed on the wall. "Now, here we have the breakdown by size of company, the type of account, the length of time they've been a customer, which as you can see," out came a spiffy laser pointer, "the longer they have been with us, the more they spend." On to another slide. "Here is the group overall," the laser made little circling motions. "And this is my group."

His chart showed the amount of money his group pulled in versus Jacques' group and three other groups in San Jose. "San Jose has a lot more customers because the company started there, but it turns out that my concentration is extremely profitable."

I was dismayed that he had skipped quickly over the slide that named his specific customers, but he generously announced, "I've sent this presentation out before, but I'll send an update." He also told us where to find the write-ups and case files for his group. He took the time to name the engineers who had helped solve the problems, including Bill. The shaggy man beamed and took a bow, albeit with his hand only, since we were all sitting.

When the meeting was over, I glimpsed my IT buddy again as I went back to my office. Maybe he had been around all along, and I hadn't noticed him, but it was doubtful. Despite what I had claimed about not taking note of a man in a darkened computer room, I tended to be watchful of who was around me. I would have remembered a slinking, long-haired scrappy individual peering around corners and over the tops of lab machines.

When in doubt, go to the source to find your enemy. Since that failed because whenever I spotted him, he scurried away, I went to Becky. "Hi Becky."

"Howdy missy!" She snapped her mirror shut. "How y'all doing? When are we doing lunch again?"

"Uh...fine. Who is our IT guy?"

"You having trouble with the damn boxes?" She smacked the stand of her computer screen. Something fizzed.

I winced. "Well, I think so."

"It's Art. You know, he used to be a hair stylist. Offered to do my hair, but can you imagine? I mean, I have my days and once, to be nice, I let him tease it back into place, but what if he butchered it with scissors right here in the office?" She fluffed her hair with bright red fingernails. "As if."

I liked to think of myself as open-minded. I've worked with a lot of computer geeks over the years and happened to think of myself as one. I knew guys that looked like they slept in a subway station, but coded six ways to Sunday, spoke flawless French and collected fine wines. Even knowing that the range of geek hobbies had no boundaries, even knowing my best geek buddy Turbo was known in certain circles for his rare antique gun collection, I was having trouble tying Art-the-hairdresser to the IT guy I had run into.

"Here, lemme call him for you," Becky volunteered, already mid-dial. "I gotta tell you though...this guy...I dunno if he can help you. Every time my computer locks up, it takes him two days to re-install the operating system."

"What?" I reached over and hit the hang-up button. "No, no, that's okay. I...he does all the IT? By himself?" If his solution for every problem was re-installation, maybe that was where all the extra money was going that Huntington was looking for. It would certainly waste time, if not money.

"If I really need help, I call Bill or Vi. This isn't a large office, you know? There's only about forty of us here even when we have contractors. Art does all the installs. He would be the one that did your computers, unless you did them yourself."

I had done my own installs, so I hadn't met any IT person officially. "Does he run the servers? The mail servers that connect us to San Jose and stuff like that?"

She looked blank. "I guess." Then a light went on and she snapped her fingers. "Oh wait, I know who you're talking about! There's some guy they sent from San Jose to handle an important data install. What is his name?" She thought pretty hard, but it didn't come to her. "Hang on. Lisa will know."

The San Jose part matched what the guy had said to me at lunch, so when she picked up the phone again to call Lisa, I didn't protest.

There was a long chat about a lot of things, but somewhere in there, she got another name. Without bothering to hang up, she put her hand over the mouthpiece. "Jonathan Taylor. She says he's a guru." Becky wiggled her eyebrows in a sign of respect and warning. Gurus were mystery people. They might prefer to work late into the night, or instead of regular holidays, they might take two weeks off for an internet gaming tournament. But they were guys that the company needed because it was their mysterious skills that kept the magic computers going.

"Jonathan." The guru part sounded right, and so did San Jose. "Thanks."

She nodded at me as I departed.

At least next time I saw Mr. IT, I could yell out his name, and he could officially ignore me.

When I got back to the lab, I had to perform the power supply testing on the Kronology case. There were two power cords that plugged into separate wall sockets. Only one cord was needed at any time. Thus if one were unplugged, tripped over or just stopped working, the other cord would still be plugged in and would keep electricity flowing. In theory.

In this case, after I started everything and unplugged one cord, the whole contraption shut down. The other cord was still plugged in, but the computer died as though I had unplugged them both.

I filled out the report. Jacques could submit the paperwork to Kronology, and we would act as liaison with the company to get it fixed. Then I'd have to test the fix and get it into the hands of the original customer who had reported the problem and asked us to help get it fixed. At least that is what was supposed to happen. Bill had already warned me not to expect much.

I was finishing the write-up when a short guy walked briskly into the lab. He came straight toward my workbench. "I hear you are having trouble with your unit. I'm trained for the productivity units." He laced stubby fingers together, stretched his arms and flexed his hands backwards. "Someone has to keep this company up and running."

I stared at him in amazement. His eyebrows were faded or plucked, I couldn't tell which. Black pants flared at the bottom, and his shirt-sleeves had extremely wide cuffs. He didn't look much older than my own twenty-six years, but his hair was silver at the temples and a very unnatural black everywhere else.

"You must be Art." He could be no one else. His belt buckle was a square LED. The name "Art" flashed, followed by the words, "On Call."

He nodded and stuck out his stubby hand. "Excellent. You've heard of me?" He gave new meaning to the word "preen."

I tried for a smile and shook his hand. "I'm not really having problems with any units."

"Oh? Are you sure? I can take a look anyway."

"No, I'm sure."

"I don't think I set your machine up. Maybe I should look just in case."

Turning him down outright was probably rude, but I didn't see any other way out. "No, it's up and running fine." I decided to get out while the going was good so I stood, grabbed my paperwork and made my way around him.

He followed. "These things are finicky. I happen to have some time now. I don't remember installing yours--I do so many. You wouldn't believe how many I do. And I'm the EMT--Emergency Medical Technician--for the building too. I like emergency work, always trying to keep computers running and trying to keep people going too."

Me going in the stairwell instead of the elevator didn't stop him. I didn't have anything on my computer that he could damage in particular, but it did not need looking at.

"I do search and rescue on the weekends too, but I try not to be on call when I'm at church. My church has hiking for singles during the summer and skiing for singles in the winter. I hate to miss those, but of course if it's an emergency," he sighed and kicked one of the steps, "I tell them to call only if they *really* need me." He almost knocked me over when we reached the second floor and he tried to hold the door open for me. "Hey, are you single? Baptist by any chance?"

"Uh no."

My left hand was conveniently hidden under the stack of papers I was carrying. That did not deter Elvis-look-a-like. He continued walking with me, but bent over and peered under the stack. "Ah-ha, not Baptist, but single!" He snorted loud enough to attract a rhinoceros from the local zoo. "Can't fool me! I'm an engineer so don't be trying to put anything over on me."

My pinned-on smile faded to disbelief. I was going to demand a raise from Huntington.

By this time, we had reached my office. The guy made a beeline for the guest chair and plopped down. I stared at him without sitting.

"Do you want me to take a look at your system now?"

I continued to stare at him for a full thirty seconds. I borrowed this technique from Turbo. When you don't have anything nice to say, say nothing. Usually other people become uncomfortable enough that they leave. I moved away from the door and sat down, still without speaking.

It worked, but it took a lot longer than I would have liked.

"Well." He cleared his throat. "Well. You call me if you have any trouble." He got up, slicked back his longish black hair and meandered to the door. He stood there awkwardly. "Hey, I also do hair." He actually swung his own greasy mess in advertisement. "Do you need a cut? I'm not supposed to do it in the office." He leaned back in and took two steps forward in order to perch on the desk. "But I make exceptions. A lot of people don't have time to get a decent hair cut these days. And since I keep my license current it isn't really illegal. If you have, you know, an emergency."

I was beginning to fear this guy, with or without a pair of scissors. As he leaned toward me, I thought fearing him with a pencil was probably wise. "I really don't think so."

He nodded and looked longingly back at the guest chair. My phone rang. He started to leave and then waited in the doorway.

"Can you close it on your way out?" I asked through clenched teeth.

"Oh. Uh, sure." Slowly, he did so. I wasn't sure he actually moved on down the corridor afterward, but at least he was gone.

I answered the phone.

"Is he still there?" Even though Becky didn't identify herself, her drawl was easy to place.

"Who, Elvis?"

"I didn't mean to sic him on you, but I had to get him out of my office so I accidentally mentioned your problem. I mean, my God, A.J. is here this week! Just because they didn't lay anyone off from the Denton office doesn't mean they aren't looking for candidates. I can't afford to have, what did you call him? Elvis? Ha! I can't have him hanging around right now making me look bad!"

"Next time tell him I'm having a problem in Ohio and fly him there," I said.

"Ha!" she shrieked.

I jerked the phone away, but the damage was done. I had to switch ears.

"Did he fix anything?" she asked.

"No, but on the bright side, he didn't break anything either."

She laughed again. "I promise not to do it again. But if you see him in my office, can you come by with something you need me to do desperately? Pete is here too, and he's upset about something. He's in yelling at the managers right now. You can't leave Elvis under my feet. He'll get me fired. You have to swear on sisterhood you'll help me."

"Only if you do the same for me." If anyone got fired, it would probably be Elvis, not Becky, but you never could tell. There was no way of knowing the powers of Elvis and what trouble he might cause.

Chapter 13

I sent an email to Kronology describing the power supply problem, care of Craig Yumen. I could have stayed late again, but since I hadn't finished the survey Jacques had assigned me, I figured, what was one more day? Besides, at five-thirty in November in Colorado it is almost dark out. It felt late, even if it wasn't.

I was grateful that Acetel had bothered to install the slanted tin-roofs for covered parking because a light snow had fallen during the day. Without the roof, I would have been stuck even later clearing my windows.

From the mass of cars leaving the parking lot, no one else was dying to stay late either. I stopped to gawk at A.J. as he climbed into a sleek yellow 911 Turbo Porsche. I noticed the Porsche again thirty seconds later because a black Town Lincoln cut it off to wedge in behind my Honda as I pulled out of the lot.

Very few computer geeks drive big, black Town Lincolns with windows tinted to hide guns.

There was no way to know for certain if the Lincoln contained Huntington's friends from the restaurant, but who else would follow me? If they were random thugs, wouldn't they go after A.J. with his much more impressive car? I mean, if I were a thief, I would put aside whatever busywork I was supposed to be doing to steal that car.

I couldn't go home. I couldn't even go to Huntington's condo because that would mark me even more clearly as someone to watch in order to find him. When being followed, all women know to go to the police station. But not all women had a lawyer brother who buddied with several policemen, including Sean's best friend, Derrick. I wondered if the fire station would work, but I couldn't quite see myself convincing a bunch of firemen to hose down the Lincoln to give me time to escape.

Filled with frustration and not just a little anxiety, I drove by Derrick's house. The police station would tip these guys off and probably make them mad on top of everything else. If I went to the police, these goons might shoot me next time instead of trying to follow me home.

Derrick's car was in the driveway. I pulled in next to it and for a wild moment considered stomping out to show my bravery. Instead, I scampered like a deranged idiot around the side of the house, hoping to make it through the gate before the Lincoln was close enough to get off a good shot. Luckily, Derrick didn't lock the gate. I wasn't even sure the back door was locked, but of course I knocked. I prayed he didn't shoot me after all the effort I had taken to escape the thugs.

He must have been sitting at the kitchen table because he peered out the back door window within seconds. "Sedona! Hang on."

He disappeared briefly, returned with keys and then took forever to unlock at least three deadbolts.

When the door finally swung open, I saw that he was not dressed casually. "I'm sorry, were you on your way out?"

"Me? No, not at all."

I rolled my eyes. Only Derrick would bother to wear pressed pants and a tucked in button down to lounge at home. He always looked professional; he walked like a cop, and he talked like a cop. Unfortunately for him, he looked like the kid next door who never grew up. It wasn't his fault, it was genetics. Cinnamon hair topped a thin five foot ten inch frame. The hair was boyish enough by itself, but worse, he had freckles. Yes, freckles.

"Come on in!" he urged. "I just finished eating. Are you hungry?" His brow furrowed in concern, that avuncular look that drives any woman over the age of sixteen nuts. I was slightly winded, but it didn't really warrant the worried arm patting.

"Uh no...actually a black Lincoln followed me as I left work and--"

Derrick stopped fussing immediately. He swung around and went straight to the front window. He closed the shades tight and picked up his cell phone from the counter. Before I could protest, he called in for a patrol car.

Gosh, it sure was good that I went to a lot of trouble to remain inconspicuous. Those guys wouldn't know I was wise to them now, no siree.

"Do you want to call the fire department too?" I asked.

He looked confused and waaay too concerned for my liking. "Did they threaten to start a fire? Did you get a license plate?" He went into his bedroom and came out with his gun. "Now, Sedona, I don't want you to be nervous. I know you don't like guns, but I need to have this out as a precaution."

I wasn't particularly fond of guns, but I wasn't about to scream either. I knew how to use them, and I knew what they were for. "Where did you get the idea that I don't like guns?"

He stood behind his front door and peered through the window shades without exposing his body. "Your brother explained it to me."

My brother Sean had a lot of mistaken ideas about me so I dropped the subject and tucked myself into the hallway out of the way. "Is your front door reinforced?"

"Of course. Back door too, steel inside of the wood. Windows have special locks."

"So, why wasn't the gate locked?"

"They could climb over that."

"Oh." It didn't take long for Derrick's cop friends to start cruising the street in front of the house. The phone whistled some song or other, and he picked up.

"No," he said. "Did you get a license plate?" he asked me again.

I shook my head. It had been impossible to see the plate because the Lincoln's lights had been shining in my rear view mirror.

"No," he said into the phone. "Yeah, the Civic is hers. Probably best." He hung up. "The patrol car will follow you home after they check the neighborhood a few more times."

I came out into the living room and sat down on his microfiber sofa. He had a matching blue chair with an ottoman. "When do you think I can leave?"

It suddenly occurred to him that he hadn't fed me. "Do you want to take a sandwich or something? I can warm up some soup." He made a move toward the kitchen, but I held up a hand.

"No, I'm fine, really. I just want to go home."

He glanced at his watch. "Probably good to go in about ten minutes. They'll make sure there isn't a Lincoln sitting at any of the intersections waiting for you to meander out." Now he looked stern. "Any particular reason this car would follow you? Having trouble at work? This doesn't," he paused and looked slightly ill, "have anything to do with that crowd you started hanging around with, does it?"

It is wrong to lie to such a naive, open, helpful face. I didn't even flinch. "No. I don't work at Strandfrost anymore. I have a new job. Maybe it was just someone from work, but I'm not familiar with the cars that go my direction since I haven't been at Acetel long." Uncertainty leaked into my voice unintentionally. "But how many people drive black cars like that with tinted windows? He cut off two cars getting out of the parking lot, and he ran a red light to stay behind me."

Derrick, for all his freckles, looked grave. "It can happen. They may have been waiting for any lone woman to walk out."

That explanation didn't make me feel better at all. Whatever happened to, "oh you're being silly, buck up?"

"Denton is pretty small, but serial crimes happen," Derrick said. "Did you get a look at the driver?"

I tried to recall if I had mentioned that I thought there were two guys. I was pretty sure that had been an unspoken impression. "No. The windows were tinted, and it was getting dark out." I swallowed and stood up. I didn't feel like sitting around listening to Derrick drum up additional serial killer scenarios. "I'm very sorry to have troubled you. It won't happen again."

I couldn't get out of there fast enough. Derrick walked me to my car and signaled the cop car, which dutifully followed me home. Derrick's final instructions were to come again anytime and report the Lincoln immediately if I saw it again.

I know the Lincoln didn't follow me home; the police presence saw to it. I waved my thanks after I was safely inside.

The only problem was that the goons already knew where I lived. I found that out for certain when the Lincoln fell in behind me right after I pulled onto Spittle road on my way to work the next morning.

Chapter 14

If the guys in the Lincoln were trying to intimidate me, it worked. Spittle Road was at the back of my subdivision one block over and three back from my house. It was far enough from Derrick's house that I didn't think they had found a way to connect the dots on their own.

They were also much more confident this time. As if they wanted me to know they could find me anytime, the car followed me all the way to Acetel before veering off at the last minute when I pulled into the parking lot.

I sat for a while, reluctant to get out of the car. I had nowhere safe to go. I wasn't driving to Derrick's house again. He might not be home this time. Besides, there were a lot more people around Acetel than in any subdivision at eight o'clock on a Friday morning.

There was only one thing to do, and it was time I met with him anyway. I waited patiently until someone else showed up to work. Hoping they would call 911 if necessary, I jumped out of my car and scurried across what now seemed like a large expanse of parking lot and huge hill with stairs leading to the door.

Once inside, I looked back out, but there was no Lincoln in the lot.

Good.

In my office, I paged Huntington. When he didn't respond, I left a message at his condo.

By the time I finally managed to get down to the lab, another surprise was waiting. "Jonathan," the IT guy, was sitting at my console. I was still deep in thought about being followed, so it took a few seconds to register that Jonathan wasn't going to run the minute he saw me. When he didn't leap over the workbench, I finally stopped my forward motion and stared at him. The situation apparently called for a good old-fashioned greeting. "So. Jonathan. How are things?"

He winced. "Radar."

"What?"

"You can call me Radar."

"O-kay. What are you doing?" I got a little antsy when anyone started playing with my equipment, especially if he was really stupid or really good. If a guy was really stupid, it could cost hours of time. If he was really smart, he could make it impossible for me to ever get the system running right again.

"You seem to know what you are doing here," Radar said amiably, turning away from my console. Without missing a beat he added, "I was looking through old newspapers and saw this." Carefully he reached into his back pocket, extracted a wallet and from within produced a printed piece of paper. There I was in all my glory, just after the break-in at Strandfrost, plastered on the front page of the newspaper with a fat lip and a bad hairdo. He had printed the article right off the web.

"I'm flattered that you recognized the likeness," I said, not pleased in the least. "Or did you break into the driver's license bureau and compare it to my license picture, one that is almost as good?"

"Nah, you had makeup on for your driver's license." He grinned. "I wouldn't have made the connection except that you didn't look so good the other night."

Hmph. Now that he was willing to talk to me, I had no idea what to say, especially since he was suddenly so at ease.

He scooted his chair over and made room for me to check the test. I sat down since I couldn't think of anything else to do.

"Where did you say that Chinese place was?" he asked.

"Tinnet. Happy Family Chinese. What do you really want?"

"Just one or two small things. What were you doing in my computer room? Who you were with, if anybody."

I actually didn't know the answers. Well, I did know why I had gone in there and who was with me, but I didn't know what had happened to start it all in the first place. "I have no idea."

"Yes, you do."

I looked around. I didn't see anyone, but then he had probably been following me, waiting for an opportunity when no one was around. I checked my watch. Too early for lunch. "No, I don't. I noticed the server had gone down. I don't know why it went down."

He considered my answer. His hair was tied back with some sort of leather braided thing, which made it a little easier for me to read his expression.

"You a gamer?" I asked, hoping to get him started on a hobby and off the subject of my nighttime scurry.

"Yeah, sometimes. Why?"

"That your gamer handle, Radar?"

He chuckled. "No, it's a nickname. I fly helicopters."

See what I mean about these guys and their hobbies? "Oh. What is your gamer handle?"

His eyes narrowed. "I have several. Mostly I use Mangusta."

"Mangusta?"

"It's a European attack chopper."

"Oh." Making small talk with gurus was hard work.

I stared at my computer, wondering how I was going to get anything accomplished today.

"Cameras," Radar leaned over and said succinctly.

"Cameras?" Puzzled, I looked up from my computer. "What cameras?" I didn't see anything camera-like in the lab.

He moved from his chair to the edge of the worktable and crossed his arms. "That is what you were doing in the storage center. Putting in cameras."

"I was?" He'd have to forgive me for sounding surprised, but I had never figured out what Mark was doing in there. "How many did I put in?" My brow furrowed. "And why?"

Radar rolled hazel eyes. "I was expecting you to tell me."

"But why would..." I stopped myself before saying "he," and had to start again. "Why would anyone want cameras in there? I assume that no one ever goes in there except you or Art. And don't you live in San Jose? So you aren't even here that often."

"Art? I don't know why anyone would point cameras at that troll." He watched me carefully and then added, "except me. Sometimes he screws things up royally, and I'd love to catch that on tape."

What could Mark have been after? "What else happens in there?"

"Do you think if Art screws up again, you could get me a copy of the camera file?"

It was my turn to roll my eyes. "I didn't put cameras in there."

He smirked. "I didn't say you did. I just asked you for a copy. You didn't deny they were there."

I wasn't certain he was on the right track. "How do you know they weren't there before?"

"I have to run cables through the ceiling from one rack to the other in order to connect the equipment. There's a lot of empty space behind the ceiling tiles. It's cleaner to run cables through the ceiling instead of across the floor. There weren't cameras in there when I ran the cables originally."

I knew about the nearly empty space behind the tiles, but I wasn't going to admit it. "When did you run the original cables?"

He folded his arms and glared at me, tired of the conversation. "I had to replace a bad cable yesterday, and that is when I noticed the cameras. I would have seen the cameras if they were there when I first installed the cables. It's obvious that the reason someone was in there the other night was to install cameras." His eyes accused me.

I blinked innocently. "I still don't know what anyone would hope to catch on camera." Unless Mark thought the equipment was going to disappear, what in the world was he hoping to see?

"I have a pretty good idea, and I wouldn't mind catching the guy either."

"Oh?"

Maybe if Mark wouldn't tell me, Radar would.

He stared at me for several moments and then gave up in disgust. "You really didn't know about the cameras did you?"

I shook my head.

"You don't have any idea what is going on, do you?"

"No."

Radar got up, spun his chair around and sat on it backwards with his chin propped on the headrest. "Okay." He pointed his finger straight up as if he were a lawyer about to make an important revelation. "I don't know what your guy is after, and I don't know what good the cameras are going to do, but recently I've noticed that someone hacked into the system with administrator privileges. Whoever is doing it can look at any file he wants using the admin ID or a fake one he sets up for the purpose." He studied me, Exhibit A, closely while he told me this.

My heart skipped a beat. Was Radar about to tell me that he had discovered someone plundering Acetel accounts? Or was it Mark that had been thumbing through the files? "How do you know this? And what is the guy looking at?"

Radar shrugged. "I don't know everything the guy does when he is on the system. I've set over a hundred tags to log files that he might be accessing. No files seem to be damaged. Nothing major even gets opened--at least not when the guy is logged in as administrator. I figured it was some cracker that got the password and did some exploring, just because he could."

"But," I said, "the guy could be stealing valuable information, couldn't he?"

"Doesn't seem that way." His reassurance was disappointing. "I'd be worried if he were accessing the names of customer accounts or the amount of money we charge. If he was doing that he could go after the customers for himself, but those files are never touched." He sat up straight and shook his head. "I've never seen the important stuff messed with. Same thing on test results--no one looks at the files that indicate whether the tests are passing or failing, so the guy isn't after selling that information. Those files haven't been opened or looked at by anyone other than test engineers."

My heart went from thinking that Radar was going to make me a hero to flat line. "Nothing?" This wasn't going to fuel Huntington's idea about customer accounts being charged on the side. The hacker would want the names of the customers. Or at least the test results to sell to customers under the table. Or maybe Radar's problem had nothing to do with Huntington's problem.

Radar said, "The only thing I ever caught being touched was employee lists and some salary information. And I'm not positive it was the same late-night guy. It could have been Art logged in as administrator trying to add new employees." He shook his head. "But I'm not sure Art is smart enough to use the administrator account."

Thinking of the great "Elvis" twisted my face into a grimace.

"What, you thinking he's going to get your user name backwards or something?"

"It's possible."

He chuckled. "Don't worry. I entered your account information when you were hired." He spun his wheeled chair around and stared at the locked door that housed the servers. "Art rarely, if ever, enters new employees. He sends me an email and says how busy he is, doesn't have time because someone's computer is down, can I do whatever it is that needs doing. That's what bothered me about whoever has been snooping through files using the administrator privileges--it probably isn't Art. He's too lazy."

"And since you've been doing the accounts for Art in order to avoid a bigger mess later, it is doubtful that he suddenly got the skills to hack into the main system," I concluded.

"Bingo. I'm not even sure Art knows how to set up a new user account. The one time he tried, the name was already in use in the database, so he screwed it up. The zonk created a duplicate name with an email address already in use. The system bumped the first name off. Then he swore up and down that he checked for duplicates, and it couldn't have happened that way."

It took me a second to remember that "zonk" was a gaming phrase that meant a stupefied character. "Meanwhile employee number one is climbing up the management chain making your life a lot of fun?"

"Yup. There's actually a couple of griefers in upper management that like to make a big deal out of nothing. But I don't sweat that stuff much; I just stay out of their way."

"Did you ask Art if he is the one who has been logging in as administrator and why he would bother?"

"We're talking stupid twink. You ever ask the guy for details on what he did yesterday or last week? Or in the morning if it's one in the afternoon?"

"No, but I'd really rather not ask him anything. Ever."

"Asking him a question is like listening to a kid with his hand in the cookie jar. He assumes he did something wrong so he starts with the excuses before you can get any information. Most of the time, it becomes a denial thesis on how it couldn't have been him because he was on the first floor in the john or something. Total zero."

I laughed and then apologized. "Sorry."

"So," he accused me, "you still denying you were in the server room?"

Oh great. Now if I made excuses or denied my involvement, I would sound like Elvis. Clever how Radar had manipulated me into either looking like an incompetent fool, a liar or someone at the top of the guilty list. Wow, what great choices.

Bill must have overheard us talking because, bless him, he chose that moment to appear from behind the racks. He was wearing the same burned pants from the other day. "Yo, Radar! Are you guys talking Everquest?"

I grinned. "I don't play, but Radar does."

Radar said, "Bill knows. We're in the same tournament at least once a month."

Bill rubbed his hands together happily. "You should join us. My handle is Wildebeest."

Come to think of it, wildebeests had beards and although Bill wasn't particularly cow-like, he had a sort of wild, beast look. I could picture him standing out on a prairie all wrinkled and casual, mowing down some grass.

I did my ultimate, social best to keep the chat going by thinking up as many inane questions as possible. "Who else plays?"

"Jacques played with us a few times," Bill said. "Right after he first got promoted. Picked the name Toucan. Can you believe it? How hard can it be to kill off a Toucan?" Bill chuckled and rubbed his belly.

Radar shook his head. He gave me a last piercing glare before strolling away. I'd probably been too obvious that I wasn't going to make myself readily available for more questions.

The minute he disappeared, I excused myself. I really needed to talk to Huntington.

Chapter 15

The phone was already ringing when I arrived in my office. I snatched it up, but it wasn't Huntington. Craig Yumen, the engineer from Kronology, identified himself. I must have entered the twilight zone sometime between the first and second floor, because Craig acted like he had not received my report or read it, but he called to talk about it.

"What do you mean you want me to run a test?" I interrupted. "The report I sent isn't a proposed test, it's a test I ran already!"

"We aren't clear on whether you pulled the power cord from the back of the computer, cut it with scissors, or whether you pulled the plug out of the wall."

"Pulled the plug out of--!" My voice was so tight, I squeaked. It took me a few more seconds to grasp that he was implying that the machine would somehow work if I pulled the power cord correctly. "The computer will fail whether you unplug the power cord from the wall or the machine. The other power supply should keep the machine working."

There was a disbelieving snort from the other end. "Does the server come back on if you plug it back in?"

"Yes, but the point of having two is so that if one fails, the other takes over."

"Of course. I'm not stupid."

"I hadn't noticed." I spoke away from the mouthpiece so he probably didn't hear me.

"Do you know if the bit is being set that detects that the power went missing?"

The best way to know if bits were being set was for him to run the test himself and look in his code and find out. I mentioned this fact. "That information would be in *your* code now wouldn't it?"

"We're not sure."

"Well, buddy, *I* didn't write any code, so we can be absolutely positive it isn't in mine."

"You probably ran the test wrong. I don't see how we can help."

Now that I had clarified that I hadn't written any bad code, he was going to blame the failure of his machine on me. I took a deep breath and started over. "All you have to do is run the test yourself. It will fail. You'll then be able to look at the code and see what is wrong. We can get this solved, and we'll both be happy."

"I'm not certain we have all the information we need. I'll call you back when I get a list of questions."

Unbelievable. I knew from Bill's warning that Kronology wasn't going to be eager to help, but the guy could have lied and said the test passed in their labs. It would have made a better excuse than to try and discuss how to unplug a power cord from a wall socket.

I called Huntington. He didn't answer. I left a message.

Since the day was in the toilet, I used the remaining time to finish up Jacques' survey.

Before leaving for home, I called Huntington again and left another message.

I drove very carefully, checking behind me all the way home, but I saw no one suspicious in a black Lincoln or any other car.

Since he hadn't answered his phone, and there was no car in the driveway, I was not expecting Huntington to be waiting for me when I arrived home. I was inside my little patio home when his disembodied voice came out of the dark. I panicked and nearly screamed. With the lack of light, Huntington didn't notice. He kept talking.

"The trouble started when the Lexus was in your driveway," he said from somewhere inside the dark region of my living room. "Mark didn't know you had been seen with me, and he left it in your driveway for me to pick up."

I quickly hit the light with my free hand. It was several more seconds before I could talk. I had to wait for my heart rate to slow. Maybe I should start carrying my gun. "You have yet to tell me why you left that car at my house." Huntington had quite possibly put me in danger before, but he had never brought my home into it. For the last case, he had provided a nice, impersonal condo, a condo that had not been mine. If someone wanted to spy on it or blow it up, it wouldn't have been my personal loss.

"Sedona…I'm sorry."

I added the kitchen lights to the mix and set down my groceries. Huntington looked truly upset. His pacific-blues were flashing against a background of a black turtleneck and matching black pants. The business casual look was almost funeral attire, and I hoped that wasn't because he had gotten my message and been worried about whether or not I'd make it home safely.

Mindlessly, I took the groceries from the single plastic bag and put a pot of water on the stove to boil pasta. "They followed me home yesterday," I told him. "Then they picked up the trail again this morning."

"You mentioned that on the phone." With a muttered curse, he stood and began to pace. "I shouldn't have involved you. These guys appear a bit more determined than just a manager scooping a couple of odd jobs."

"Yeah, I'll say. I saw that Mark put some cameras in the lab. What's that all about? What is he hoping to catch?"

"Whatever we can."

That kind of vague answer didn't sit well with me. Any guilt he felt over putting me in danger hadn't made him more inclined to discuss facts openly. I crossed my arms and waited.

After pacing back and forth once, he noticed my silence and offered, "We want to find out if someone is using the machines to log on and get the customer lists. Mark put the cameras in there to see if we could catch someone who didn't belong."

"They don't have to access the accounts from the machines in the locked room," I said. "All they have to have is the right permissions and they can access the information from any machine." I told Huntington how things could be hacked without mentioning Radar. Huntington didn't know how much I did or didn't know about computing; let him think I was a good hacker.

He shrugged and defended his strategy. "There are other cameras in other places. We want to know if someone is on campus who doesn't belong-- sabotaging, stealing, whatever. Although watching people is probably how our two friends started following the Lexus. Mark was watching a few homes here and there."

"He put cameras in people's homes?"

"No, Mark put the cameras in various offices. The homes we're keeping an eye on in person. We need the cameras because we can't keep watching everyone. Unfortunately it appears that someone is already onto us. That is going to hamper our progress even more." He shook his head. "Look, it might be best if you opt out of this one. I owe you for changing jobs. But it would be a good idea if you got out of the line of fire. Maybe you could go on an extended vacation until we clean this up."

"I thought you deposited the money in my bank account already?" I think I was being fired. Twice in one month. That had to be some sort of record.

"I deposited the money, but you can't keep working at Acetel. You've already been seen with me. That may have made you a target."

"They may have seen me with you, but that isn't when they found me. How did someone happen by to see the Lexus in my driveway?"

He watched me through hooded eyes for a long moment before deciding to answer. "It's really pretty simple. You live very near Piney Oaks."

"And?" My subdivision was actually split into three sections; my patio home was in the middle section. Sean lived over in the newest section, and I didn't know anyone in the oldest section. When the builders began building across Spittle Road, instead of it being a fourth part to the subdivision, it was all custom homes and larger lots. That subdivision was Piney Oaks.

"Mark and I are keeping an eye on someone who lives there."

"Who lives there?" I couldn't believe he had a suspect and was keeping it from me.

"That isn't pertinent."

"Are you crazy? It sounds to me like you've got the goods on the guy-- you're watching him, and he doesn't like it so he's been sending people after you. Why not have him arrested for attempted...attempted something."

"Those guys in the Lincoln haven't caught up with any of us so what are we going to charge them with?"

I thought stalking me was a good place to start, but apparently Huntington didn't agree.

"Granted, someone fingered the Lexus as a problem, but the place in Piney Oaks isn't the only one we have under surveillance. The guys in the Lincoln could have followed us from any one of the locations we're watching." He grinned a little, almost a proud smirk. "Your place was a good exchange location. We can walk into Piney Oaks in a variety of, shall we say, disguises, and keep an eye on whatever we want. We only used your driveway the one time, but apparently that was enough to get your place pegged."

"Who is it you are watching?" I demanded.

He raised empty palms in a not-so-convincing display of innocence. "If you knew who it was, you'd get complacent. You might not notice suspicious activity from someone else."

"Riight. And if this guy happens to invite me to lunch, there I'll go like a lamb to slaughter, never suspecting he has been up to all this suspicious activity." Angrily, I drained the pasta, nearly burning myself when it splashed.

"He isn't going to invite you to lunch. You don't get asked out to lunch much."

That did *not* win him any points. "Huntington."

"And you never go when you are asked. I had to practically beg to get you to go to dinner with me." He had the nerve to pout over a meal he hadn't even eaten and a date that wasn't a date. I closed my eyes and tried to ignore the urge to smack him with one of my pans.

He continued, "The best thing at this point is for you to leave town for a few weeks. Mark and I will get this straightened out and then you can come back. You should certainly leave Acetel. I don't want to try pulling strings to get you back on at Strandfrost, but you have enough money, as promised, to give you time to look for another job."

"Sure, no problem. I'll tell my family I'm going to be gone for Thanksgiving and Christmas. That will go over big." Of course, my family would prefer me alive and somewhere else than dead in Denton. I sighed and finished throwing ingredients in a bowl for the noodle casserole I was making.

Huntington came back into the kitchen and peered over my shoulder. I put it in the oven. It wouldn't take very long since the pasta was still warm from the boiling water. "I suppose I could show back up at Strandfrost and avoid you and Mark. If those goons catch me, I'll tell them I dumped you."

"I can't get that job back for you, not for a while anyway. I'm sorry."

Huntington was used to being able to manipulate events to his satisfaction, but this time I didn't need him. "I never quit. I went on vacation."

There was a funny little pause before he grabbed the counter top as if he were trying to keep from falling over. "You *what?*"

"Went on vacation. They were going to fire me anyway, right after they rehired Gary Marcus, you remember him?" Huntington was too startled to nod so I kept talking. "Since I didn't quit, I could show up at Strandfrost and give them a run for their money. It would get me out of the picture for a while." Of course, I did have the bonus Huntington gave me, and Hawaii would be nice and warm this time of year.

Huntington started laughing. There might have even been tears in his eyes. "Sedona, you are priceless. Absolutely priceless. Do you even want the job at Strandfrost?"

I shook my head. "No."

He chuckled all the way back into the living room. He put on his leather jacket and at that moment, the back door opened wide. Huntington had either unlocked it for Mark, or Mark was a very quiet lock pick.

Mark's eyes gleamed wickedly when he saw me jump halfway across the kitchen. "Hi." He came in and shut the door. Like his brother, he was dressed all in black. His eyes narrowed when he smelled dinner. He raised an eyebrow at his brother. "Cozy, huh?"

Huntington grinned and moved back into the kitchen, slapping his brother on the shoulders. "It's in the oven."

I didn't even know for sure I was having a guest, and if so, I had assumed it would be Huntington since he conveniently met with me around dinnertime. I grabbed an extra plate from the cupboard.

I turned back around in time to see Mark hand Huntington keys. Without another word Huntington was gone, out the back door the way his brother had entered. My first thought was, how was Mark going to leave without keys?

Mark grinned at me, a very suggestive look in his eyes. He moved over and leaned on the edge of the dining room table. "How've you been?"

"What exactly have you caught on those cameras in the server room?" I countered, checking the casserole. I grabbed a soda from the fridge and when he nodded, I handed it to him. His hand brushed the edges of my fingers. He let his grip linger.

"Do you want ice?" I asked nervously.

He raised his eyebrows and looked wicked again. He set the soda down. "I didn't come for dinner. I was just changing shifts with Steve on the stakeout." His arm snaked out and captured me against the counter before I could move back to the relative safety by the stove. "You have an interesting way of distracting a man."

"Uh...does this mean you've cleared me with Huntington?" My voice squeaked. I was having trouble getting enough air into my lungs.

He frowned. "Why? Haven't you?" He went from teasing to irritated in a hurry. For some reason it made me laugh.

"I don't go around asking him for clearance for much of anything. I just never knew for sure what you were talking about."

"Me either," he said. When he finally did kiss me, I was awfully glad he was holding me up. His left hand caressed the back of my neck, gluing me into place, moving me where he wanted to go. I was in no mood to resist. Ever since I had been plastered against him that night in the lab, just the thought of white t-shirts made me break into a sweat. After this, I could add black t-shirts and if we kept going, no t-shirts.

Wow.

"Do you still want to know about the cameras?" he asked while nuzzling nerve endings near the pulse at my throat.

Speaking was out of the question. I was breathing hard and feeling weak in a very energized sort of way. "Listen, Mark," I managed faintly.

He nibbled ever so slowly up my chin before pulling back. Seeing my dazed expression, he grinned one of those guy smiles. "How about we move this to another room?"

That got my attention. What was I thinking? Mark was as dangerous as his brother--no, make that more so. I decided to put my legs to some use other than trying to turn into water. He let me get my balance, but one hand continued to span my ribs. He never stopped moving his fingers.

"Maybe I should make some coffee," I suggested dimly.

His beautiful brown eyes were like coffee, giant pools of mystical beverage, pulling me closer until I forgot about the coffee. Truthfully, I don't think he was as calm as he pretended. When he slid away from the counter and onto a kitchen chair, bringing me with him, I was positive.

I sprawled across his lap in a very unladylike position, and his hands moved and oh, it felt good. I really needed to stop him, but my own hands were reveling in the feel of muscles rippling across his back. His fingers skimmed the lace edge of my bra. I stopped breathing. Before I could think, the back door made a sound like it had been hit by a cannon.

We both froze. Time stopped. Without pulling away from me, Mark rolled, taking me with him to the floor. He continued the momentum until we were behind the bar-counter between the living room and kitchen.

He crouched and hit the lights, stuffing me behind him. My legs weren't any better than they had been a few moments ago, but I managed to slither further back across the carpet.

The back porch remained ominously quiet.

"Where is your gun?" he asked.

"Where's yours?" I thought I heard a groan from outside the back door. "Never mind." I scrambled on hands and knees toward the bedroom even though I had to make it across a stretch that included exposing myself to the back door. The gun was in the bedroom closet. That seemed like a safer place to be anyway.

Before I got halfway there, Mark cursed and jerked the back door open.

I froze and spun around, still on my knees. My mouth fell open.

Mark dragged his brother in the door.

Huntington was covered in blood.

Chapter 16

Mark got Huntington through the door and slammed it shut. Without looking up, he asked, "Did you get the gun?"

I turned and ran.

With the phone in one hand and the gun in the other, I started to dial 911. Mark grabbed the phone and shut it off. "No. No cops, no hospital. We're working on a case at the hospital. He isn't going there." He set the phone down on the table and stared at my semi-automatic twenty-two. "You call that thing a gun? Shit."

He ignored the weapon and reached for Huntington. Using one of my kitchen knives, he cut away what was left of Huntington's leather jacket. I winced.

"Is...what do you mean no hospital?" Frantically, I grabbed kitchen towels and stuffed them in Mark's direction. He didn't answer, but used the towels as a tourniquet. I ran to the bathroom for a couple more big towels and my entire basket of medicines.

Most people have a medicine cabinet; I keep toothpaste in mine. The rest of my cures were stuffed into a basket with a lid.

Mark ripped at Huntington's pant leg, trying to tear the cotton twill. Out of the basket came a pair of scissors that were actually for cutting my bangs. He grunted and started cutting the heavy twill pants.

"Uh, Mark, he sort of looks like he's been shot..."

I tossed aside an ace bandage, a bottle of aspirin, an entire package of night-light bulbs I had been looking for last week and finally found the alcohol and peroxide. A lot of alcohol in an open wound might kill him if he wasn't already dead. The peroxide might clear the wound site, but I was fresh out of sutures. The band aides were looking mighty small. "Uh, Mark..."

"We'll get him to the condo. One of the guys there is a doctor."

I didn't live close to the condo. Since I had pretended to live there, I knew very well where it was. It was further than the hospital. "We could take him to Sean's house," I suggested very, very weakly.

"Sean?"

I nodded and gulped. Sean was going to kill me. "Brenda's a nurse. She works at the hospital. There's this one doctor she says walks on water..."

Mark looked up at me for the first time, fire in his eyes. "Call Sean then."

I had already reached for the phone, but then I changed my mind. Sean was very good with emergencies, unless they were mine. A phone call would result in nothing more than a marathon of questions. It would give him waaay too much time to think about all the people that could be sued.

"Let's just go," I said. "Get Huntington--Steve, in the Mercedes." I cringed at the blood on my floor. Mark finished wrapping Huntington's leg and arm while I backed the Mercedes into the garage so we could put Huntington in the back without being seen. I added a blanket in the cargo area. By the time I was finished, Mark had him in the hallway leading to the garage.

I ran back into the kitchen and grabbed the gun.

Mark would have driven, but I was already in the driver's seat by the time he got his brother loaded. I handed him the gun when he jumped into the passenger seat.

"What do you want me to do with this thing? Spit peas at them? Don't you have a real gun?"

I pulled out. Sean's house was only a few blocks away. "You and Sean can go through his gun collection when we get there. In the meantime shoot anyone that looks like they are following us. I'm *not* endangering Sean and Brenda because of Huntington's shenanigans. She's pregnant for God's sake!"

"Shoot them with this thing?" He honestly looked as though he couldn't imagine it doing any real damage.

"Think of it this way," I said through clenched teeth, "the twenty-two has longer range than a thirty-eight. You can shoot them before they get too close."

I would have glared at him, but I was too busy checking the mirrors and wondering if Huntington was dying. What if he died? In the back of the Mercedes?

Blocking all thought, I pulled into Sean's driveway. "I'll get Sean and have Brenda call the doctor."

"You sure he's clean?"

"Sean?"

"No, not Sean!" He almost ripped the back door off the Mercedes getting to Huntington. "The doctor."

I had no idea what Mark was talking about. Deciding to ignore his ramblings in favor of trying to save Huntington, I ran inside and started explaining things to my disapproving brother and his calm wife. Gone were Brenda's unorganized, unfocused kitchen tendencies, replaced by training and several years of hospital work. She took charge as though we were in the ER instead of her living room.

By the time we had Huntington inside and arranged on a blanket in the kitchen, Dr. Taylor had pulled in next to the Mercedes. He was less than happy when he saw the gunshot wounds. "I have to report this," he snapped, opening a large zippered bag.

For some reason I thought he would have a black bag like in the Western movies. His was more like a giant gym bag and had enough stuff in it to take care of four or five head-on collisions.

Brenda reported, "Two bullet wounds, one still lodged in his leg muscle. Didn't go all the way to the bone--I don't think. The arm injury looks like it went straight through."

Dr. Taylor made his own assessments. "He should have surgery to remove that bullet even though its shallow. I'm not taking it out here."

Mark shook his head once, sharply. "Do you work at the hospital?"

"ER, why?"

"Are you aware that some of the doctors there seem to be charging for services not rendered?"

Dr. Taylor looked up. "What?"

"Steve and I have been investigating a problem there. Patients get checked out, but there are discrepancies in the records. Some records show patients are admitted for longer than they were actually there, that type of thing."

"Insurance scam?" Dr. Taylor guessed. He never stopped working on Huntington's wounds. Brenda was right beside him, keeping everything organized and monitoring Huntington's pulse and breathing.

Mark said, "Most of the patients are either elderly or victims not likely to notice an extra charge tagged on their bills. The bills are covered by insurance."

Dr. Taylor sewed two pieces of flesh on Huntington's arm. "I still have to report it."

"As long as you don't know his name," Mark said agreeably.

Dr. Taylor would have protested, but my darling brother got there first. He shouted about lawsuits, sisters and something about a horse that nearly killed me. It was his favorite story when he was trying to prove that I was either unhinged or unsafe to those around me. Unfortunately for him it wasn't making any sense in this context.

It was almost two hours later when Dr. Taylor leaned back and pronounced his work, such as it was, finished. He didn't stay to argue with us either.

I wrote Derrick's name and number down on a piece of paper and handed it to him as he was leaving. "Derrick's a cop. Maybe you can tell him." Sean would tell Derrick anyway, so I saw no reason that Doc Taylor couldn't use Derrick as his official report line.

Mark started to hoist his brother back towards the door, but Brenda was having none of it. "Leave him here. Now that he's not bleeding, let's get him into the guest room." She led the way down the hall, past the baby's room. "You take Sedona home and let him rest. I'll monitor him until morning."

Sean's house was probably safer than my house, and Brenda would keep a professional eye on him. I was pretty certain from the look on Sean's face that we weren't all going to be invited to stay.

Mark was more than a little reluctant, but I nodded my agreement. "It's a good idea."

Mark didn't look convinced, but followed Brenda. As soon as he put Huntington on the bed, Brenda pushed him toward the door. "Come back tomorrow. I'll watch him."

I grabbed his hand. "Let's go." I led the way back out, holding his hand in mine.

When we got back into the Mercedes I thought about the fact that the shooter knew where I lived. "Why didn't whoever shot him follow him all the way back to my house?" *And keep shooting?*

Mark never looked at me. "They could tell they had hit him; maybe they figured they didn't have to follow him all the way to the end." He slammed a fist onto the dash.

My blood ran colder. "You're guessing that whoever shot him didn't expect him to make it back to my house."

He didn't answer until I pulled into the garage, and the door was shut behind us. "I'll make sure that if they knew he was headed here, they won't come back tonight."

I didn't have to walk into the kitchen before I remembered the casserole. "Uh-oh." I was lucky the house hadn't burned down.

Mark checked the rest of my humble home while I turned off the oven. Thankfully it hadn't been on high, and though it was a charred mess, it had just started to smoke, so the kitchen was hazy rather than blackened.

With a sigh, I turned to find Mark using the already ruined towels to clean up the floor.

I pitched the casserole, bowl and all. Some things weren't worth cleaning. I made myself a cup of tea and asked if he wanted coffee. He didn't answer so I made some anyway. "Huntington, I mean Steve, says I was followed home the other night because I was seen with him at the restaurant. But...they picked up my trail at work, Mark. I know you guys are watching someone near here, so maybe they found my house because of that, but it's starting to feel like someone knows that I'm involved in the investigation."

I handed him a large green trash bag. He loaded the towels in it. I picked up Huntington's discarded leather coat and shook my head. "What a waste. This was such a great jacket." Even if the arm could be sewn back onto the jacket, the blood and giant gunshot hole more than ruined the thing.

Mark found the cleaning solutions under the sink. He turned back around and caught sight of the jacket in my hand. Unconsciously he aimed the cleaner in my direction, his knuckles white.

We stood that way for a long time, him staring at the jacket and me frozen in place. Not knowing how to break the deadlock, I dropped the jacket and stepped forward, blocking the sight of it with my body. "Brenda would call immediately if Steve's status changed," I said. "And despite your investigation at the hospital, she'd get him straight there if she thought he was picking up something as innocuous as a cold while in her care. Trust me."

His tortured brown eyes finally found my face. "Yeah." The agreement exploded out around the breath he had been holding. He walked over to the jacket and stuffed it into the garbage bag. "It was his favorite jacket."

"Mine too," I said softly. I had no idea how to offer comfort. The muscles across his neck were strung tight. His jerky movements were like those of a disjointed puppet.

He finally stopped cleaning and changed the subject. "I don't know if anyone has marked you as a plant. The guy making the deals could easily be a board member, in which case he would know you were there to investigate."

I would have been more reassured if he had told me that I was in no danger and that no one knew I was involved. Since he wasn't going to lie to me, I plunged into the mess. "The board members aren't involved in the day to day. How could they be skimming? How could they control which engineers worked on what?"

He shrugged. "Someone on the board could have mentioned the investigation to the wrong person. The entire board knows about the investigation because they gave the okay to hire Steve. The chicken knows the fox is in the hen house and will fly the coop without ever leaving town." He rested his hands against the counter. He was still breathing hard. "We'll be left with nothing but a few rotten feathers and no idea where they came from."

I poured him a cup of coffee and set it down on the counter before taking the garbage bag out to the garage.

When I came back in, he was on the phone. He put his hand over the mouthpiece and said, "I'm going to make sure there are a few people watching your house tonight to keep you safe."

I didn't know what to do with myself so I took my cup of tea into the living room and sat down. Dinner had been ruined, but for a change, I didn't feel like eating.

When Mark finished his calls, he turned to me. "Steve mentioned he was coming over here to make sure you quit this one. It sounds like a good idea, especially if someone has decided you're not just another engineer."

I shrugged noncommittally. "Yeah, he mentioned it." I got up and rinsed my cup out. There was no point in holding the cup of tea; I wasn't going to drink it. I realized that Mark was getting ready to leave. He hadn't been wearing a jacket, so there was nothing to collect. The long sleeves of his black t-shirt didn't look that warm. For some reason, I thought about the sword tattooed across the muscles of his upper arm, but couldn't remember seeing the tattoo in the lab when he had been wearing short sleeves. Then again, the light hadn't been very good.

He saw me looking at his arm. He folded both of his across his chest and frowned down at me. "You should take Steve's advice. This one is ugly." He moved closer. He looked down at me, all at once stern and...something unfathomable. "I'll keep an eye on the place tonight, but Steve probably wouldn't have come back here unless he was certain he had lost them."

Like a deer in headlights I couldn't move my head away from the beam. He reached up to touch my cheek, but stopped shy of the mark. "This is way out of control." His hand only stopped shaking because he grabbed the doorknob.

As quietly as he had come hours before, he was gone.

Chapter 17

I wouldn't have had the courage to do what needed to be done if it hadn't been for the ego boost Mark unknowingly gave me. It would have been a lot easier to slide back into Strandfrost and fight the status quo than continue to work on Acetel's problems. Huntington originally seemed to think I had it in me. Then again, he wasn't smart enough to keep from getting shot so what did that say about his judgment?

Checking in with Brenda confirmed that Huntington had made it comfortably through the night and was gone with Mark first thing in the morning. Derrick came by Sean's to get a statement, but Mark had planned his visit well. He whisked the evidence away long before Derrick showed up.

Sean, of course, directed Derrick my way, but I wasn't answering the phone, so I had some time.

Before leaving my house, I called Huntington at his condo. I left a message inquiring about his health and basically demanding an update. He picked up as I ranted into the phone.

"I'm fine." His voice was hoarse, but otherwise normal.

"Thanks for thinking to let me know."

He sighed. "I called your brother and sent them flowers and a gift certificate to the restaurant at Whispering Pines Resort."

Since he was ill, he was the one that should have been receiving flowers, but where Huntington was concerned, everything was backwards. "Oh. You could have called me too. Are you following the doctor's orders?" It occurred to me that he had been out cold and suffering from loss of blood so he hadn't heard any instructions.

"There's a guy here that looked me over."

Mark had said something about one of the other condo owners being a doctor. "And did he say you would live?"

Huntington waited a heartbeat. "Concerned?" he purred.

"You do pay my paycheck." I was admitting nothing.

"Ah, but you quit, remember?"

"Yeah, yeah." And I was going to quit, as soon as I had Radar verify one or two things. "I have a couple more questions. I assume you'll be home the entire weekend resting up?"

He grunted. I took this as an invitation to stop by whenever I wanted. With Huntington it was as close as I would get.

After I hung up, I printed out my resignation again. I tried not to make the letter too personal, but I did say I was leaving with "great regret and felt I was forced to leave." The words were mostly for Turbo. Since he had been my boss before the promotion, that was where I delivered the letter. He met me in his office even though it was Saturday.

When I handed him my resignation, he stared at it in disappointment. "You like the job at Acetel?"

"No," I admitted. "But I like the idea of coming back here and fighting with Gary a lot less." I had made a deal with Huntington, and he had paid me. I didn't have to do anything overt; I would just get Radar to verify Huntington's theory one way or the other. Besides, Huntington's hoodlum friends already knew where I lived. Unless I literally went to Hawaii, they could find me. I also had a feeling it would take Huntington a lot longer than a couple of weeks to figure things out, especially now that he was laid up.

"You aren't going to wait until after your vacation?" Turbo asked.

"I want to give two weeks' notice. If I wait until my vacation is over, I'd be in a pickle when I was supposed to be showing up here and at Acetel."

"Are you going to tell John personally?"

The thought of having to look Strandfrost's esteemed vice president in the eyes made breakfast rumble in protest. "I suppose I could. I don't owe him anything though."

Turbo didn't disagree. "How's the new case going?"

I told him a little about it, describing my new boss and the stupid people at Kronology. Turbo knew more about Kronology than I.

"What did you say your boss's name was?"

"Jacques Cardin."

"That's funny." He turned to his file drawer and shuffled through it. "Hang on a second..."

It might have taken longer than a second because although Turbo was very good about labeling things and saving every scrap of paper that came his way, he wasn't that keen on actually getting the things filed properly.

"Well, well, well. Isn't this interesting." He handed me a resume with a business card attached. My mouth dropped open.

Turbo shook his head in disapproval. "I guess maybe this is why Jacques is so interested in helping the Kronology customers, huh?"

I stared in fascination at the resume and business card. Jacques name and "Senior Engineer, Kronology Servers" stared right back at me.

"He interviewed here, gosh..." Turbo leaned back and started thinking. "We were working on the Gummy Bear Project and that was during that really bad winter...I'd guess five years ago." He sat forward again. "Kronology has been known to buy some very, very good small companies. I knew a couple of guys who started a server business that was bought by them. Kronology has trouble keeping talent though. The ones left behind don't have enough history with the acquired technology to be able to add features or fix problems."

"The Kronology people certainly give no impression that they know what they are doing." I pointed at the resume. "Jacques doesn't strike me as being into low-level engineering."

"I could call my old buddies for you, see if they knew Jacques and find out what he did for Kronology." Turbo rubbed his hands together. "It would be interesting to discover what his current ties are to the company. Maybe he has stock options and stands to get rich if Kronology does well!"

That was an intriguing thought. In the engineering industry, it was common for publicly owned companies to give engineers stock options. As the company grew, the stock price was also supposed to grow-- making the stock options a valuable part of compensation. Jacques could be sitting on stock from Kronology hoping to make money--if his old company did well. "How has the stock done over the past few years?" I asked.

"Let's have a look." Turbo punched keys on his keyboard and after a second or two, turned the monitor on his desk my way. "Down."

The stock chart showed a pretty steady decline over the last five years with occasional bursts of hope, one of which was occurring right now. The price had climbed about five points in the last month. "If Jacques has options, he has reasons to help Kronology succeed even though he doesn't work for them anymore."

Turbo shrugged. "If he bought the options outright when he left, he might now be sitting on a loss--and maybe he figures helping Kronology is a way to try and goose the stock back into the money."

Jacques could help Kronology until the cows came home, and it might not make any difference. That didn't mean he wouldn't try. In addition to stock options, if Jacques was solving customer problems and charging the customer on the side, he could be raking it in on all sides. "I guess it wouldn't be a bad idea to hear what he did for Kronology."

I left Turbo looking happy with his self-assigned task of contacting his old friends to dig up dirt about Jacques' background. I was less pleased with my own remaining chores. Before I left Strandfrost for the final time, I went to my old office and sent an email thanking the guys that had reported to me. Even though I hadn't been officially fired, the grapevine would know. I pitied myself enough without seeing it in anyone else's eyes. I was grateful Turbo had agreed to meet me on the weekend.

I consoled myself with the thought that it would probably take Mr. Vice President and his ward of suck-ups two more weeks to figure out I was gone. Turbo would mention it and turn in my resignation, but the big-wigs wouldn't pay any attention until they got desperate. Oh well. Maybe if I got killed, Strandfrost would somehow end up paying out the life insurance policy.

I went to karate practice to get rid of some adrenalin, and then after a quick shower, drove over to Sean's house. Much to my annoyance, Derrick was there.

He harassed me immediately.

I waved him away. "Look, the guy showed up at my door with wounds. I have no idea how it happened. I brought him here because I was hoping Brenda could help. It was an emergency!"

"Address?" Derrick asked tersely.

Dutifully, I gave him my address. "He lives with you now?" Derrick compressed his lips. I thought Sean was going to swallow his tongue.

I rolled my eyes. "I thought you wanted *my* address, you goof! Huntington lives in the condominiums in Alpine Hills. I don't know the exact address." A total lie. During the three weeks of pretending to be the condo owner, I ordered more merchandise than I ever had in my life. I knew the address very well.

"Is he still working with Federal Agents?"

That, I honestly didn't know. "He showed up on my back porch. I brought him here. I don't know where he was going or where he was coming from." The loser hadn't told me. I couldn't even give Derrick the address of the home Huntington had under surveillance.

"Uh-huh. I expected you to be more cooperative, Sedona." Derrick tapped his pencil against his notebook. "I bet your brother can advise you on why it is smart to help the authorities."

His genuine enthusiasm and belief in the system was touching, but I still wasn't going to tell him I was working for Huntington again. What good would it do anyway? "I have no idea who shot him. I saw no one on the porch and no one on the way over here. In fact," I said recklessly, "I made sure no one followed us here."

Sean's eyes bulged. Uh-oh. He hadn't thought of his own personal danger until my big mouth pointed it out. My feet rolled toward the door.

Brenda caught my arm before I could make it through the living room. "Us girls are going to have a nice little chat now, so you leave Sedona alone. I need some advice with this pregnancy thing, and you two are taking up all her time."

Sean's mouth dropped open. He looked at Derrick for help, but Derrick was busy frowning and flipping through his notebook to see if he had any more rude questions.

Sean sputtered, "But Brenda!" He implored her with his hands. "Why in the world would you want her advice?"

Brenda sniffed. "Because she's a professional."

I'm pretty certain that didn't really explain why she was asking me for help. Nonetheless, neither of them was going to take on a dangerously unpredictable pregnant woman.

Brenda dragged me into what was fast becoming a nursery. The walls were a brilliant shade of yellow that nearly blinded me. A new changing table and crib were parked lovingly in the corner.

"Now," Brenda whispered. "Tell me how you think I should lay out this little pregnancy problem to my boss."

Uh-oh. Straight from the fat into the fire. "What makes you so certain I know?" Suzy had replied to my email, but pointed out that she hadn't had a job when baby Maureen came along because she was already a stay-at-home-mom for Jimmy.

"Simple. You lie to people all the time. It's all that undercover work you do. This should be easy. All you have to do is lay out a plan for how we keep the entire hospital fooled."

Oh...boy.

Chapter 18

Sunday morning I visited Huntington at his condo and told him to expect a visit from Derrick. I also mentioned Jacques' previous job history. Since I didn't think he would be any help at all with Brenda's problem, I left that out of the conversation.

Huntington must have taken painkillers because he didn't seem to be focusing too well. He split his gaze between me and the ceiling. He sat on the couch with his arm in a sling. I couldn't tell how bad his leg might be because he was dressed in dark blue pants. There was a cane propped on the couch next to him. He smiled for no reason that I could see.

Maybe it wasn't such a bad time to ask him some questions. I started with an easy one. "I think it would be a good idea if I had Mark's cell number in case of an emergency." I had a list of good reasons for needing it, but before I could mention a single one, Huntington recited a number in an almost sing-song voice.

"Oh. Great! Thanks." Since he was so cooperative, I plunged ahead. "I'd like to meet the accountant that put you on the case in the first place. I mean, I know I'm not working on the case anymore, but just to clear up a few questions."

Huntington didn't even look at me. I plowed ahead. "Ben something? Remember? Do you know his phone number?"

His eyes drifted to his briefcase. I helpfully offered to look it up.

When he didn't protest, I opened his briefcase and quickly located a smartphone tucked inside. It was quite tempting to take the phone and mine it for information, but I settled for the one phone number. "Now then, his name was Ben...?"

"Martineeez," Huntington had gone from mellow to slurred.

I found the name Ben Martinez without further help from Huntington. "How about we meet tonight if I can get hold of him?" I figured my luck would run out if I waited to get Huntington's agreement after the medication had worn off, plus the guy probably had to work tomorrow, and I know I did.

Since Huntington didn't say a word, I said, "I'll just call him." I pushed the number to make the call. Sadly, Mr. Martinez was out. I took a huge chance and left a message. "I'm calling for Steve Huntington. I work for Mr.

Huntington and was wondering if you could meet tonight..." I wracked my brains for a good place and then settled on the condo. "Can you meet at Huntington's condo to discuss the Acetel account? Say five-thirty or six? Here's a phone number where you can reach me if you're unable to make it." I could bring Chinese. We would all be one happy family while I pumped Mr. Ben Martinez for the information that Huntington was so fond of leaving out.

I hung up and went into the sparkling stainless steel kitchen to make some coffee in the little four-cup pot. Huntington looked like he might need some later. I would have offered him some right away, but when I turned back around, his head had fallen back against the plush leather couch. He was snoring very softly.

I snuck into the bedroom and stole a pillow. I tried to gently coax Huntington over sideways, but it didn't work. Finally, I put the pillow down and shoved him over, making sure his bad arm was on top. He was dead to the world, so I put his feet up on the couch and took off his silly dress shoes. Man was sick at home on a Sunday and dressed for business.

With his eyes closed and his face relaxed...it was amazing how much he looked like Mark. My heart skipped. Bad direction to be thinking.

I left Huntington a note about the meeting at five-thirty since he probably hadn't heard the phone call, and if he had, he wasn't likely to remember. I checked his breathing one more time and was quite satisfied that he wasn't going to die immediately. Since I had been visiting the poor and sick, I figured I could skip church. Well, I had visited the sick, anyway.

After grocery shopping and house cleaning, I was a nervous wreck, afraid to answer the phone in case it was Huntington, but scared not to in case it was the accountant. Even if Martinez called to cancel, I wanted to talk to him.

By four o'clock, I had worn a groove in the carpet and worked up a sweat. I took a shower and dressed in a nice professional pantsuit, one of the leftovers from helping Huntington the last time. It was a rich dark purple and brought out the depth in my gray eyes.

Not wanting to be late, I hurried along, picked up food at Happy Family Chinese and made it to the condo with five minutes to spare. I breezed past Michael, the attendant, with a casual, "No need to announce me."

Michael wasn't fooled. He had his hand on the phone as I darted into the elevator. He probably had special instructions where I was concerned.

Huntington was less pleased than I anticipated. The door was open, and he glowered from within, one hand on his cane and the other holding onto the door hard enough to break the wood.

"Hungry?" I queried, holding up the peace offering.

He stared at me, a muscle in his jaw working. "You drugged me."

"I most certainly did not!"

My honest denial seemed to throw him. He backed off slightly, allowing me entrance.

"Why exactly did I want to meet with Ben? And I thought you weren't working on the case any longer?" Huntington would have towered over me, but I skipped on into the kitchen. He leaned heavily on the cane and had to gimp after me. He stopped at the couch, but since I was busy setting food out on the little glass breakfast table, he forced himself to walk to the kitchen nook and sat there instead.

I gave him my best professional smile. "We need to discuss the case. Remember, I told you that Jacques used to work for Kronology, and he is really pushing their client case hard--more so than it deserves. It's possible Jacques is our prime candidate for getting paid on the side." I laid out my theory with enthusiastic detail. "Jacques may be lining his pockets by taking on Kronology cases and getting Acetel employees to help with the problems for his own gain. Once Kronology publicly tells Acetel there is no solution, Jacques probably gets one of his old buddies to provide the customer with the solution on the side, and he pockets the money from the customer."

It was pretty obvious that Huntington didn't remember any part of our earlier conversation. It was also clear that he didn't trust me. The knock on the door saved me from further embellishment. Since he was already sitting, I helpfully answered the door.

"Ben?"

The man at the door was not the expected bald little fat stereotype with round glasses. He was businessman polished, and although he was probably in his late thirties, he still had most of his dark hair. "Hi, you must be Sedona?"

His long stride brought him forward, and we shook hands. He set down his black leather briefcase and shrugged out of a dark wool trench coat. A gold Cartier watch briefly snagged on the lining. "What's with the sling?" he greeted Huntington. "You been up skiing already and take a spill?"

Huntington grunted some sort of response while I slid into the kitchen. "Can I get you something to drink? I hope you like Chinese. It's dinnertime, so we thought it would be nice to feed you since you came all this way on your day off."

Ben looked a little perplexed, and I realized that except for the trench coat, "all this way" could have been the downstairs condo for all I knew. He looked at Huntington who said, "Help yourself. Bar is right behind you."

Ben did, and I served the cartons of food. "I was just telling Huntington a few things that I've learned, but nothing is concrete. I was hoping we might brainstorm a few ideas and figure out areas that need a closer look."

Ben missed the tension in the air despite the fact that Huntington glared at me every time he looked my direction. "I never had much more than suspicions," Ben confessed. "The numbers look good, but a few quarters back, I started getting a bit of run around when I asked the managers for particular files. It's standard procedure to dig into greater detail every now and then to make sure the company is keeping proper records and can back up their write-offs. I wanted to see some of the original expenses broken down by unit and project." He shrugged. "When I finally asked Pete, the CFO about it, everything was turned over properly. Like I told Huntington, I wouldn't have thought anything of it except I happened to notice the file attributes."

My mind went racing. "Attributes?"

Ben wiped his mouth with one of the cloth napkins and explained, "After Acetel gave me access to their database, I was sorting through the list, comparing file names with some I had already looked through when I noticed in the file folder window the author of several of the official files showed up as "Silvanus" instead of A.J., Pete or one of the managers."

"Silvanus?" That didn't sound like anyone I had met or heard of. "Silvanus what?"

Ben chuckled. "There wasn't a last name, but the file attribute did list Acetel as licensing the software so at least it looked as though the files had been created at Acetel by someone who worked there. I actually thought it was kind of comical. Since when do the project managers use Roman gods as their ID?"

I swallowed and choked. Roman gods? I could think of a few personality types, that might use a Roman god as a name. I didn't like the implication. "Which files had this name on them?"

Ben helped himself to another serving. "About half of them that I requested, maybe more. It really doesn't matter who created the files as long as they are accurate. It was one of those little things out of place."

Huntington finally put his two cents in. "The most obvious files were customer account files, which is why you're supposed to be sniffing through the customer accounts."

But Radar had told me that the customer files weren't being tampered with. Had he been lying? Was one of his gamer IDs a Roman god?

"This is excellent Chinese," Ben said. "Where did you get it?"

"Happy Family Chinese. Were there any other clues in the files?"

"Only the fact that if someone isn't skimming, this is one poorly run company. Other companies in the industry are on solid ground, and Acetel has plenty of work. Acetel charges hefty prices for the work that they do. There's no excuse for things to have gotten so bad they had to lay me off."

Ben managed to hide most of his annoyance over being laid off, but it did make me wonder again about his motives for suggesting the investigation. Not all whistle blowers were innocent--and some might be after revenge. Regardless, I went after more information. "The only work I know of that Acetel has been providing, but not being paid for is when Acetel works on Kronology problems. Acetel tries to find a solution for the customer, but Kronology won't supply one so the customer never pays Acetel. What if a guy like Jacques were to provide a solution to the customer on the side? He could then talk the customer into paying him under the table."

Ben shook his head. "The kind of losses we're talking about have to be more than one customer. If it were a single fifty thousand dollar contract missing now and then, it would be a blip on the balance sheet and wouldn't require layoffs."

I pushed food around on my plate. "Kronology is the only company that I've come across so far that supposedly doesn't fix their problems, but there could be more."

"The balance sheet has some unpaid accounts, but no huge red flags. It has to be subtle, whatever it is." Ben leaned back. "I don't think I can eat another bite."

Huntington said, "The inside guy must be deleting records because there aren't enough unsolved cases to explain the losses. Whoever is guilty doesn't want the customers or Acetel to know. The only way to do that is to delete the evidence. Sooner or later our cameras are going to catch the guy with his fingers typing the keys on the wrong computer at the right time."

I wasn't sure about that, but we had already discussed the cameras and their limitations.

Ben got up and helped himself to another drink. "It's possible the company is just very poorly run. Little things don't make sense though. It appears they have more work than they can handle and plenty of large contracts. It should be more profitable."

Huntington half closed his eyes. He was quiet for so long I wondered if he had passed out.

"Huntington?"

"No, there's definitely a problem somewhere," he said. "Because if everyone involved is so innocent, why did someone come after me with bullets?"

Instead of feeling triumphant, I was even more dejected. "There is that," I agreed. The new facts didn't offer any additional hints that Jacques was involved either. Worse, Silvanus sounded like a really good gamer name, and I knew of at least two people at Acetel that fit that description. One of them also happened to be a very good hacker.

Chapter 19

Having officially resigned from Strandfrost, Monday morning, I marched into Acetel intent on getting some answers. Of course I still had company assignments, so I headed to the lab first. Before I could gather the data from the weekend performance run, I got lucky and saw Radar unlock the server room. The door was a whisker ahead of slamming when I nabbed it. Sliding in, I whispered, "Where are the cameras?" I looked up, but didn't see any. "Are there bugs too?"

He looked amused. "No, but if you're worried stand this way and don't move your lips."

To his surprise, I did as he suggested and then asked furtively, "I know you said you can tell if someone tampers with the service contract records, but have you checked to see if they deleted any records completely?" I told myself one more time that I was only substituting for Huntington until he recovered.

Radar exhaled hard as if I'd punched him. He glanced up at the ceiling before leaning over to tie his shoe. "Those records aren't kept on these servers," he hissed.

"I didn't ask you where they *are*," I clarified, uneasy in my own right. "I asked if you could look at them. I need to know a couple of things." When he didn't refuse, I continued. "First, how many contracts are completely unpaid. For example, how many times has a customer hired Acetel to obtain a solution for non-working equipment from Kronology, but never been paid because Kronology refused to admit there was a problem?" Ben wasn't convinced there were enough unpaid accounts to be the cause of the layoff, but I still thought Jacques might be running an illegal side deal, especially if solving Kronology problems might help his stock.

Radar looked at me askance. "Why do you want to know how many failures Acetel has? Thinking of solving the cases to make yourself look good?"

I ignored his smirk. "I also need to know if anyone is deleting service contracts entirely either before or after they have been paid." If an inside guy filled out a service contract, got the problem fixed and then somehow diverted funds to his own account, he could delete the record and he'd be home free. No one would notice that money was missing, because the whole case would be missing.

Radar sat back up, but he fidgeted. "I told you, no one that shouldn't be is accessing those files. What are you looking for?"

There were several holes in my theory, but Radar was going to be a lot more help than any cameras so I took a deep breath and plunged in. "I'm really not sure. I know you are tracking certain files, because you're wondering who is accessing them, but what if someone that has legitimate access goes in, creates the contract, but then later deletes part of the record or the entire record after the work has been completed?"

He thought for a long time about it. He even sat down at the console and did some typing. I got more and more nervous while I waited. There was one big problem with asking Radar for help. He was good, and he was obviously a hacker. A very good hacker could mess with the service contracts any time, in any way. I didn't think Radar was guilty. He was the one that had mentioned to me that he thought something weird was happening. If he were guilty would he do that?

Plus, I doubted that he carried a weapon. Unless he strangled me and left my body behind the computers, I was probably safe. That and there were cameras watching even if they didn't pick up on what we were saying.

He finally answered. "I don't see how that could work. Why would the inside guy bother? He'd have to siphon money from a lot of contracts over time to make it worth his while. And he'd have to convince the customers to pay him under the table." Radar shook his head. "Plus, if he deleted the whole contract, someone might notice the missing contract eventually."

"I don't see how it can work either," I agreed. "It would probably be safer for a thief to take money from part of a contract rather than delete the whole thing, but I don't want to overlook any possibilities."

Surprised, he faced me again. "If you don't think the scheme would work, then why bother to look through the contracts?"

I shrugged helplessly. Because if I didn't know how an inside guy was stealing money, maybe I could prove how he wasn't. And if Huntington happened to be right about the method, maybe I'd stumble across the proof he needed. Of course we'd still have to figure out who was changing or deleting the reports, but Jacques was an excellent candidate.

"Who are you working for? The cameraman?"

I pressed my lips shut.

He rolled his eyes. "Okay, I can check file dates and see if there is a pattern of some contracts that started out huge and then later had stuff deleted. I haven't actually looked for deleted records either, but I can pull some things from tape backup to see if records are missing."

"That would be excellent." I could tell he thought I was crazy.

Radar shook his head. "The customers would have to be handing this guy a check or cash. You'd think that would make them a bit suspicious in this day and age of electronic payments."

He was right. I could see Kronology paying Jacques on the side, but if he tried to work private deals too often, one or more of the companies would smell a rat and complain. "Maybe he gives them a fifty percent discount to pay him in cash under the table. Might make it worth it for some."

I didn't want to stick around and give Radar time to shoot even more holes in my theories, so I scurried out and tried to look innocent when Vi saw me coming out of the server room.

She waved hello.

I waved back and meandered to my station.

Once there, I calmed down. The day wasn't looking too critical, and I was proud of myself for getting things moving in the right direction. That good feeling lasted about forty seconds, right up until Art shouted at me.

"Hey, babe!" He charged across the lab, straight down the aisle leading to my station. Since he was looking straight at me, I could only hope he somehow died before he reached me.

I scrunched down in my chair and prayed for gunmen, a lightning storm or a miracle.

No help arrived. He strolled over with his thumbs tucked into his jeans and his rhinestone studded boots, yes, rhinestones, clacking on the concrete floor. His pants were tucked inside the boots. His belt buckle was now seasonal; not only did it have shiny crystals around the border, the text screamed, "Happy Holidays!" before scrolling to, "Art. The man!"

"Your computer still working okay?" he asked.

"Don't *ever* call me babe. Not in the grocery store, not in private, not at work, not anywhere."

"Huh?"

He couldn't hold a thought long enough to remember shouting out the phrase only seconds ago. I glared at him.

"Wowza!" He leaned over my terminal. "That's some impressive performance numbers you're getting there." He mashed his hand on my computer monitor and left smarmy fingerprints. "You're going to fit in here nicely, aren't you? Maybe we'll have a chance to work more closely together. I should put in a good word for you with Jacques."

I had no earthly idea what he was babbling about. "I need to go help Vi," I said.

"Is this the baby putting out those numbers?" He was dangerously close to my setup.

"Uh..."

"It really rocks, doesn't it?"

Bill happened around the corner of the racks and spotted Art. Like a wary wildebeest, Bill stopped on a dime. He spun around, but not quite before Art caught the movement from the corner of his eye. "Bill! How are you? I was wondering, man, did you have a chance to put that stuff out on the website for me?"

Wasn't it Art's job to make sure the website was up and running? "I thought you maintained the website."

"Oh well." Art hung his head in an attempt to look bashful. "Bill offered to help me, and I couldn't turn him down. You wouldn't believe the upkeep on the thing."

Bill looked like he could believe it and knew the pain rather more intimately than Art. While Art was facing me, Bill seized the moment of distraction and ran. Without a sound he was gone behind the racks of equipment.

Art turned back and leaned over my server in order to try and see where Bill had gone.

"Art," I yelled, "watch--"

Too late. His hand smashed down against the surge protector power button. The whole system spiraled down to...silence. In dismay, I watched the screen blip to black. I stared at it, willing the run of weekend results to come back. It took *hours* to run those tests, and now I was going to have to start over. In slow motion, I turned to face the enemy.

Murder.

Apparently there were some vestiges of survival instinct left in the Neanderthal brain because Art backed away, stuttering. "There...there was a power failure. Or surge. Could feel it," he babbled. I followed him with my eyes and clenched and unclenched my fists. As I took a step toward him, he turned and fled full speed out of the lab.

I slammed my hand on the table instead of following him. With a groan, I plopped down into my chair. The screen remained miserably blank.

A few seconds of silence reigned before Bill dared poke his furry head tentatively around the side of his rack. "Is he gone?"

"Not far enough!"

Bill came out of hiding. "I *offered* to update the website? Griefer. If he comes in again looking for me, tell him I left for the day." He shook his fist at the lab door before retreating behind the machines.

I doubted Art was actually smart enough to intentionally cause trouble, but like griefers--gamers that went after other gamers' characters even when it wouldn't help their own score--Art was severely annoying. With no other option, I reached over to turn the power back on. If only I had copied the results to a file before Elvis-the-idiot had shown up. I needed to automate that part and soon.

The tests weren't that hard to restart, but I hadn't finished doing so before Jacques called. The Kronology guy had emailed and asked for a phone conference to get the "real" information they needed. Jacques was less than pleased with this development. He squawked into the phone, demanding my presence in his office.

I hurried upstairs.

"I told him how to duplicate the problem," I defended myself. "Although from the customer report, it's pretty darn obvious. My report or the customer report should have worked for them."

Jacques sat behind his desk, looking stern. "He mentioned that you gave him some information, but that you were unable to really help him. Our job is to help the parties arrive at a solution. This may mean finding the root of the problem by going the extra mile."

I tried to be patient, but I was embarrassed and frustrated at the way the Kronology guy had made me look incompetent. "If the server is shutting down this easily, all they have to do is duplicate the problem and check the parameters themselves. I would define his response as a smoke screen."

Jacques tapped his desk with a pencil. "No, no! I am certain they are merely confused. The phone conference is in ten minutes. If you can have a complete picture by then, it would really help."

Help? Why not give me the code, and I could fix it myself? I slammed back into the lab. The Kronology guy should be able to obtain the information he needed in his sleep. Jacques had to be in on something illegal. There was no other reason to ignore the obvious unless he was a bigger idiot than I could imagine.

I pulled one power cord. The server shut down. I rebooted the server and noted the stupid parameters again. Not that any of the data mattered in this case because a server crash was a server crash.

I made it to the conference room fifteen minutes late. Jacques had already started the conference call. His forehead was beaded with sweat and the table in front of him was full of pen marks. He was also backpedaling fast enough to take out the wall behind him. "No, no, we're not saying you have a bug. No, we duplicate the customer problem. We don't tell the customer what you did wrong." Dazed, he beckoned me into the room. "Sedona! Here she is now, she can explain the test."

I took a seat and started talking. I explained the sorry details carefully. Whoever was on the other end of the line either didn't understand English or didn't want to.

"This is Craig. Why did you pull the power cord?"

This was not supposed to be a chicken crossing the road joke. "That is what the customer did."

"Was there something wrong with the machine? You shouldn't go yanking power cords out of the back of things."

I pinched the bridge of my nose and gave a slightly nasal reply. "The customer was testing your claim that the system could run with one cord plugged in and the other for a backup. My guess is that when one side gets unplugged, you record the system as not having power and this causes the server to crash."

"Impossible." This was a new voice. "We just monitor the system."

Doggedly, I kept trying. "A program somewhere has decided the system is in critical condition unless both cords are plugged in."

Jacques tried to placate them. He droned on about his belief in their company and products. He reiterated that we had not told the company with the complaint that we had duplicated the problem.

"That would be libel," an unidentified voice snapped. "We certainly hope you aren't publishing false reports."

I butted back in. "Let's concentrate on getting the customer an answer that solves his problem. I spoke with Craig about duplicating the test. Have you done so?"

There was a lot of whispering on the other side of the phone. Finally Craig spoke up. "Tell me again what you did to crash the server."

Okay, there went my patience. "I did not crash the server. I didn't write any of this inept code. All I did was pull a power cord. The server shut off. There are two power cords. The server should have continued running."

"After you pulled the plug, then you started the server?"

"No, the server was powered on and working fine. I pulled the cord. Then the server crashed."

"You shouldn't go around pulling things."

"So you're saying that pulling one of two power cords is not supported." Their much-advertised feature was a lie. "Maybe the machine won't even start unless both cords are plugged in."

Craig's voice got happy. "Oh, we've run that test. We're sure if you start with one power cord, all will operate normally."

Someone in the background muttered, "I could bench press twice her weight with half my brain tied behind my back."

No one said anything for a few seconds, and my slow burn ignited into an inferno. "Did you take into account that I am six two, weigh two hundred thirty pounds and am a black belt in karate? I'm not all that keen on the idea of being bench pressed, and doing so will not help solve the customer problem." I had to stretch to reach five seven. With my lax attendance at karate, I was lucky I had made it to green belt in three years.

Jacques tapped his pen so hard against the table, the laminate chipped. He sputtered. I took a deep breath and cut him off. "Listen guys, if you can't duplicate the problem there, why don't you visit our lab? Perhaps if you see it happen, you'll be more comfortable troubleshooting the problem."

There was a lot of paper rustling on the other end, several below the mike mutterings and finally the unidentified voice agreed. "You guys could use some training on our stuff anyway. How about we visit your lab and show you how the system is supposed to operate? Then you can file your report."

"That would be great." I failed to keep the irritation out of my voice. "I'll show you the test I ran. You can tell me if you're able to fix it."

More silence and then Jacques finally spouted polite goodbyes and dates for the visit and other political nonsense. By the time he hung up the phone, I was as annoyed with him as I was with the Kronology people

Without a word, I got up to go to lunch. He called out after me, "Sedona, we need to talk about this!"

It was probably best that I not kill Jacques, at least not yet. If I got myself arrested, I would be protected from Beefy and Buns, but I wouldn't be doing Huntington any good.

Lunch normally gave me time to reflect and calm down, but this time all it really did was quell the growling in my stomach. I hadn't even had time to make peace with having to quit Strandfrost before the rest of the morning had taken on the beauty and serenity of a tornado.

The day didn't settle as fast as a tornado either. When I returned from lunch an email from Jacques requested my presence in his office. Great. Maybe I could get fired a third time this month. That trip to Hawaii was looking awfully good.

Jacques was calmer in his own territory. He wasn't sweating anymore. Ensconced safely behind his neat little desk, he waved me to a chair. He steepled his stubby little fingers, and then changed his mind about sitting still. He tapped a pencil on his desk. I thought about grabbing it and snapping it in half.

"The call didn't go very well," he said.

"Maybe in person they won't be able to deny the problem."

He tapped harder. "We can't alienate these vendors. We need their help to solve the customer problems. Without them, we have no service to provide."

"Okay," I agreed. "I can write the report for the customer and explain that both cords must be plugged in. But they aren't going to be very happy about it since they paid for backup protection and they got a giant boat anchor."

"Uh…but…" He couldn't counter my very logical idea, so he changed the subject. "Why did you have to mention that you know karate? That isn't a good way to start vendor relationships. This is a very, very important computer company."

No one had been attacking his skills and threatening to use him as a barbell. Men didn't make asinine comments like that to other men. "I wasn't the one on the phone call who changed the subject to sports."

Jacques' only response was his little owl blink.

"Look at the bright side. We were able to move on from sports after I clarified my talents."

"But, you lied! Why did you tell him you weighed two hundred pounds?"

Einstein was missing the point. "Because I only weigh one hundred twenty-five on my fat days, and didn't want him thinking he could actually bench press me!" No way was I admitting that if I totally pigged out, the needle on the scale edged a lot closer to one-thirty. I gave Jacques an evil eye and stood up. "I'm not good with being threatened."

As I walked out he called after me, "You're not six two! Whatever will you tell him when he comes here?"

My arms flapped with frustration. "I'll tell him that I've been dieting. Women are always dieting. I'm more successful at it than most."

His pencil tapped.

I left.

His actions were definitely suspicious. There was no logical reason for him to defend Kronology or to continue to bend over backwards to keep them happy. He was up to something, all the way to his beady little eyes.

Radar caught me in my office as I was contemplating throwing in the towel for the day, even though it was early.

He came in, shut the door and sat down. "Your buddy keeping an eye on you in here?"

I shrugged. I hadn't looked to see if there were cameras in my office. Since I wasn't that interesting, I couldn't imagine why Mark would bother, but who knew?

"You should work late," Radar suggested, looking me in the eye.

"Oh?" I asked in dismay.

"Yeah. In the lab."

I tried to think of an excuse. Of course, Radar was probably more help than anyone else would be, but my day was not going well. I didn't need to add any more disasters. "Why?"

"Heh, heh, heh," he laughed.

I always worried when engineers were happy. It usually meant they had figured out how to fix something, how to destroy something or a strange combination of the two. "What will we be working on?"

"Answers. I'd rather do it with a witness present just in case."

"In case?"

He stood up and put his hand on the doorknob. "This way if we find anything and something happens to one of us later, your buddy will have it on camera, right?"

I didn't like the sound of that. Radar being enthusiastic about the idea of cameras wasn't good news.

Chapter 20

Unfortunately, I had more than enough work to stay convincingly late mainly because my weekend test had to be redone.

I started the test and then typed up an outline for the report, leaving space for the final results. Vi was still working nearby when I finished with the outline. Since I didn't want her to see me knock on the server room door, I double-checked the companies that Arnold had sent around against Huntington's master list, but found nothing out of place.

When Vi finally did get up to go, she asked if I wanted to walk out with her.

"No, I want to finish this stuff." I pouted, and that wasn't even faked.

"I heard you arguing with Jacques. Are you going to switch out of his group?" she asked.

Uh-oh. I wasn't supposed to be making waves. "Probably not. It was just a Kronology case thing."

"Arnold's great. If you're thinking of switching, let me know. I'll put in a good word for you. I think he's the best, even though Jacques' spends a lot more time, you know, talking up projects and stuff. Arnold's usually pretty quiet."

"I know a guy like that." His name was Turbo.

"I heard they were talking about making Arnold the manager of the whole Denton office. I kinda hope they don't. Then again, maybe he'd be better than Jacques."

I wasn't sure either of the managers could run the Denton office without causing a revolt from the other one. For half a second, I forgot I was undercover and envied her because at least she wasn't working for a boss that was using his employees for possible personal gain.

After she left, I managed to wait thirty seconds, but only by counting out the seconds slowly.

The server room was eerily dark when Radar let me in. The only light came from the computer monitors, painting everything a weird blue hue. Radar had set up an extra monitor that hadn't been there before.

"I didn't think you'd be showing up," he said.

"Why not?"

"You took forever. Pull up a chair."

"What are we looking for?" I asked.

He peered through his long hair. "Aren't you supposed to be telling me?" He turned back to the keyboard. "I looked through the service contracts, but didn't find much. Of course if someone wants evidence gone permanently, our best bet is to get backup tapes and hope there is a discrepancy. But honestly, the customer contract records don't look like anything has ever been deleted out of them."

"I was afraid of that. And if the guy is really good, he's going to make sure any evidence is completely gone, isn't he?"

Radar nodded. "But I thought of another way to get started. We know someone is accessing the system even if we don't know what the guy is up to. With that in mind, I ran a search to find files that were being accessed at strange times--like after midnight. Odd timestamps were how I first noticed someone using the administrator privileges. The admin is usually me, and since I hadn't been logged in during some of those nights, I got suspicious. Of course, if the guy is any good, he will have created a false identity with the correct privileges."

"A "Joe I-belong-in-customer-contracts" account?"

"Exactly. But my method should catch anyone mousing around where they don't belong because the worm is still probably doing his lurking at odd hours. Once we find the activity, we'll track the login ID."

"What if he is using someone else's ID?" I asked.

He shrugged. "My program will still catch the activity. If the ID comes back as someone unlikely--say yourself, you can tell me if you really have been accessing the files that late at night."

"You're so funny."

"Watch this." Radar started a program. The human resources database came up, the payroll database and a mess of Word files. "So far these are the only accounts that met the weird hours. A lot of that stuff is probably okay to be accessed, but we have to start the chase somewhere."

I peered over his shoulder at the list. "What are the Word documents?"

"I dunno. Look through them and see if they contain anything interesting."

He had already set up the extra computer, so I sat down in front of it. The information didn't look particularly interesting, but I opened about five of the files and started reading. Two of them were related to hiring; there was a list of grade levels and salaries. One of them appeared to be a ranking of every single employee in the company, a file most likely related to the layoff.

Inspiration hit. "How can I tell where these employees live?" Okay, it was none of my business, and Huntington was probably right; knowing which employees he was watching near my neighborhood might not be of great benefit to me. But since I had stumbled across the employee list and

Huntington *had* been shot in my neighborhood, using the opportunity to find out who lived in Piney Oaks seemed like an excellent plan.

Radar glanced at my screen. "We'd have to look them up. I've seen that list you're looking at. It's just a list of all the employees pulled from the employee database. The red names are the guys that got the ax."

"Oh." I scanned the list. "I see the two names of the contractors are red-lined. The job titles for those that got laid off are all over the place, aren't they? I wonder where they live." If Radar wouldn't show me how to look up addresses, I was out of luck because I wasn't going to be able to hack into the proper records on my own.

Radar wheeled his chair over. "Why do you care where they live? Here, I can show you how to look up addresses."

He must have gone into the human resource database using a back door because no password was required. I was pretty sure there was supposed to be one. Otherwise, people like me could willy-nilly change their salaries and titles and maybe even give themselves a retention bonus.

Since he was watching over my shoulder, I started with the contractor that Becky had told me about. Stella didn't live anywhere near me. Of course, as I was looking up names, it occurred to me that more than one person at Acetel could live within walking distance of my house and be a resident of Piney Oaks. Then again, Piney Oaks was at least a notch or two above my neighborhood. The houses were new and had been designed by a custom builder. I was looking for...someone with a legal or illegal income who could afford such digs.

Radar was still watching, so I gave him a tight smile. I knew the name I really wanted to look up, but I wasn't sure I wanted Radar to know that I was looking for Jacques' home address, so I checked the next two people on the layoff list instead. They had post office boxes, one in San Jose and one in Denton. The next person also had a post office box listed in Denton.

Radar looked down at his cell phone and flipped open the handset. Since it had buzzed and he didn't talk, I assumed it was a page, not a call. He ignored me and sat down at his console quickly.

Good. Now that he wasn't looking, I looked up Jacques' address, not only because I was suspicious of him, but because the guy had annoyed my last nerve today. Sadly, he didn't live in Piney Oaks. Arnold wasn't above suspicion either, but he lived over in Alpine Hills near Huntington. A very nice neighborhood and easy for Huntington to keep an eye on if need be.

Hmph. Maybe Huntington was watching every person in the company and figuring out who lived in Piney Oaks wouldn't be all that informative.

Still...I went down the list, hitting three more people who had been laid off. Two of them had post office boxes in Denton and one had a street address in San Jose.

I started to look up Becky's address because she was next on the list, but seeing Becky's name reminded me of the contractors. Why were there so many laid off people with Denton addresses? Hadn't Becky told me that only the contractors had been laid off in Denton?

I scanned down the list and checked another laid off person. Another post office box in Denton. Maybe I had misunderstood Becky about where the laid off people lived, but it seemed strange that most of them had post office boxes instead of street addresses or apartment numbers.

I checked another one. Alvin Nygen had a post office box in Denton as well.

I spotted the other contractor's name: Ben Martinez. Maybe he lived in Piney Oaks. Maybe he had started this entire investigation because he was a disgruntled, laid-off employee.

I didn't get a chance to find out where Ben Martinez lived. Radar looked up from his computer. "What are you doing!?!" His chair rolled close to mine so he could stare at my monitor.

"Huh? I just finished looking at the name Alvin Nygen. To see if he worked in Denton or not. And he did."

"Troll dung," he muttered. He pushed himself back to his computer and typed furiously. "Get out of there."

I obeyed, and then sat and waited. He kept typing. "That page I got-- someone tagged us looking. An email got sent after you opened one or more of those files. It looks like the email is going through one of the IT mail accounts to somewhere else." He typed some more. "Yup, several emails."

"What?"

He didn't stop typing. "When I have a file tagged--when I'm watching the file--I get an email if that file gets accessed. It looks like someone else had a tag on one or more of the files you opened...and bam, we've been caught. There was a program executed to send an email to whoever was watching. What were you doing?"

I blinked. "I was looking at employee addresses. Mostly the ones that got laid off. Do they have all the laid off employees tagged?"

"*Don't* try that yet!" He started to type, stopped, then started again. "Troll crap in a dungeon."

I sat quietly, letting him think.

"I should be able to figure out the name on the mailbox that is being notified, but it's going to take more time. The guy was clever and used a forwarding mechanism rather than going straight to a single name. Meanwhile, someone knows we've been in here. Crap. They probably knew the first time I was looking around."

"Why would anyone care if we accessed someone's file that isn't even working here anymore?"

"Who knows? You're the genius that is looking for something."

"How do you know someone tagged you before?"

He scrunched back in his chair. "Not sure if they did. I've been in and out and all over the place. I didn't have it set up as carefully as I do now. I wouldn't have figured it out now if I hadn't started getting paranoid and tracking certain other activities."

"Can I open another one? Can you stop the email notification from going out?"

He thought about it. Without answering, he wiggled his fingers over the keyboard and then did some typing. "Okay, what is the next name?"

I found the name of the next person on the list who had been laid off. "Sandra Garcia."

"Why couldn't I have a normal job? No, I have to get involved with genius wander around." After several minutes of frenzied typing, he ordered, "Okay, try it."

I opened it. Bingo. Denton, Colorado, post office box. That made at least six people that had supposedly gotten laid off in Denton, and they all had post office boxes. I was pretty sure Becky had told me only contractors got let go. I hadn't been keeping track of the San Jose addresses, but there had been a lot of post office box listings there too.

I was able to glimpse Sandra's over fifty-thousand-dollar salary before Radar shouted, "Close it!" Then he slumped over. "Too late."

"It sent another one?"

He shook his head. "Not exactly." His cell phone buzzed again indicating an incoming page. He didn't look at it.

"What?" I whispered.

"The mail server went down because my little setup wasn't quite sophisticated enough." He chewed on his nails. "I bet that email notification got stuck...I wonder if I can track the forwarding when I bring the server back up. Of course, all that it is likely to tell us is his fake account name. He could go in and delete that before I get a chance to trace it too."

Network accounts were very complex, but in general, it sounded like the hacker was tracking the hacker who was tracking him. If someone was watching activities that closely, something was very wrong. "If the mail server is down, can I access these other accounts?" I still didn't know what I was looking for, but if someone was interested in us looking, I figured I should look some more.

He didn't look happy. "You could, but that's not going to stop the program that sends emails. They will queue up somewhere. This guy is going to know we were looking at these files. This was not a good idea."

"How are they going to know it was us?"

He glared at me. "They won't know because I'm not using my real name. The only way anyone would know is if you told someone. And you are not going to tell anyone."

In the dark, with the blue light from the monitor illuminating only one side of his scraggly hair, he looked very unsavory. His tone of voice wasn't exactly sweetness and light either.

I felt a need to remind him that cameras were watching. "I guess the only person that will know is the guy with the cameras."

He glanced up at the ceiling. "Yeah, whatever." He glanced back at me, a grumpy slit to his eyes. "Look, I'll have to work on this some more to be able to tell you whether or not we can keep netting around. But you were right about one thing."

"Oh?" I was ridiculously pleased to have any good news.

"Someone is up to something. People don't set traps unless they are running some sort of game."

I thought long and hard about that, but it still bothered me, no matter how I looked at it. I finally asked, "So, uh, why exactly do you set traps?"

He looked back over at me. Out came the grin. "Heh, heh, heh," was all he said.

Chapter 21

I tried to call Huntington both when I got home and then again the next morning. For an injured man, he sure was out and about. I didn't want to leave a message since what Radar and I found seemed awfully important.

At work the next morning, I called Becky. I fully planned to pump her about the layoffs again. "Are you free for lunch today?" I asked.

"Absolutely. We can leave now. I'm starved!"

"Except that it's eight in the morning. That would be breakfast."

"Okay, okay. We can wait until noon."

Since she didn't seem to be in a hurry to get off the phone, I asked the first of my questions. "Are you sure that no one from Arnold or Jacques' group got laid off? Some guy in the lab said something about a bunch of layoffs here in Denton. I hope no one thinks I took a job out from under someone."

"No way! We were really lucky here. We only lost Ben and Stella, but Stella doesn't count because they hired her back. I'm sure no one is looking at you like you took someone else's job! Maybe if they knew about you in San Jose, but not here."

"Thanks, you're probably right. Twelve for lunch?"

"Excellent. I'll come grab you from the lab."

What were the chances that six other people had been laid off and that Becky knew none of them? Not...likely.

I headed for the lab to get some work done. Before I made it to the stairwell, a voice hailed me. "Sedona!"

Arnold was standing in the hallway with Pete Saget, the CFO. "You have a minute? I wanted to introduce you to Pete while he's in town."

That seemed quite unnecessary, but I marched over and stuck out my hand. "Hi."

Arnold pushed his glasses high on his nose and smiled wide. "Sedona has been working on a Kronology case, if you can believe it. She's making some headway. I've been so impressed I've been thinking she'd make a great addition to my A-team."

Well, that was news to me. My eyes narrowed.

Pete gave me a football coach evaluation look. I did my best to remove the distrust from my face. I didn't like being a pawn in other people's power games, especially when those people didn't bother to talk to me first.

"How are you liking Acetel?" Pete asked. "Finding it challenging?"

"Yes," I responded to his second question rather than his first.

Arnold punched my shoulder playfully, "What do you think, are you ready to move to the A-team?"

Oh, a trick question. If I said no, it made me look like I didn't want to excel. If I said yes, Arnold would assume he had my blessing. Now see, this was not good. Being cornered made me ugly. My hair stood on end, and I was positive my fingernails grew an inch. It was possible a little forked tail whipped around behind me. "I'm confused," I said, looking first at one man and then the other. "I thought I was hired onto the A-team working for Jacques. I mean, I was told you needed a specialist-- a top person in this spot."

CFOs don't get to be CFO's without political acumen. "Absolutely. All of our positions are top-notch. We want keen investigative minds, ones that grow, become team players, but still think outside the box."

What? Garble-gook. I put on my very, very sweet face, the one that made Sean worry. "Jacques has quite a reputation. I noticed that he takes on cases that no one else will touch. I heard he is up for a promotion to head up the whole Denton office because he is so good at coaching individuals on their career goals." And wasting my time, but I left that part out.

Arnold pushed on his glasses again and glanced sideways at Pete.

See, that was the problem with politics. You think you're maneuvering and making headway only to find out that last left turn was a u-turn.

Arnold's neck got red as we waited for a response from Pete.

Pete's dark eyes bored into me, making me feel like a scummy beetle rather than a potential member of the football team. Perhaps he didn't care for my brand of self-defense.

"Jacques is a good manager, isn't he?" Pete said. "I'm very lucky to have good managers in Denton. They keep the ship steering in the right direction." He slapped Arnold's shoulder and moved away, down the hall. "It was nice to meet you, Sedona. Keep up the good work."

"Nice to have met you too." Arnold would likely bomb my office later. At worst he was probably hoping to tout his stupid A-team and at best plotting to get an additional employee out of it. Maybe I should have told him I was working undercover for Huntington, and I didn't care about any of his petty little games.

Riiight.

I really needed to find Huntington and give him an update. My mind was still chewing over the post office boxes in Denton. Why didn't any of them have street addresses? Anyone could open a post office box. And that same anyone could pick up a paycheck. But…who were the employees? And why didn't anyone here seem to know about them?

I thought of the size of the write-off for the quarter. Was Acetel paying an entire team that worked on a different campus? A secret workshop that solved customer cases, but instead of that payment going to Acetel, it went straight into an embezzler's pocket?

I closed my eyes, but could only vaguely remember Bill saying he was happy he hadn't gotten laid off. He might have said something about San Jose, but I couldn't swear to it.

Before lunchtime, even with half my brain on something else, I managed to record the performance numbers and start another test. I finished up the report for the Kronology customer and sent it to Jacques for approval. Instead of answering my email with glowing praise, he sent me a meeting request for three o'clock to go over my employee improvement survey questions. What a pain in the posterior.

Becky came down early for lunch, but I was ready.

We headed to the parking lot, walking single file down the stairs that graced the dormant grassy slope outside the building. We were halfway down when the black Lincoln screeched up and Beefy got out. His New York accent hadn't improved. "Youz needs to come with us."

Of course, I should have expected my buddies to try again. It was terrible luck they picked lunchtime when I was on my way out with Becky.

"Run," I screamed at Becky and shoved her back up the stairs. Mr. Beefy had a gun under his jacket. He showed it to me, but kept it relatively hidden from the world at large.

Becky did not run. What she did was let out a scream that nearly shattered the windows on the Lincoln.

I faced the enemy and grabbed the railing on either side of the stairs as Beefy came my way. I jumped and let loose a kick. He leaned away. I would have missed completely except that with my hands on the rails, I had extra reach. My flailing leg caught his nose on the way down rather than on the way up.

His nose popped, a quiet but distinct crunch. I guessed that his nasal accent was about to get worse.

Panicked by the continued screaming from behind me, and the fact that the driver was getting out of the car to help, I followed the kick by launching myself away from Becky towards Beefy. The palm of my hand smacked his already bleeding nose. He went over backwards like the side of beef he resembled.

Sadly, the driver didn't hesitate. He took the stairs toward me three at a time.

I jumped the rail and ran, sliding across the frozen grass slope. Thank God I never wore heels to work.

Contrary to my thinking that Becky was no help at all, her unabated screaming brought people to the door. Before the Bun-dozer could run me down, three and then four guys poured out of the building. The Bun-dozer reversed. He started to jump back over the railing and grab his buddy, but there wasn't time. He changed directions again. With a flying leap, he sprawled inside the passenger side of the Lincoln. For a moment, he looked like a beached whale trying to swim his way to the steering wheel, but he managed to slam the passenger door shut and step on the gas.

My rescuers ran to Beefy just as the guy started to get up. I recognized Bill as he shuffled in a funny lope down the steps. With a loud *plop* and a dull cracking noise, he sat himself proudly atop Beefy.

Still, Becky did not stop screaming. "My God, my God, Sedona!" This was followed by another banshee wail, and an operatic screech of, "Are you okay?" She got a leg up over the rail and then ran my way, flailing her arms like a windmill.

Dazed, I sat down hard and hoped she didn't run right over me. The cold ground went straight through my jeans, but was real and somehow comforting. Becky took a couple more woozy steps in my direction, her hand to her heart. "I don't feel so good. Spots. Black spots." Her head searched around like a drunk looking for car keys. "Help!"

Like a bad omen, a very bad omen, someone answered her prayers. "I'm here, I'm here, EMT training, someone call an ambulance, clear the way, I can help!"

I didn't even have time to turn my head before Elvis lost his footing.

In a dazzling, rolling swoop, Elvis took Becky's legs right out from under her. The two of them slid downhill, almost onto the tarmac before Becky came out on top. She let out a roar and smacked Elvis on the head with her forty-pound purse.

"Get away from me, you lunatic. Someone get him away from me!" She made a mad scramble to her knees, trying to escape. "Don't touch me! I'll die first! I'll kill you if you touch me. Anyone lets you give me mouth-to-mouth I'll kill them too!" Relentless, she beat Elvis with her purse.

I honestly don't think the guy was still trying to help her; he was just trying to get up, but disoriented, he couldn't get away.

Radar poked my shoulder tentatively. "You okay?"

I nodded. "Someone should calm her down."

He looked at me like I had lost my mind.

Well, okay. She didn't look very approachable. She was still screeching, and she had tears running through her makeup. None of the rescuers, not even Bill, who was still firmly mashing the prisoner, looked willing to take on Becky in order to save Elvis from sure destruction.

With a sigh, I hauled myself up from the ground. Becky was considerably taller than me, and at the moment she was a lot angrier. There was nothing to do but put my arms under hers and pull her backwards. If I had been below her instead of above, it wouldn't have worked. "Becky, Becky, it's over," I shouted, trying to haul her backwards up the hill. "Rebecka!"

She sobbed hysterically and nearly slipped out of her jacket. "I've been attacked!"

"It's me!" I tried again. "Stop Beck! You're okay now. No one is going to hurt you." Since she was unable to hit anyone now that I had her arms, she hurled her purse in Elvis's general direction.

"I'm not letting him touch me!"

"He's not going to. Honest." I confided this promise in a loud shout into her ear.

"I mean it," she shrieked.

"It's okay. Really."

She struggled until I managed to get her several feet away from Elvis. Unbelievably, like some sort of headless chicken, he kept on coming until Radar came down the slope and blocked him.

Becky panted heavily once or twice and then, finally, the fight went out of her.

I loosened my grip, letting her fall forward so I could help her sit down. "It's okay, Becky. They're gone."

Well, not everyone was gone. Police cars pulled into the parking lot, lining the curb. More flashing lights pulled in as we sat there.

Radar meandered lazily back up the hill and disappeared inside the building, but three other guys began telling the police what they witnessed. Someone carted a handcuffed Mr. Beefy into an ambulance. The ambulance personnel came over to soothe Becky. I left her to their careful attention.

Wow, that woman had a short panic switch. She probably shouldn't hang out with me anymore. The guy that had driven off wasn't going to be so nice the next time he caught up with me.

I didn't have much time to worry about it though. The cops started asking a lot of questions. Someone figured out in a hurry that I was Sean's sister. Then Derrick showed up, followed shortly by Sean.

I had already given my statement, and as soon as Sean arrived, he stood next to me, defying anyone to ask me more questions.

Radar came back outside and approached us. He dumped a sandwich in my hand. He had gone to the Subway across the street, bless him.

"Aren't you going to give me any of that?" Sean wanted to know.

"No," I said, protecting the sandwich from his greedy hands. "Half is for Becky."

Becky didn't look too interested in food. She was still mad and a little hysterical. She had hold of Derrick's arm and was demanding Art's arrest. Art, dumb though he was, belatedly figured out that it was time to clear the disaster area. He scurried back inside when Becky started detailing his crimes.

Jacques and Arnold finally appeared and began to "manage" the situation. Arnold approached one of the officers and wanted to know if Acetel could get round the clock protection. Receiving a non-committal answer, he began quizzing one of the police officers on their methods for catching the crooks.

Jacques bustled over to me. I was ready to brush off his concerns when he asked, "Do you think you'll make our three o'clock meeting or should I reschedule?"

Sean looked at me and recognized the spark in my eyes. He backed away. "Since you're doing okay, I'm going back to the office. Don't hesitate to call if anyone gives you any trouble." He stared at Jacques rather pointedly. "Must be some important meeting." He turned and made his way carefully back to his car.

On the way, he rescued Derrick from Becky. I ignored Jacques and took half of the sandwich to Becky. "Let's go get a soda," I said.

She sniffled. "With caffeine. And real sugar. None of this diet garbage stuff today. I'm too stressed." She took a huge bite of the sandwich as we headed inside. Right before the door closed behind us, I heard Jacques and Arnold arguing about who would turn in the report to upper management. Arnold was texting someone on his cell phone, no doubt the absent Pete and A.J.

We bought sodas from the vending machine and sat in the cafeteria. "I still think they should have arrested him," she muttered. "Bastard almost killed me."

It would have been tacky to ask why someone as annoying and incompetent as Art hadn't gotten laid off when the company had the chance. I sent the hamster in my brain spinning away, but I couldn't think of a polite way to bring it up. "Who does Elvis--I mean Art, work for now? Did his boss get laid off so he skated through the whole layoff mess and kept his job?"

She sniffled pathetically, still feeling sorry for herself. "Nah, Art reports to Jacques, and Jacques didn't have to lay anyone off. And even though Jacques is a total pain, I don't think he had the heart to fire that big loser. When he first ended up with Art, Jacques sent him to every improvement course he could think of. Art has been to "Seven Habits of Highly Effective People" four different times. Jacques finally gave up and sent him to EMT training. I think Jacques was hoping he would change careers."

"Guess it didn't work."

"No kidding." She crumpled the sandwich wrapper with one hand. "He's going to need more than an EMT if I see him again today."

I grinned. By the time we walked back upstairs, I barely had time to plan my next test before it was time to meet with Jacques about the employee survey. After what I had just been through, how bad could it be?

Chapter 22

Bad bosses are like bad dates, only worse. With a really bad date, you can call a taxi. With a bad boss, you can't even get up and walk out.

Considering the narrow escape I had experienced at lunchtime, I wasn't in the mood to deal with twenty questions that might or might not save a job I didn't even want.

Jacques was blithely unaware of my conflict. He insisted on reviewing the employee improvement survey in painful detail, including the parts I had left blank. "Are these your only hobbies?"

I didn't have time for many hobbies. Telling him I was working two jobs at once probably wouldn't help. "Yes."

He cleared his throat and then listed my spare-time activities in case I had forgotten. "Karate, nunchucks...and shooting at the range..." his voice trailed off.

Now that it was read back to me, I could see that jotting down the first few things that had come to mind might not have been wise. The narrow list might leave a mistaken impression that I leaned toward violent hobbies. "Shooting is a family pastime," I said. "My brother takes me."

"Oh, does he live here in town? Was that him out there today at lunch?"

"Yes."

Jacques seemed to be waiting for more, but I wasn't going to volunteer any additional family nuances.

"I noticed that you didn't completely fill out the twenty-five things you wish to do before you die. That shows you aren't a very focused individual. I see you also left your spiritual goals blank, although that is personal and optional."

My eyes crossed. "I listed eleven goals, and you're right I wasn't entirely comfortable filling you in on my spiritual goals." Especially since one of the goals would have to be to make it to church every week. Shoot, I could have filled in at least two lines because not only should I make it to church, given my occupation and friends, praying more frequently should be a number one goal.

He moved on. "Going to Hawaii as your top goal seems..." he hesitated. He steepled his hands together, an indication he was giving this one all his formidable brainpower. "The purpose of this survey is to help me help you reach your work goals, but also blend with your home life. All goals are worthy of course, but some of them are more...supplemental...than others."

So the Hawaii thing was a little lame. But I really did want to go and had been thinking about it a lot, especially with winter coming on strong. "I wasn't certain you could really help with loftier things like getting a date, winning the lottery and world peace so I tried to stick to more attainable goals."

To my surprise, he looked pleased. "Oh! You could have listed marriage and children under spiritual goals."

My mouth dropped. He made some notes on the paper. "You have to set your goals high even if they don't seem feasible!"

"I didn't mention children." I hadn't even mentioned the "M" word.

"What?" Overcome by his own enthusiasm, he missed my comment. It was probably for the best.

"Nothing." I stifled a large sigh.

He skimmed through the survey again. "You didn't say what sorts of things you would like said about you at your funeral. This is very important, you know."

"It is?" Maybe he thought it was especially important because of the attack. If so, it was extremely rude of him to bring it up. Shouldn't a boss offer comfort after such an ordeal? Telling me to plan my funeral arrangements was...ominous. Maybe he had sent the thugs, and this was his way of letting me know he would get me sooner or later.

Should I leave now, while I still could?

He leaned over the desk, his beady little eyes almost rabid in their eagerness. "If you focus today on what you want people to know about you, then ultimately in life you will be a success! All you have to do is figure out the ending, and then you'll know the entire path!"

I blinked. "What?"

"Profound isn't it?"

I clamped my mouth firmly shut. I didn't correct his misinterpretation of my astonishment. The man was loose a few network connections.

"Think hard on what you want said, Sedona. Perhaps as a starting point, it would be easier if you consider what you want said about you when you leave here."

"Leave here?"

He sat back and tapped his pen. "Of course. You won't work here forever, will you?"

Why do my bosses always say things like that to me?

"I'm going to graph these goals and align them with some self-help classes for you to take, including the personality test, Myers-Briggs. You should sign up for a few more classes than the usual five I recommend to most people."

My eyes crossed, but he babbled on.

"You also need to pick up more projects now that you're almost done with the two you have."

"Almost" done was stretching things, but I didn't have a chance to protest.

"It's time for you to take on a full load. Select up to seven more projects and we'll go over them." He handed me a sheet of projects and a sheet of classes. The prices of each class, at five per employee, were probably enough to bankrupt the company without additional pilfering. And if I were taking all these classes, when did he think I'd have time to take on seven new projects?

I escaped back to my own office, very certain about one thing. Jacques may have found a way to bilk money from Acetel, but he was not running several hidden employees on the side. He simply didn't have time for it, even if he didn't assign them self-improvement courses. Jacques might very well be redirecting work to Kronology, but the man couldn't manage the work at Acetel, let alone extra employees in Denton and maybe some in San Jose.

Who did that leave?

Arnold could probably pull off such a scheme from a technical and organizational standpoint. Or maybe one of Arnold's people could do it.

The problem was that even the most focused manager would have cases blow up in his face. Those cases would require phone calls, new equipment, and re-assignment of people for testing and retesting. Said manager would have a heck of a time showing up to work at Acetel and managing a hidden team via the internet and phone.

I started typing on the keyboard, not sure where I was going, but moving anyway. Who had the skills to slide work to someone else, trust them to get it done and take a cut?

Instead of finishing one of my lab tests, choosing improvement classes or new projects, I trolled the company web. Radar could access anything I couldn't, but what I was after was simple and public: I wanted names. I wanted to find out who could run employees and projects on the side. He'd have to have access to company projects and data, as well as potential clients. He was probably a manager or wanted to be one.

The company organization charts weren't hard to find. I started with the Denton one because Denton only had fewer employees.

The first thing I noticed was that the contractors who had been laid off were still listed. The names stood out because they were in blue and had a "c" after the name. There were more contractors than just the two names I had heard; one HR name was listed as being a direct report to A.J. Stella reported to Pete and still had the "c" next to her name. Ben Martinez, with the title of "financial manager," reported to both A.J. and Pete. The way he was placed on the org chart made it appear as though Jacques and Arnold reported to him or at least through him. "And wouldn't he have had access to all the records? And even if he did, so what?"

The names of the people I knew were easy to find. Everyone was still working for the same manager they worked for now. I only remembered two names from my illegal search of the employee database. Alvin with a last name that started with an "N" and Sandra Garcia. According to the list Radar had accessed, they had been laid off.

Neither name was anywhere on the organization chart even though it still showed Ben and Stella. It was possible I didn't remember the names correctly or maybe the post office boxes had been in San Jose, but I didn't think that was the case.

I pulled up the San Jose org charts. Neither name appeared. Hmm.

I double-checked the dates on the files; they were pre-layoff. Stella and the other contractor were listed plain as day. So where were the two employees that I saw on the layoff list? Maybe the organization chart had been partially updated?

Radar said the client files and test results weren't tampered with. But someone was watching the employee database. When I opened those files, Radar got paged. An email was sent. Goons showed up and tried to kidnap me the next day.

I pulled up every org chart I could find, regardless of the dates. I couldn't find the name Alvin or Sandra Garcia anywhere.

I thought about calling Becky and asking her where the latest charts might be stored, but before I picked up the phone, I remembered Arnold's presentation. It wasn't an org chart, but it listed all the projects and the people.

Since he had emailed it to me, I didn't even have to search for it.

My heart beat a little faster as I read down the projects and names. Neither Alvin nor Sandra was listed.

Maybe Arnold had updated his files and deleted laid off employees. After all, he was using the information to try and get promoted or paid more. Listing old employees wasn't likely to help.

I stared at the screen, picked up the phone and called Becky. She was happy to help.

"Do we have a new org chart? I'm trying to figure out who to call in San Jose for a new project Jacques gave me."

"Just use the old charts. We haven't done new ones yet because the reorg hasn't been finalized. Well, maybe it has been in San Jose, but that's why A.J. and Pete are here now. Yanno, move all the players. I'll send you the ones I have."

"Okay, thanks." It didn't take long for the file to make it through the ether. I scanned it quickly. It was exactly the same as the one I had already seen. No sign of either Alvin or Sandra.

I spent the rest of the day looking through old project files, some in San Jose and every file I could find in Denton. Neither Sandra or Alvin was assigned to anything. There was no trace of either of them except the post office box address I had seen. It was looking more and more as if they didn't exist at all.

Chapter 23

When I got home, I still hadn't heard back from Huntington. He wasn't waiting in my house either. I could sit around and hope he called or I could try catching him at his condo. Pretty simple choice and this time I wasn't bringing food.

One foot was already in the garage when the phone rang. It wasn't Huntington. I had almost forgotten that Turbo existed, never mind that he was "researching" for me. "You almost missed me," I said.

"Is the case keeping you busy?" Turbo asked, as if there was absolutely nothing else in my life besides Acetel and working for Huntington.

"Something like that." I really did need to broaden my activities. My attraction to someone as dangerous as Mark had to be due to some sort of deprivation, didn't it?

"I contacted my buddy, Daniel," Turbo said. "Are you on your cordless phone? You know that most cordless phones aren't secure."

"Of course I'm on my cordless phone." Since he had called my landline, that was the phone I had answered.

"Anyone sitting outside your house could easily pick up a conversation on a cordless phone with a scanner unless you've bought one of the new cordless digital phones or have one that works on the new frequencies."

Apparently I wasn't keeping up on my super spy techniques. "Turbo, I have had the same phone for five or six years. It's not something I replace every year!"

"Does it use the old forty-megahertz frequency?"

I felt a headache forming at the base of my neck. "Do you want me to get my old phone with a cord and call you back?"

The pause was long enough that I could have gotten the old phone, gone to the bathroom, made tea and cookies and taken a nap.

"Uh, well. Perhaps you don't recall the product spec if you bought the phone so long ago." He didn't sound like he thought it was possible to forget such important details.

I was an engineer, but I was not as obsessive-compulsive as all of my friends. Turbo, being at the very far end of that spectrum, frequently obtained the company electronic specifications when it became apparent that, gasp, the schematics of the inside wiring and voltages had not been included in the consumer box. Me, I was lucky to read the bullet points on the box telling me whether or not the phone had speed dial.

Rather than continue the ridiculous conversation, I simply hung up. Grumbling, I called him back on my cell phone.

He answered on the first ring. "Domino's pizza."

"*What?* Turbo?"

"Is the line now secure?"

And if it wasn't, he had sort of blown it with the whole pizza front question. I held back an urge to scream. "Secure as it's going to get."

"Okay." I could picture the look of supreme satisfaction he wore. "Here's the scoop. Jacques was an engineer, but it equated to a low-level management position. He was at Kronology five years and guess what that means?"

I chased the carrot, my mind churning. "Vesting?"

"Bingo. According to Daniel, everyone at the company got stock options when they were hired on, and those options vested after five years. Daniel also mentioned he had been offered twenty thousand stock options when his company got bought up."

"Whew. That's a lot for a grunt engineer."

"Jacques was there long enough and played the game well enough that he probably had the opportunity to get even more options. Jacques may be sitting on them waiting for the stock price to go up."

"He would have held them for seven to ten years now." Maybe he had gotten tired of waiting for Kronology to get its act together and decided to step in and help Kronology customers. "I guess good old Jacques has a lot of reasons for wanting Kronology to succeed, doesn't he?" No wonder he got so hot under the collar when I didn't mollycoddle Kronology.

"Absolutely. Daniel also said he was pretty certain that when Jacques left he got at least two Kronology customers to go through Acetel for support rather than straight to Kronology."

That would make him look very good to his new management--and could he be getting paid on the side for the work? But there had been no evidence of that in the database. And how did the layoffs fit in? It still didn't tell me who the people were that had supposedly been axed from the Denton payroll.

I thanked Turbo for researching the information and hung up. It was time to tell Huntington my suspicions about the post office boxes and inform him that he was watching the wrong guy. I wasn't certain of exactly what Jacques was up to, but he wasn't completely on the up-and-up. He was a much more likely candidate than whoever lived in Piney Oaks. Well...except for the shooting.

I drove to Huntington's condo carefully, watching behind me the whole way and taking a circular route. Eloy, the doorman, parked the car. If someone had managed to follow me, they wouldn't be able to track which condo I went into. Additionally, since Eloy parked the car, the goons couldn't attack me in the parking garage.

Michael, professional greeter, master of the elevator and general "watcher over all things" was working behind the little lobby desk. His face fell when he saw me.

I smiled. "Is Mr. Huntington in?"

"I'll be happy to announce you."

I didn't wait. Let Michael warn Huntington that I was on my way up. Michael probably treated reporters and cops the same way he treated me. Vermin. I was low-class vermin.

When I knocked, Mark answered the door. He let me in and gave me one of his less wolfish greetings, but that didn't stop me from getting a silly grin on my face.

Huntington looked like he could have easily answered the door, despite the sling still around his arm. The cane was no longer in evidence.

"How are you feeling?" I tried to start out on the right foot.

Huntington grunted. "I've been better."

Since I couldn't head for the kitchen and start cooking to get rid of my nervous energy, I perched on the opposite edge of the cream leather couch where Huntington was sitting.

Mark brought me a soda and helped himself to one.

"I suppose you probably heard about the, uh, disaster at work today?" I asked.

Huntington grinned. "Did you really attack some guy with your purse?"

"No," I said irritably. "That wasn't me. I was going to lunch with Becky, and she had an issue with one of the EMT guys."

Mark pulled around a kitchen chair to face the couch. "I've been watching the camera data from yesterday. Any chance the stuff you were looking at is the reason those guys showed up?"

I nodded uncomfortably. "I would guess so." I told them quickly about the files I had accessed and the automatic email warning that was sent. "I was looking up various employee addresses. It's too coincidental that those guys attacked the day after we were looking at those files."

"And why were you looking up addresses anyway?" Huntington demanded. Mark hid a grin behind his soda.

"What difference does it make? The point is, you're watching the wrong guy. You should be watching Jacques. Let's look at the facts here. Ever since you gave my resume to Jacques, I've had people chasing me."

Before I could continue, Huntington interrupted. "You were seen with me in the restaurant. That doesn't point to Jacques."

"When exactly did you give my resume to him? Was it before or after that night in the restaurant?"

Huntington squeezed the side of the couch with his good hand. He opened his mouth to yell at me. Instead he muttered, "Dammit."

"That's what I thought. You had already given him my resume *before* we went to the restaurant, so the resume told him where I was currently employed and where I lived. Those guys could have picked up our trail based on my work history because you picked me up at Strandfrost."

Huntington growled, "If he is up to his eyeballs in this mess, handing him your resume might not have been the smoothest transition into the job."

"And," I added crossly, "He's using company employees, mainly me, to enhance his own pocketbook." I explained rapidly about his probable ownership of stock options in Kronology Servers. "He not only stands to gain if the stock goes up, he is in the best position to make side deals."

"Did you find solid evidence of side deals?" Huntington was finally starting to pay closer attention.

"Noooo, not exactly. I actually found something even more confusing." I hated to get shot down, but I plunged forward. "The layoff list included a lot of people with post office boxes. I looked through the org charts for a couple of the laid off employees, but I couldn't find them. If those people exist, they don't appear to have worked on any project I can find. Yet the payroll and address database show they were being paid by Acetel and laid off by Acetel. Unless Jacques or someone else had them working on the sly, there's no evidence the employees existed at all, which makes no sense."

Huntington sat back. "They have to exist if there are records for them."

"I know it sounds crazy, but no one talks about anyone that has been laid off. Becky is positive the layoffs were mainly in San Jose, but the files I saw indicated several people in Denton."

Mark summarized. "So we've got some files being watched and possibly tampered with. We have employees who don't appear to have permanent addresses and may not exist. We have a guy that may or may not be trying to line his own pockets with Kronology customers. Bottom line, we need to know who has looked at those files and why they were being watched."

"Good place to start," I agreed.

Mark continued, "The cameras aren't going to help us much. We put those in mainly to see if any ex-employees came back to either sabotage systems or try to access data that they might need to continue customer relationships. Whoever is hacking into the system probably isn't using an office machine."

"No, and they definitely aren't using their own login account. It would be stupid to do so. Radar can easily track a login to a particular office machine regardless of what name is used. Whoever is hacking the files is likely doing the work off-campus and off the clock."

"That does bring up an interesting point," Huntington interjected. "Who the hell is Radar?"

Mark started laughing. He obviously knew about Radar because he had been watching the camera files.

My face fell, and my cheeks flamed. Since I was busted, I confessed. "Radar is the guy that has been helping me track down who has been opening certain files." I glanced over at Mark to try and gauge how much he had already told Huntington. He looked back at me with a charmingly innocent expression.

I mumbled onward. "Radar...uses a back door into the system to find out when files are being accessed. He has also set some traps to monitor certain things. Before I even got involved, he noticed that someone was using the Administrator account to crawl around Acetel's systems. I just borrowed his skills."

Huntington narrowed his eyes. "It sounds illegal."

I squirmed. "It wouldn't be illegal if you, representing the board or the company, hired him to track this type of information and keep records. I think it would be a very good idea to copy the files we looked at to a nice safe place. We're dealing with someone who could easily change what I saw yesterday to something completely different."

Huntington gave a sharp nod. "That is actually an excellent idea."

I frowned. He could have sounded less surprised. "The point," I emphasized, "is we need to legally get our hands on those files. Whether you hire Radar to do it, or you know someone you can trust enough to get them, we need to have them."

I looked from Mark to Huntington. Mark watched me closely. His brown eyes were warm, sharply intelligent...and concerned. "There is one other possible culprit you haven't mentioned," Mark said.

I had thought about it, but didn't like the idea. I looked down at the carpet, but that didn't stop Mark from spelling it out. "Whoever is doing this is a very good hacker and is probably stashing a lot of money. And there's at least one person we know for sure who is an excellent hacker. Not only that, this excellent hacker has *legitimate* administrative access privileges that he can use without raising suspicions. Your buddy Radar can also wander into any of the computer rooms whenever he pleases."

I nodded an agreement of sorts, because he was right.

Mark leaned forward intently, his forearms on his knees. I felt obligated to meet his gaze. "Whoever is doing this is incredibly smart,

Sedona, and it's past time to be careful. Maybe Radar is leading you on and laughing up his sleeve."

Before I could decide how to answer, Huntington added, "The setup this afternoon could be the kind of egomaniac thing a hacker would pull. Show you the files, and then silence you at lunchtime the next day."

Since I couldn't readily dismantle their logic, I attacked elsewhere. "Yeah, and the pristine guys that hired you are all above board. Sure, it could be Radar, but since it appears that everyone in the company knows I'm at Acetel undercover it could also be any of the others we've just talked about that set up the attack."

In his own way, Mark agreed with me. "Chances are very good that at this point someone has us all made." He exchanged a look with Huntington.

"There's nothing to be done about it now," Huntington said.

Mark didn't look convinced. "Time to get rid of the obvious enemies."

Huntington gave an exasperated sigh. He glared at his brother, and I had the feeling this was ground already long covered. Without taking his gaze off Mark, Huntington asked, "Sedona, if I buy the ticket to Hawaii, will you go?"

I thought about it. "After the holidays."

"I'm hoping this case will be over by then."

"It is very tempting." How often did one get a chance to vacation for free in Hawaii anyway?

If I had known what the next several days were going to be like, I would have made him get the ticket delivered to the condo and grabbed it from his hand.

Chapter 24

Meeting Radar at Happy Family after work on Wednesday felt more clandestine than meeting with Huntington. Maybe that was because Radar handed me a note with the time and location, and then whispered that I should eat the piece of paper after reading it. Mark's warning about Radar drifted in the back of my mind like yeast, growing on its own.

I didn't eat the note. I mailed it to my home address. If something happened to me, someone would eventually open it. Sean probably, because he was so nosy.

The folks at Happy Family were always glad to see me. There was certainly no point in me trying to appear in disguise. The more stressed I was, the more they saw me; they had seen me in all of my moods, from bag lady-stressed to celebratory happy.

Since this visit was the second one this week, Evie Chang, the motherly owner, was very eager to make sure I was okay.

"Oh, I'm fine. I'm here to meet someone." The restaurant was small and did more takeout than sit-down business. Only half of the ten or so tables were full. I wouldn't have seen Radar had he not stuck his hat in the air. At least I assumed it was his Gatsby hat that waved.

Evie grinned and bustled along behind me with the menu. By the time I reached the table, Radar had the hat pulled low over his eyes.

"Here, here, take menus. I know, I know, not need them, take anyway. Never know, might try Peking duck today, yes?"

She winked and sped into the kitchen.

"Yo," Radar saluted as I sat. His hair was pulled back neatly under his hat. He would have looked quite dapper except for the fact that he was scrunched against the wall of the booth in order to stay hidden from anyone coming in the door.

"Hi." Only one other couple was nearby since Radar had chosen the booth closest to the kitchen door. There were red candles burning on the ends of the table and chopsticks already out.

Evie put a water down in front of me to match whatever Radar was drinking. We ordered.

"So," I said.

"So." He grinned. "I looked up the service contracts, the reports that got sent to the auditor, and hunted around for deleted reports as well. We can be pretty sure that you aren't looking for altered customer reports."

"Did you bring the files for me?"

"Of course. They're in the car. That's why I figured you'd be willing to buy me dinner." His smile was gigantic.

"Oh." I blinked and feigned concern. "Then that makes you an accessory."

His eyes narrowed.

I nodded solemnly. "If you did it as a favor for me, you could probably get off easy. But if you take payment, that makes you an accessory."

"I don't think it is illegal for you to see these reports." His smugness was replaced by eyebrows drawn in a tight line.

"My brother is a lawyer." Sean was always accusing me of being an accessory to something. I wasn't sure reading the reports was illegal, but I was very sure that the way Radar had obtained them was way over the line.

"How about I just bring them in and you can look at them, then?"

I would probably need to take anything he gave me home, but I shrugged agreeably.

He scooted out of the booth, and returned very quickly with a package the size of two large phone books. The stuff I had asked about was on top. I thumbed through it. He was right--the sample reports didn't look like they had ever been illegally altered. There were updates, but every one of them contained additions, not deletions.

He pointed to another section of the pile marked with a post-it tag. "I grabbed some files from backup, but from the date stamps, you can tell that once entered, they are left alone. The only ones that changed were when customers asked for more work. But even then it looks like Acetel usually did a whole new entry rather than change an existing record."

Radar had retrieved all kinds of information, including the layoff files I had been trying to look at. "Sixty-five people got laid off." The company had been at about six hundred fifty. He had not gotten me every employee file, but there were several lists. The first thing I checked were the two names I remembered: Alvin Nygen and Sandra Garcia. Both Denton post office boxes, as I thought.

The food came, but I ignored it for the moment. Perusing the other addresses, I noted that fourteen of the people that had been laid off had addresses that were post office boxes. Most of them were in Denton.

"No one seems to know very many of the laid-off people. Well, except these two." I pointed out the contractors. Neither of them had post office boxes. In fact, Ben Martinez lived in Piney Oaks, the neighborhood near mine where Huntington had been shot! I kept that little note to myself, but found it very interesting. Maybe Huntington hadn't thought Mr. Whistle-blower had been free of ulterior motives.

"It's funny," Radar said. "I work mostly in San Jose, and I only knew one of the people on that list. I thought most of the layoffs had been done in Denton. Another strange thing is that I don't remember adding any of those post office names to the database. I must have added some of them because their start dates are all over the place, going back about five years."

Five years? Aha! Right when Jacques started working for Acetel!

Of course, I had no idea when Arnold or Ben or anyone else had started. My head reeled a bit with the data. I flipped back to the quarterly report. "Acetel took a huge charge for the layoff. They ended up with a loss for the quarter, supposedly related to the layoffs--including paying these people severance."

Radar shoveled food in around his next comment. "Everyone in San Jose assumed the layoffs were here, and you assumed they were in San Jose."

"Post office boxes can be opened by anyone--or the same someone over and over."

"All to pick up a paycheck."

"If these people don't exist, how do we find out who has been collecting the paychecks for five years? And who got their severance?"

Radar looked as perplexed as I felt. "No way of knowing at this point. I already looked to see who deleted these people's privileges when they got laid off. I was expecting someone from HR or Patel, a guy that sometimes works with me out in San Jose. I even looked to see if maybe Art had done the deletions. Funny thing was, I couldn't tell who did it. Whoever it was logged on as the network administrator, which isn't all that unusual, but it means that there isn't a trail tied to a particular name. No way did Art do it because there weren't any obvious errors. Patel wouldn't have done them because I was in San Jose at the time of the layoffs. He only does network stuff when I'm not there."

"Who else knows the administrator password?"

He shrugged. "It's not necessarily the same everywhere in the company because the network is broken into subnets, but in general, all three of us; Art, myself, and Patel. Oh, and my boss, Ramon Gonzales, knows the passwords. His boss too if he ever bothered to ask."

"Or anyone that weaseled the info out of someone stupid enough to give it out."

We both said, "Art" at the same time.

Radar paused in his eating to take a gulp of water. "The real answer is probably even dumber than Art. I got curious, so I looked closer at the setup. The administrator password on each system hasn't stayed the same over the last five years, but from what I can find, it was probably the name of the company for a long time. That means that someone could have guessed the password too, because it is the same password that HR uses to enter payroll information."

"Oh boy."

"You going to eat that?" He indicated my fried rice.

My mouth gaped. "You cleaned up that entire General Tso's Chicken!"

"So? Are you going to eat it or what?"

I thought about trying to look pathetic. That never worked on Sean, so I settled for disgruntled. That never worked with Sean either, but it fit my mood. I put a huge helping on my plate and then passed the serving bowl his way. Radar ate more than my brother and was still skinnier than a rail.

After helping himself, he continued, "And there's one other small problem with all of this."

I had a bad feeling I knew what he was going to say. I fiddled with my chopsticks, but couldn't wait for him to finish chewing before asking, "Did you figure out who was getting email notifications when we were in the system?"

He left me hanging while he ate a few more bites and drank some water. He accepted a refill from Deke, Evie's son, before answering. "That's the problem I was referring to. I had to make sure I could look at these files without any warning emails being sent. That took so long, I didn't have time to trace back the email account. If the guy wants to move around fast and count on getting notified when certain files are accessed, he can't be using the administrator account. There has to be at least one false account that this guy can use whenever other, legitimate accounts won't do."

"Do you think the guy is using one of the laid off employee accounts?"

He shook his head. "Nah, none of those have global privileges."

"What about Jacques or Arnold?"

"They shouldn't have all the right privileges either. No need for them to."

"What about someone above them like this Ben Martinez guy?" I pointed to the name on the layoff list. "He was near the top of the org chart."

"He might have had such privileges when he was at Acetel, but his account would be deleted now."

I stared at the list of employees, including the laid off ones. "Does this pile of stuff happen to have a list of the hiring dates for the employees?"

He nodded. "Sure, but I looked it over. It's not as though the ones with post office boxes all got added at once. Would have been too obvious." He sat back and looked very, very full. He grinned at my worried expression. "Don't worry. I'm well-mannered. I promise not to belch at the table."

"I was more worried about you exploding."

He laughed. "This has fast become my favorite place. You know any other good restaurants?"

"It's my favorite too." I thought about Anthony's Grill, but that wasn't really his style--or mine for that matter. "I like Italian, but haven't found one that fits."

"You been to Italy's Canal?"

I shook my head so he told me where it was located. "I'll have to go there." I thought some more about the information I had gathered so far. "Has someone really found a way to collect a lot of extra pay, including severance? How is the guy collecting the checks? He can't pick up fourteen checks and deposit them in bank accounts with all those different names..." My mouth remained open as a thought struck me. I gaped at Radar like a guppy.

"What?" he asked.

"Do you use direct deposit?"

"To get paid? Sure."

I reached into my backpack for my wallet. It took another second to extract the check that Suzy had written to me. I hadn't gotten around to depositing it. There it was, her mismatched name and signature.

"What's that?" Radar asked.

I showed him the check and explained how Suzy was using checks that had a different name than her account. "Maybe the post office boxes are needed because the HR form requires it, but what if the addresses aren't used to pick up a check? What if each of these employees has a different name and a unique post office box, but their bank deposit account numbers are all the same?"

He stared at the check and then back up at me. Wheels turned.

I dared to ask, "Can you look at payroll accounts? Can you tell if the deposit numbers for those on the layoff list all go to one bank account?"

Radar squirmed. He obviously hated to be pinned down on his hacking activities. Without much enthusiasm, he pushed his plate to the edge of the table. "Maybe."

"Radar..." my voice trailed off. It wasn't a good idea for Radar to be involving himself. "Don't leave tracks."

"You know I was recently offered more stock options at Acetel," he replied. "I guess I'd better ask for paper copies of the stock options. At least that way, if the stock turns out to be worthless, I can sell them as a collectible."

Evie brought the bill and put it next to Radar, of course. I grinned. He scowled.

"Oh, I'll pay for it," I said. "I owe you for the sandwich the other day, anyway."

He grabbed it before I could. "No, I ate most of it. I just wanted to bug you, actually."

Just like Sean. Always trying to yank my chain.

Chapter 25

Do not ask me why I promised Sean I would help Brenda with Thanksgiving dinner. Usually, I roast the turkey and invite them over, but my brother wouldn't give up on the silly idea that his darling wife would one day be able to cook. Brenda was too unconcerned in the kitchen to follow recipes--and that was before she was pregnant. She had an amazing knack for substituting ingredients and thinking it would turn out fine.

It rarely did.

Now that the time had arrived to pay the favor, I was grumpy and nervous. I loved Thanksgiving, particularly the food part. It was unsettling to think I might somehow be cheated out of creamy gravy over succulent turkey, mashed potatoes and all the trimmings. To add to the pressure, my parents, after learning of the impending grandchild, had decided to make the drive.

Sean had, as promised, done all the shopping. When I arrived, a lump of a turkey sat on the counter top, still wrapped. Sean was nowhere to be found now that his part was done, but Brenda was thrilled to see me and eager to get started. When mom heard where the cooking was being done, she declined an early arrival, so I was on my own.

Brenda had recently grown out her hair. The new style made her look a lot like Annette of the Mouseketeers. Her dark shoulder-length curls bounced prettily with no effort on her part. Probably a good thing too. If her cooking skills were anything to judge by, I didn't want to see her hairdo after she got a hold of a curling iron.

"This is going to be sooo fun, don't you think?" With great enthusiasm, she grabbed my arm and tugged me forward. "I have already started on the stuffing. I've been saving breadcrumbs and letting them dry for the last three months!"

I was a big fan of stuffing, but my recipe didn't call for dried breadcrumbs. I'd have to improvise. "Do you have regular bread? I like the bread to be soft."

She frowned. "No." Then she brightened. "We got the Pillsbury rolls you told us about. We could use those!"

"Well, uhm. If we did that, we wouldn't have bread to serve with dinner." Plus the stuffing recipe called for almost an entire loaf of bread. The Pillsbury canister made only eight medium-sized rolls. "Don't worry about it. I'm sure we can figure something out." Maybe Betty Crocker had a dry breadcrumb recipe or maybe we could use the same recipe I normally used even though it called for soft bread.

"Why don't you start on the stuffing, and I'll clean out the turkey?" I wanted to be very sure the giblets and other parts were properly discarded.

She nodded and pointed to a pan of onions and celery. "I already cooked the veggies for the stuffing. I put in all the herbs you listed too."

I sniffed the air. I couldn't smell any herbs. "Did you use fresh herbs?"

She nodded.

"Okay." I wasn't sure what could have happened to the herbs. Maybe she hadn't put a lot in or maybe I was used to smelling them because mincing them made my hands smell like thyme and sage all day. "Go ahead and put half the breadcrumbs in and then toss all of it in a bowl. I add one egg after the butter is all mixed in."

I started on the turkey.

Brenda hummed along happily. "I can't wait to do the pie. Sean just loves your pumpkin pie."

"That reminds me. We should stick the pie crust in the oven." I finished cleaning the inside of the turkey and then washed and dried my hands before grabbing a pre-made crust from the freezer. "That way we won't have to wait to put the turkey in once it is stuffed." I turned the oven on and happened to glance in the bowl she was stirring. I looked twice to make sure I had seen what I thought I had seen.

"Uh, Brenda...I thought the breadcrumbs were dry?" She was stirring a bowl full of soggy bread. Bits of celery floated in the goo.

She nodded. "Yeah, they were. The trouble was they were still dry even after I added the egg, so I added milk. Look," she tilted the bowl, nearly spilling its contents onto the floor. "It looks much better now. I would hate for the stuffing to be dry."

I would hate to have to eat that stuffing period. "Milk?"

She noticed the squeak in my voice. "Do you think I should have used water?"

I could answer quite truthfully to that one. "No." Maybe a tablespoon or two of chicken broth, but not water and not an entire gallon of milk. I put the pie crust in the oven. I thought as hard as I could, but saw no clear avenue that would lead to delicious stuffing. "Maybe we should try it again with the rolls." I dug them out of the back of the fridge. If I only used half of the other ingredients it might work. Or I could try to find my idiot brother and send him to the store for bread. "Where's Sean?"

"He didn't want to interfere with our girls' day so he went to the office." She started humming again. That should have warned me, but I ignored the sign and headed for the study for privacy and called him on my cell.

Sean answered on the third ring. "You need to bring home a loaf of bread." I considered other things I might need. "And get some fresh thyme and sage. If you can't find fresh stuff, get the dried herbs from the baking aisle."

"Why?" he asked.

"Why do you think?"

He didn't say anything for a moment. Finally he asked, "There hasn't been a fire? The kitchen is intact?"

I closed my eyes and tried to rein in some semblance of patience. "Did you get a bag to put the turkey in? I haven't asked Brenda yet and no, there is no need for any emergency rescue personnel at this moment."

"The oven bag is in the pantry."

"Oh, bring some celery. I don't know if she has enough. We can always use the extra with peanut butter or cream cheese."

"I only like peanut butter on them."

"Yes, but I like celery with cream cheese."

"Do you think Mom and Dad will be impressed? It will be the first Thanksgiving we've cooked."

I bristled at the "we've cooked" part. Shopping for groceries was the easiest duty, and I didn't think he should be taking credit for making the meal. Then again, at the rate things were going, there might not be any harm in sharing credit for the actual results. "You might want to bring a frozen pizza or two just in case," I said.

I heard the timer go off. "I gotta go, Sean. The pie crust is done. Will you hurry with the bread?"

I hung up and raced back into the kitchen. Brenda had sense enough to get the crust out. It was a good thing because the sight that greeted me froze me in my tracks long before I got to the oven.

"Crust looks good, doesn't it?" She held up the evenly browned crust, dragging my eyes from the turkey.

I swallowed hard. "Uh, yeah." I trailed over to the counter, focusing on the bird that we were to partake of in a few short hours.

It oozed. Milky goo dripped around the sides. A slimy path leaked across the plate and onto the counter. Closer examination found a pool of smarm resting in the previously empty bird. Mounded little breadcrumbs floated in the opening.

"Oh," she exclaimed.

I thought she had finally realized the error of her ways. "It's okay," I tried, but my voice cracked.

All she said was, "I need help getting the turkey legs clamped together. I stuck the skewers in a few times, but the legs won't close right. The stuffing keeps trying to come out."

She was right about one thing. The stuffing was trying to come out. Maybe if I stayed in the kitchen the rest of the day without even taking potty breaks, I could salvage the rest of the meal. I'd have to warn Sean against eating the stuffing. It was too late to save it now, unless I could get her to leave and then rinse the bird out and start over.

I looked at her gleaming face. Not a chance.

With a sigh, I found the oven bag, bagged the sad bird, and got it into the oven.

"I know Derrick is going to be impressed. He's bringing his partner and wife. Adrian's wife, not Derrick's wife. Derrick isn't married." She looked my way slyly, as if maybe I hadn't noticed that Derrick was single. I had news for her. Only my brother would be foolish enough to marry someone that was this big of a cooking disaster. If Derrick thought I had participated in this mess, he would run if he had any sense at all.

"Does Sean have his cell phone?"

"Why, did you miss him at the office?"

"Something like that." I went back to the study without leaving her any instructions. Hopefully she would bomb the place, and we could go to Luby's or something.

"Bring some Stove Top," I ordered when he answered.

He didn't say anything for a long while. I let static fill in the space. Finally, he grunted a reply. "Too late to save?"

"Yup." I hung up and returned to the kitchen. We made the pumpkin pie and after Sean arrived, we created mountainous appetizer plates with little pickles, celery, carrots and mixed nuts. Once that was all done, I decided to run home.

"I'll make the potatoes and bring them back over here."

"Oh, but I want to help," Brenda protested.

"You've made mashed potatoes before." I didn't mention that they were usually lumpy or soggy. "Besides, you need to take a nap. If I'm here, you'll just run around and worry. That bird has hours to go. Just leave it in there, don't touch it, and don't change the oven temperature. In fact, you don't even have to look at it." I thought really hard about what else she might try, but my mind couldn't begin to imagine what she might do.

I left Sean in charge and Brenda resetting the china on the table for the fifth time. She might not need the nap, but I did.

I slept like a dead person for over an hour before showering and making potatoes. As I loaded the car, Mark showed up. "I'm on my way to Sean's for dinner," I explained.

"I see. What's in the bag?"

"Mashed potatoes on the top, maternity clothes on the bottom."

He raised a questioning eyebrow.

"Brenda, my brother's wife, is pregnant. These clothes are from my friend, Suzy."

He didn't say why he had shown up on my doorstep. His eyes were warm and friendly. Even though we were standing feet apart in my driveway, I remembered drowning in those eyes. I couldn't resist. "Do you want to join us for dinner?"

"Is she a good cook?"

"Not…exactly." Then, I brightened. "But Sean did buy pizzas just in case.'"

His eyebrows went up again. "Pizza? For Thanksgiving?"

I wasn't going to put any money down on Brenda not having touched anything since I had left. "Don't worry. My mom is going to be there, and she will have cooked up a bunch of sides. I'm bringing potatoes so we can always eat those."

"That bad?" Now he looked amused.

"We're pretty good at filling in. Although…nah, I'm sure it will be fine."

Mark finally came along, following me in his vehicle.

Derrick's partner, Adrian Williams, and his wife Sarah were already there. They brought a wonderful German chocolate cake. Derrick managed some sort of cranberry concoction. I tried in vain to substitute the Stove Top stuffing, but ended up lamely telling Brenda there wouldn't be enough regular stuffing. The only really tense moment was when Sarah commented on the "bread pudding."

I quickly advised eating it for dessert. I hoped to be able to somehow get the soggy mess off the table by then.

My mother decided to take more immediate action. She grabbed the serving spoon out of the bowl and rushed off as though it had suddenly sprouted dog hair. Sean, thinking it was an opening, came around the other side of the table, grabbed the whole bowl and yelled, "I'll get a serving spoon."

I'm sure what happened next was an accident because my brother would never intentionally risk my mother's wrath. She must have been on her way back out of the kitchen when Sean turned inside the kitchen entryway.

"Sean O'Hala, what--" my mom sputtered. Sean stepped back, but the damage was…extensive. Soggy stuffing dripped in large clumps down the front of Mom's shirt.

There was one of those funny little family silences before Sean sputtered out an apology.

Brenda made a fuss. "Give me that! Sean, you've wasted half the stuffing! It's a good thing Sedona made Stove Top." She bustled into the kitchen and grabbed the spoon mom had just rinsed and put in the drying rack. "My first Thanksgiving dinner, and you spilled half of it."

Plop, onto the table went the remainder of the goo.

We all milled about again, pretending to be busy while Brenda showed Mom into the bedroom to change clothes.

During the confusion, Mark leaned over and whispered in my ear, "I take it I am to avoid the, uh, bread pudding?"

I nodded emphatically and whispered back, "Very avoidable."

We said a blessing and passed the food around. Naturally, someone asked how the pregnancy was evolving. Brenda launched into an account of her worries. "I'm so nervous about everything; the baby, my job, gaining weight!" She passed the mashed potatoes without taking any. "I know I'm going to balloon into an impossible size!"

She looked coyly around the table, expecting the usual, "of course not, not you, you'll be great." Instead, Dad took the bowl of potatoes and gave himself an extra large helping before offering her the bowl back. "Go ahead, you know you're eating for two. You probably won't get too fat. Maybe medium fat."

Brenda looked from the bowl to his face. She sniffed. "How do *you* know?"

Mom's eyes widened. I gave Mark a tight smile. He looked rather interested in the conversation, but he didn't know my family very well.

"Now, dear--" Mom, as always, tried.

Dad, as always, was not about to be deterred. "You can always tell. I grew up on a ranch, you know. That's how I became so interested in agriculture."

For a scant moment, I thought he might stop there, but he was only pausing to pour gravy over the turkey and potatoes. "Some cows get bigger than others. They carry the calf real sloppy, low the whole time and they look much, much fatter. They tend to be the ones with wide hips. Now you, you've got medium hips so you'll only get medium fat. And you're young yet. The older cows learn from the first pregnancy to push the other cows out of the way so they can eat heartier. Since this is your first, you won't gain as much weight, but you'll sneak in enough food that your feet will disappear. By and by all you'll see is tummy no matter how you look at it."

I swallowed. I was sure Dad shouldn't be telling her this. I spoke louder than normal. "Uh, I'll take some potatoes."

Dad, oblivious Dad, continued. "The whole ordeal is an absolute mess, of course. You're lucky you don't have to give birth right out there on God's earth. Not that you'll be looking much better than the cows do even though you'll be in a pristine hospital room."

Brenda's chin turned red. "You're comparing me to a *cow*?" The color crept slowly up her cheeks.

"It's not all that different, you know. During birth, the cow moos, the woman makes a God-awful amount of noise that sort of sounds like mooing now that I think of it. Don't you think so, Mom?"

My mother, unlike Brenda, had gone white. She held her fork at a rather dangerous angle. "I *do not* recall mooing."

I decided to try and keep the family alive. "Uh, well, yes, we're all so very happy about the baby. Dad is overcome with…emotion. He doesn't mean to compare you to a cow."

"No emotion in the cows, although they bellow like they are going to die. 'Course when those gangly long legs start pushing out, I'd guess a bellow is called for. Looks like it's mighty painful." Dad stopped to eat a bite. "Now at least pigs lie down when they give birth. More comfortable. Come to think of it, the little piglets are smaller too. Course pigs have to give birth to lots of piglets at one time. I'm sure you'll only have one," he nodded encouragingly towards Brenda.

Brenda didn't look the least bit comforted. In fact, tears were imminent. Her lower lip trembled.

"The turkey is really delicious," I mumbled. "I better try the stuffing. Brenda this meal looks fabulous." Now I found myself stuck with the bowl of slop in my hand. I thought about faking a spoonful, but Brenda's eyes were suddenly glued to the bowl.

"We're very excited we're going to have grandchildren," my mother said, leaning over to wipe invisible crumbs from Dad's mouth. She dabbed much harder than necessary.

Dad glared at her, but might have finally gotten the hint.

Brenda took a deep breath. "I don't think I'll have piglets."

I smiled tightly, put two spoonfuls on my plate and prepared to set the bowl down. Mark touched my leg under the table with his knee.

I dared a glance at him. His eyes twinkled madly, as if gales of laughter were being held back by sheer force of will. His hand was out. I passed him the bowl.

He put two very small spoonfuls on his plate and set the bowl down.

Our efforts were enough. Brenda's face went from red to pink. She sniffed, but only once. Her eyes looked as though they might contain tears, but they didn't spill over.

I took an extra roll and positioned it so that Brenda couldn't see the stuffing on my plate. Maybe I could hollow out the middle of the roll and hide the stuffing inside when she wasn't watching.

When I passed the bread to Mark, he took an extra one as well. His leg brushed mine again.

We all ate as though our lives depended upon it. I refused to watch Brenda's face when she tried her stuffing.

I didn't even pretend to eat the goo, but Brenda must not have thought much of that first bite because she didn't ask anyone else for an opinion.

I thought the rest of the meal went rather well. I was able to smash my extra roll on top of the stuffing. Mark left half a roll strategically placed as well. I made a point to take his plate when it was time to clear the table, but no one save Brenda would have held the hidden stuffing against him.

Mark made his excuses right after dessert so I walked him to his car. I wasn't certain, but I thought the gun-metal gray Lexus SUV was one of the new hybrids. He glanced at the house and looked amused when I stayed carefully out of reach. "I owe your sister-in-law and brother," he said.

"No, you don't. Brenda takes care of people for a living."

"Good thing she's better at that than cooking."

"Damn straight," I agreed.

"Interesting family you got there." His hand was on the door, but I guess since I was a little too obvious about not being noticed or making a scene, he snaked his other arm out and snagged me. "Afraid?" he murmured, his lips hovering near mine. "Shouldn't have brought me home to meet the parents if you were embarrassed." He then proceeded to convince me that I didn't care what anyone else thought about it.

From my response, I think he could safely dismiss any real concern. He smiled smugly and left me trying to catch my breath and find my knees.

Chapter 26

The next morning, Derrick showed up at my door dressed in his detective uniform. He had a decidedly grim set to his mouth. Neither he nor his partner, Adrian, looked like the carefree friends they had been at the Thanksgiving table.

I ushered them inside without bothering to ask if it was business or pleasure. Derrick's freckles stood out on his face possibly because of the cold, but more likely because he was upset. Adrian always looked calm. His dark hair contrasted sharply with Derrick's red. There was a small balding circle on the back of his head that would probably expand with age, but both of them were in their early thirties, so it wasn't very noticeable yet.

"Larry Bartholomew showed up at headquarters this morning," Derrick announced, staring stoically at my forehead. "He refused to say how he had been bundled and delivered, but he is claiming that after following Mr. Huntington into your neighborhood, his partner shot Mr. Huntington. You wouldn't know anything about this matter would you?" He finally met my eyes, accusing me.

"Larry who?" I blinked rapidly and tried to remember any Larry I might know. Then again, if he was claiming he knew who shot Huntington, I wasn't sure I wanted to know him.

"Fits your description of a certain guy that may or may not have been driving a Lincoln the day you were attacked at Acetel."

"Oh! Mr. Buns. White whale of a guy with sausage-like appendages? His partner was the black guy that Bill sat on?"

Derrick rolled his eyes towards Adrian. "We prefer to say that his partner is likely of black or mixed black heritage, five-eleven, and two hundred sixty pounds. Larry was delivered to the station in a parked, black Lincoln. He was duct-taped from head to toe. He had been shot in the shoulder and in the leg, clean wounds from a short range. Because of the duct tape, the victim did not bleed to death. His hands were taped to the steering wheel. The medical team had to shave his head, including his eyebrows, to get the duct tape off."

My eyes bugged out. "Wow." I knew Mark's idea of first aid needed work.

Derrick wasn't finished. He pulled out a small notebook and flipped it opened. "I checked the police report from the other night. The attending physician, Dr. Taylor, told me that Mr. Huntington had two bullet wounds. One in the shoulder and one in the leg."

I shook my head in denial. "No, one was in the arm. The fleshy part." I demonstrated using my own, not sure how to get Derrick's attention off what appeared to be wounds that mimicked Huntington's injuries.

Adrian almost smiled. "His question was more of a mobility one."

"Oh." I looked down at the carpet. "I don't think Huntington really has the mobility to be duct-taping anyone."

"Uh-huh." Derrick jotted down a note in his little book. "Wasn't it a black Lincoln that followed you the day that you stopped by my place?"

This wasn't the first time I chastised myself for that little action. Sean had heard about it, and of course reported it to my parents. "What happened to Beefy?" It suddenly occurred to me that I didn't know.

Adrian did grin this time. "Other than the broken nose he sustained when you kicked him and the broken forearm from being sat on, he's fine. He has been safely sitting in jail. Won't say who it was that hired him or why he was at Acetel. Maybe you could give us a few names that we could throw at him. He might break down if we had the right info."

Dare I say Jacques? Oooh, Huntington would kill me. If the detectives hauled Jacques into custody and risked the investigation, Huntington would be sending me somewhere, but probably not Hawaii. "I have no idea." I put my palms out in an innocent shrug. "I never knew why they followed me in the first place. Maybe now you can get them to tattle on each other?"

"Maybe," Adrian agreed amiably. "Mr. Buns, er, Larry, seemed very eager to point out that it was his partner who shot Huntington. He claimed he was just the driver and doesn't know who hired Beefy."

"That's Trevis Smith, not Beefy," Derrick corrected stiffly.

I ignored him. "Buns was the guy driving that day at Acetel. I can't tell you if he was the one in the Lincoln who tried to follow me home because I never saw who was in the car. Do you have enough to lock him up?" I was a little worried about fingering the guy. He already had it in for me.

Derrick pressed his lips together so tightly they disappeared entirely.

Adrian knew his partner well and since Derrick wasn't going to answer my question, Adrian did it for him. "They both have some pretty interesting outstanding warrants. For one, The Lincoln was stolen, and there Larry was sitting in it like a duck. In general, Larry doesn't have a reputation for stalking women or even kidnapping, but they both have extortion charges pending against them and one burglary charge."

"Oh." Nice, all-around American guys.

"Based on your telling us that Beefy was trying to get you in the car, and you do have witnesses, we can probably get attempted kidnapping or attempted assault if we need to go that far."

I still wasn't sure why Derrick and Adrian were really here. "What do you want me to do?"

Derrick grunted. "Where were you last night?"

"At Sean's house. With you guys!"

"After that," he snapped.

"I came home."

"Were you alone?"

I glared at him. It was none of his business. And I knew he'd tell Sean the answer. "You are so rude. You were at dinner with us, Derrick. I left at what, eight or nine last night--long after Mark left."

"Where did he go?"

"I have no earthly idea."

"Where were you this morning?" he continued.

My eyes narrowed. "Was Mr. Buns left in his car last night or this morning?"

"We're just constructing a time frame."

"Wait just a hairy little minute here! He can't have been sitting out there very long without some police officer noticing, even if you guys went out for donuts before going to the office." Not to mention that duct-taped or not, his wounds wouldn't have been in very good shape if he was left there long. "Why did you ask about last night if you found him this morning?"

Derrick shrugged defensively. "If Mark came over here then he couldn't have been out tracking down Larry Bartholomew last night."

Derrick was fast becoming a worse problem than my brother. I tapped my foot. "I don't have an alibi. I was here, I slept and I woke up. Now it is," I looked at my watch, "eleven o'clock. I can't provide an alibi for Mark or for Steve." I thought about it. "Although, as I mentioned, I don't think Huntington, that is Steve, was in any shape to go roaming about. When I went to his condo, he still had a sling on his arm."

Derrick almost snapped his pencil in half. He looked up at me full of disapproval. "And when were you last in the condo?"

I could almost hear the, "and does your brother know about this," on the tip of his tongue.

Adrian waved a white flag by putting a hand in front of my glare and saying, "Okay, you two, enough." Then to me, "Did you talk to either of them last night or have any reason to believe they might have been out prowling around after this guy?"

Huntington was going to have to pay me overtime for this. It was embarrassing to have a policeman digging into my non-life. Worse, that policeman thought it his personal duty to report my every possible infringement, legal or not, to my brother. "I have no idea if either of them were after Beefy and Buns. Mark left from Sean's house, and I didn't ask where he was going."

Derrick wasn't finished. "And Mark lives where, exactly?" The pencil was ever at the ready.

"I think he's staying with Huntington. Steve," I clarified before he could point out that they both had the same last name.

Derrick must have figured out where Huntington lived because neither of them asked me for the address. Calling Sean to act as my lawyer to get out of their interrogation would only make matters worse because Sean would be asking even *more* personal questions.

Adrian must have decided the interview hadn't gone particularly well because on the way out, he let Derrick go first and held back. He stuck his head back around the door and said quietly, "Next time someone chases you, do me a favor. Stop by my house or go to headquarters."

Yeesh. No kidding.

Chapter 27

What with Friday morning being rudely interrupted by the police, chores and generally goofing off, I didn't sit down to go over the documents that Radar had given me until late on Saturday. The papers warranted more than the cursory inspection I had given them. There could easily be clues that tied the missing employees to one or another manager, and I was determined to find said clues if they existed.

Radar had the information sorted into two main categories: customer reports and layoff information. I ignored the customer reports and attacked the list containing every employee that had a post office box.

The start dates were in a column next to each employee record. Radar was right; there didn't seem to be a pattern except that in many cases several employees with post office box addresses were added at one time. I scribbled the dates down until I had the hire dates broken into neat segments. The only obvious pattern was that whoever did the hiring did it almost every quarter over the five-year period.

At first the hiring appeared arbitrary, but as I looked at the last two years of post office boxes, the hiring consistently occurred about a month after the end of the quarter. It appeared as though someone was using earnings to determine how many people could be hired. That wouldn't be all that unusual, but in this case, the hiring dates were exactly four weeks after earnings. It would be difficult to hire real people that consistently.

Ben could have told me the actual earnings results for each quarter, but I didn't entirely trust him. Luckily, Acetel was publicly traded, so the information was available online.

A quick search revealed my theory had holes. "Rats." There was no direct correlation between free cash flow and the number of people "hired."

But why else would the additions fall right after quarterly earnings were released?

Perhaps the number of fakes was related to the amount of money the embezzler needed. But whoever had been doing it had been very careful. There was never a huge influx of people all at once, just a few employees added each quarter.

Unfortunately, after five years of adding people, the company's bottom line suffered. If the guy paid attention to earnings, he should have been able to spot the fact that he couldn't keep adding people--fake or not. After five years and fourteen extra people with salaries ranging from fifty to a hundred and twenty thousand, the revenue couldn't keep up.

But if the employees weren't real, how were layoffs done?

The guilty party, say Jacques for example, must have deleted the employees--or put them in the "layoff" pool so that severance checks could go out. But how did he keep management from figuring out that the employees didn't exist? Even if he tinkered with the master layoff list...hmm. Had he taken real employees that were about to be laid off out of the list and added in fake ones?

It was a risky strategy unless he was in charge of the layoffs. Of course, in Denton, most HR activities were done by a contractor. Not as easy to track. Had Jacques changed the list at the last minute? Paid the HR contractor to keep her mouth shut?

I pulled up the org charts again. There were sixteen...no seventeen employees not on the chart. Two employees had regular addresses, but one of them wasn't in the layoff pool or the org charts. Maybe she had quit earlier, but not been taken out of the database. What a mess. If nothing else, Acetel's records were shoddy, especially when it came to the employee database.

After studying the org charts more, I noticed that the contractors for human resources had changed three times in the past five years. It was a wonder the records weren't worse. Some database details were obviously never checked carefully or updated properly.

I thought hard about the evidence, because I really did think Jacques was guilty--of something. The problem was that neither of the Denton managers--and probably none of the San Jose managers had real-time access to the layoff information.

Only Pete and A.J. regularly traveled between San Jose and Denton. Either of them could set up phony post office boxes. Either of them could delay sending Ben reports until after they had been manipulated. They were also the only two who would see the entire layoff list or have any say in changes. Of course, neither of them would need to hack into the system. They should have complete access to all records if they needed them.

I was fairly certain this new idea wouldn't sit well with Huntington. But A.J. and Pete could both manipulate information undetected. Neither had really hired Huntington; the board hired him. Once under that kind of microscope, A.J. wouldn't dare say no to a close inspection.

I was completely stymied. Radar had better be able to look up the automatic deposit data, because I couldn't do that on my own. That would tell me if my hunch about the money being funneled into one account was correct. It still wouldn't tell me who was guilty. Nor would it tell me how to convince Huntington once I knew. Even worse, Huntington would probably point out the one other person who commuted frequently between San Jose and Denton. He was a gamer and a hacker. And Radar was either helping me or playing me for a fool.

Chapter 28

Sunday morning I had to put in an appearance at church because Brenda had naturally assumed we would meet there before shopping. It served me right that I had to help her shop. When she had asked me again after Thanksgiving dinner for advice about hiding her pregnancy, my smart mouth made the teasing suggestion that she dress as Santa Claus until Christmas. For some insane reason, she thought I was serious and demanded that I help her shop. "I'll tell everyone that I'm dressing in the Christmas spirit to cheer up the sick children!"

Brenda didn't work in the children's ward, but pointing that out hadn't helped one bit. She had it in her head that dressing as Santa Claus would buy her some time. As a bonus, visiting the kids might help her promotion chances.

First we went to a uniform store, but they said they would have to special order the maternity uniforms.

"Maybe you should still get a couple of uniforms in bigger sizes than you usually wear. If you're going to add the Santa disguise to each outfit for the next five weeks or so, you'd better plan on being a Santa of different colors. It will amuse the kids and keep your supervisor from concluding that you never do laundry."

Brenda dithered back and forth. "I really don't want to buy larger sizes. What will I do with them after I have the baby? And," she said loftily, "I'm going to be Mrs. Santa, not Santa."

What was the difference between larger sizes and maternity clothes? She wasn't going to be able to use either after her pregnancy. "Yeah, okay, but I still think for now you get some of these larger sizes with elastic. Then you can put stuffing under there until you no longer need it."

"Do you think pink is close enough to red?"

"Absolutely." I nodded emphatically and then waited while she tried on the pants and large shirt. She didn't need all the room yet, but it wouldn't be long.

"Wow, these are a lot more comfortable than what I have been wearing."

Wisely, I kept my mouth shut.

"Do you think I should get these or wait and see if we find something else?" She posed in front of the mirror.

"Get a couple and let's go see if we can find some real maternity clothes. Maybe you can get overalls and a green felt hat. Then you'll be able to mimic one of Santa's elves." The words were out before I could stop them. Me and my big mouth.

Penney's only had normal-sized overalls. The other three stores we checked didn't have anything like that at all. Finally, although Brenda was loathe to shop there, we went to an actual maternity store, "Expectant Mothers." There were cute little goslings following a mother goose in the window display. I clamped my lips shut tight before I could joke about her dressing as a goose.

We found some denim coverall things that had a giant expandable panel under the tummy part. She could tighten the thing or let it out. Since the coveralls were loose anyway, they really hid her condition.

She also found a huge red poncho that made her look more like Little Red Riding Hood than Mrs. Claus, but since it fit her ideas, I just shoved the purchase under my arm with the rest.

On the way out of the store, I almost knocked over Ross from Strandfrost. I had forgotten that Ross was married, but vaguely remembered meeting his wife at the party I had thrown at Huntington's condo. I tried to shift bags around to shake Linda's hand, but with the latest "gosling" purchases, my hands were too full. I ended up just nodding at her.

"How are things at Strandfrost?" I asked Ross. What else was I supposed to chitchat about? My resignation? His part in getting me fired?

"About the same, about the same." In obvious desperation Ross looked around wildly for a way out of the socially awkward situation. Finally, he hit on the season and practically shouted, "We're getting ready for Christmas. I promised Linda we'd get the shopping done early this year, except for her present." He grinned kind of sheepishly and ran his hand nervously across his straight-top.

"Oh yeah, Merry Christmas." The thought of coming back to shop for Christmas caused me to hold my breath in a bit of a panic for a second.

"Absolutely, Merry Christmas to you too. Good luck." He waved at all my bags. "Looks like you have a lot to do." He grabbed his wife's arm and hurried off like a deranged idiot.

I looked around for Brenda. She must have ducked back into the store. I looked for her inside, but still didn't find her.

Exasperated, I finally spotted her coming from Auntie Annie's pretzel counter with a giant lemonade and a pretzel coated in cheese sauce. "Do you want one too? I'm exhausted. I thought we should have a snack."

No way was I going to fight a pregnant woman for half a pretzel.

I got my own before we walked back to the car.

We had to stop at a Barbette's Bobbins, which was not only a sewing store, but a costume shop as well. Brenda found a white wig immediately. The place also had a perky green hat for the elf outfit and a typical red one for Mrs. Claus. Brenda found some stuffing that would round out her belly and make it look fake instead of pregnant. She planned on attaching some cotton to the ends of her uniforms for a cuffed look.

I felt a bit of a cheat when all was said and done. She might make it through Christmas, but not much longer. In the meantime, her coworkers were going to think she had lost her mind.

She was hungry again so I suggested we try "Italy's Canal," the place that Radar had recommended.

"I love Italian," she gushed. "But I am supposed to be learning to cook. I promised Sean. Of course we're both kind of tired so maybe today isn't a good day."

"You should never cook when you're tired," I said. Shoot, the woman really shouldn't cook *ever,* and I couldn't quite fathom what might happen when she was worn around the edges like she was now.

"Well, then! It's decided. I'll treat you to dinner since you helped me so much. I can't wait to do this again. Do you think Suzy can come with us when I have to register for the baby shower? I didn't want to go that route, but my mother insists on it. Since I'm not going to tell anyone about the baby until way late, no one will know what to get if I don't register. You don't think it's too…forward to register do you?"

"You don't have to take me out to eat, and yes and no."

"Yes and no? You don't think I should?"

"Yes, Suzy can probably help and no, it's not bad to register. How else will people like me without children know what to buy?"

"Oh, you're right. I hadn't thought of that."

The restaurant was a quaint mom and pop's place with little red and white checkered table cloths. The food was freshly made, including the bread. All in all, it was quite possibly worth raving about much more than Radar had done. As I dipped bread in the succulent tomato sauce I was even happier that Brenda had decided against cooking.

A girl can only take so much domesticity.

Chapter 29

Monday morning I wasn't ready to face work. I felt even more strongly about it after I arrived. First thing, Jacques informed me that the Kronology folks had decided to visit after lunch. I had shelved the Kronology server by pushing it under an unused lab bench. No one in the lab wanted the thing, and I had assumed the Kronology engineers would never show their faces.

My entire morning was spent wrestling the server out of the dustbin and getting it set up. Whenever visitors came in the lab, a notice was required so that everyone kept confidential conversations quiet. I sent the notification out, and because Vi was working on a proprietary, unannounced design, we had to wheel out partitions to place around her workbench.

"I was going to do this anyway," Vi said as we dragged equipment around. "Arnold said that Ben is back to do some consulting, and he wants all our projects kept away from wandering eyeballs."

"Ben? The finance guy that used to work here?" *The guy that lives in Piney Oaks? The one who caused this whole investigation to be started, and a guy who may have had access to all the employee files?* I stopped mid-drag on my end of the partition.

"Yes, the contractor. We never had to watch what we worked on when he was here before. Besides, he never comes into the lab. Arnold is just super paranoid about my current project."

Hmm. Huntington was right. Knowing that Ben lived in Piney Oaks, I couldn't help but wonder if I was in danger. Had Ben weaseled his way back into a job because he knew we had found the files he had been watching? Of course...whoever was watching those files had a back door into the company. He didn't need to work here. It might make things easier for him to watch all players if he were here...but it was completely possible A.J had hired him back without any prompting. Companies were routinely careless about hiring and firing. Strandfrost had barely waited for the ink to dry when getting rid of Gary before they hired him back. Apparently Acetel was no different. In spite of all that was going on, management couldn't wait to hire.

I didn't have time to worry about it, at least not today. Unless Ben showed up in the lab with a gun, I had to deal with the real job of Kronology.

I made sure the Kronology test still failed because I'd rather kill roaches for a living than be embarrassed in front of that particular team of engineers.

By lunchtime I was prepared to do battle. Jacques called me from his office before escorting the Kronology guys upstairs to one of the conference rooms. I met them at the doorway to the meeting room. The tallest guy muttered something about "short."

I could have worn heels to make my frame taller, and maybe I should have put a pillow around my middle, but I wasn't going to look six feet tall or two hundred pounds anyway. "Good afternoon," I said with a serene smile.

"This is Sedona." Jacques coughed into his pen. "She's been dieting."

I stared at him. The man was an idiot. I offered my hand to the guy closest to the door.

"Craig Yumen. I'm the project manager. This is Rob Mandell. He wrote the code, and he's an excellent trainer."

We shook hands all around and then got down to business. I went over the reports. We went down to the lab where I demonstrated the error. I was grateful that Art was now afraid to enter the lab when I was in it, so I doubted I'd have too much trouble from unexpected chaos.

The server failed three times in a row. Rob tried to tell me how I should have shut the server down. I ignored him. "Do you want me to tell the customer he'll have to buy a product from another company if he wants to have a backup power cord?"

Jacques sputtered and so did Craig. "No, no. We can add that functionality since the customer requested it," Craig said.

I was kind. I didn't point out that the marketing advertisements said the functionality was already there. I did ask how long it would take.

Craig turned to Rob. "What do you think?"

Rob was a tall man, but he had let himself go around the middle. His physique wasn't helped by the fact that he stood like a wrestler in one of those funny poses designed to show off muscles. Instead of answering the question, he sat down in front of the machine. He looked at various parameters, changed the values and muttered. In his anger, he slapped roughly at the keys and accidentally entered a negative number in the temperature warning column.

Like a bomb in free-fall, the server shut down. It was impossible to miss the telltale whirring noise as the fans slowly choked themselves to a stop, but Jacques kept right on making pleasantries as if he hadn't noticed the splattering silence of the dead server.

I suggested helpfully, "You should probably change the code so that if the customer accidentally puts a negative number in that spot, it doesn't cause the server to crash."

"Bitch."

Jacques gargled and stopped mid-sentence.

I couldn't believe it. "What did you say?"

Rob stood up, clenching his fists the way he had before, but instead of posing, this time it looked as though he was trying to keep himself from attacking. "Bitch."

I didn't bother to swallow my anger. Rob probably wouldn't try to bench press me in front of all these people. I crossed my arms, but made sure I was clear of the lab bench and any other obstacles in case I needed to run. "That's what I thought you said. What does me being a bitch have to do with errors in your code?"

His eyes bulged. "It's connected all right! If you weren't such a bitch, we wouldn't have this problem!"

Having two brothers, I had been called names before. Having two brothers, I knew that when a guy took a cheap, stupid shot, logic was not involved. I felt my lip curl, but tried not to snarl. "Of course you would still have the problem. Just because I happened to find the problem doesn't mean that if I didn't exist, the problem wouldn't exist." I waited for him to get his breathing in order or die from hyperventilation. I hoped for the latter.

Craig spouted what might have been an attempt at a half-apology. "No one means to be nasty." He put a hand on Rob's arm.

My manager tapped his pen along his leg and looked like a gaping fish.

"So, uh," Craig said. "You, uh, what should we do next?"

I had a lot of suggestions, but because the dead server was a better insult than anything I could propose, I said, "How about you fix the problem, I'll test it, and we can give the fix to the customer."

"The temperature thing too or just the power supply feature?" Craig asked.

"If the customer enters an invalid temperature, it shouldn't crater that way." Meanwhile, I was wondering how to persuade Jacques to let me tell the Kronology customer to purchase a different server. Maybe I wouldn't wait for Jacques to grant me permission. He hadn't exactly been supportive here.

"Uh, yeah," Craig nodded.

This seemed to signal Jacques to get his mouth moving again. He uttered polite noises about how glad he was that they came to see us. Craig followed his lead and echoed the sentiment, shuffling Rob toward the door.

Rob still looked mad enough to throw something. I deduced that my buddy Rob needed anger management classes. He was probably the main reason that nothing would ever get fixed.

I could have followed them to demand a concrete schedule for getting the "feature" added, but that would have been bitchy.

I turned the server back on. Out of the corner of my eye I saw Radar watching. He smiled, a really amused grin. "Are they coming back?"

"I doubt it, why?"

"Looked like you had them won over completely, your new best friends."

I gave him my best glare. "Any progress on your end?"

He swung his head back and forth, making sure no one was nearby. "Some things are harder than others. With all the tagged files, it's a mine field. Limited excavation looks like some direct deposit numbers are going into the same accounts. I'll keep you posted." He started to turn away, but Bill appeared from behind the server racks.

We both looked at him, wondering if he had overheard.

Radar said, "That one guy was really warming up to you. He'll probably fix all the bugs now."

As cover, Radar's remark wasn't much, especially since there had been no warmth whatsoever from any of the Kronology folks. We both watched Bill for any kind of reaction, but he just said, "I'll bet not even Aphrodite could get them to fix it."

What did that mean?

Radar noticed the confusion on my face and said, "Character in one of the games from last weekend. Powerful."

"Oh."

"Those Kronology folks are idiots. Lock them in a room with a troll," Bill advised as he shuffled off towards the lab door. "I heard Ben was back on board. Since they're hiring maybe they'll find money for profit sharing. If you want your share, you're gonna need to have a high percentage of solved problems."

Profit sharing? At this point, I was probably lucky I still had a paycheck.

I turned to ask Radar what else he had found, but he was gone.

I went back to my office and called Huntington. If he didn't know already, he needed to know that Ben was back. For certain he needed to know that more than one paycheck was going into the same direct deposit account.

Finding out about the direct deposit checks made me think that some of my other ideas weren't so far-fetched either, but I wasn't ready to tell Huntington that maybe A.J. and Pete deserved a closer look.

Some things were better left to the right timing.

Chapter 30

I had conveniently forgotten that the weekly project meeting had been moved to Tuesday because the week before we had been out for Thanksgiving. Pete and A.J. attended to remind us about the company party on Wednesday and rally us with their enthusiasm. Oh goody.

Management didn't disappoint either. They did everything except wear clown suits.

Jacques started by lying outright. "The Kronology Server project, thanks to Sedona, is a success."

Arnold didn't let that sit for even a heartbeat. He adjusted his smarmy glasses and interrupted rudely, cutting his eyes to A.J. to make sure the CEO was paying attention. "Do you have the actual fix in hand?"

Jacques nodded and embellished his lies. "Yes, we're getting great responses from those folks. I want to point out these successes--my group follows the company motto. Who here can recite the company motto?" He held up a hand as if he was leading a band, but the band didn't start playing.

I was going to claim ignorance because I had only been around a total of two weeks. Of course, I was also the most recently hired so I should be able to recall the big, bold headers on the paperwork, but I hadn't actually read the material. No one read it, and no one paid attention to company mottoes except the marketing people that came up with them to impress management.

"I propose we put the motto on the back of our company business cards!" Jacques exclaimed. "It would be a great way to remind all of us that 'Acetel is where customers come together!'" He beamed. Perhaps he interpreted shuffling feet and muffled groans as support.

As CFO, Pete must have decided it was his job to respond to such a silly financial drain. "Great idea. I want everyone to know that even in these tight times, we will spend money where we need to. We need to rethink the paradigms and find new ways to generate revenue and synergy."

And waste it on business cards with logos. I carefully kept my eyes on the table in front of me.

Jacques babbled through some more interesting "facts" and then Arnold stood up. He said, "Welcome back, Ben. Really glad the company is doing well enough again to be able to hire a few people." He glanced at me when he said it. I was busy trying to overtly study Ben, who sat three people away from A.J. The only difference from the first time I had seen him was that he was now wearing glasses. He had an electronic device, either a phone or small tablet in his hand, but with attention on him, he moved it under the table. His eyes swept the room with a vague friendly look. He did not stare at me even though I was rudely staring at him.

Arnold began his presentation. He mentioned his group's profitability, which should have given management a clue, but the real message didn't become apparent until Arnold talked about how profit sharing could be better split up between groups--giving groups that brought in extra revenue more of the profit.

A.J. interrupted the speech as soon as it became evident that Arnold was not-so-subtly trying to redirect cash to his own group. I thought A.J. might reassure us that profit sharing wasn't going to be canceled, but all he had was excuses at the ready. "We do want each and every one of you to share in the success of the company, and as soon as we're able, we plan to re-instate a new profit sharing plan. The manner in which that is done can always be improved upon."

There was some grumbling, and I distinctly heard Bill say, "Everyone didn't get a retention bonus." The executives had a sudden attack of earwax blockage. No one acknowledged the remark, so of course, the elephant was not standing in the room, no siree.

It didn't help any when Arnold asked, "When do you foresee the company being profitable enough to reinstate profit sharing?"

People leaned forward in their chairs, scenting blood or meat. A.J. made soothing motions with his hands and continued politicking. He started with, "We intend to be one of the best places to work in this entire industry," and followed it immediately with typical management proof. "We have always kept up with industry standard benefits."

If you're only "keeping up with standard" benefits, how does that equate to being the "best" in the industry?

A.J. was smart enough to continue talking so no one could ask any more questions. "The sooner we focus, the sooner it will happen. We fully expect within the next year to be able to have some profit sharing for at least parts of the company." He raised a cautionary hand. "Good work always needs to be recognized and rewarded."

A.J. quickly turned the conversation back to work accounts, wanting to know specifics about the cases that were currently being tested.

Not surprisingly, all of Jacques customers were "completely happy" and all cases were "eighty percent resolved." When asked, Arnold gave a summary of each customer and the exact technical problem in excruciating detail. Eyes glazed over at first, but the room got downright desperate when he announced, "I suggest that we go around the room and let each person discuss his or her case load. It might give you a good idea of just who is contributing the most."

Pete stood up so fast he nearly knocked his chair over. "This has been exceptional. With this trip to Denton, I can happily say that all reorganizations are now in place. We have a lot to be proud of. There isn't another company around that could so quickly get reorganized and focused.

In a Herculean effort to blend, I kept my expression neutral. Do not ask me how a company can label a reorganization as "progress," especially when the new organization charts looked the same as the old ones. Maybe I was missing something, but to win the game, didn't you have to do more than move chess pieces aimlessly?

From the tight set to Arnold's mouth, he was disappointed to hear the reorganization was complete. It meant he had no near-term chance of getting promoted to head the Denton office. Then again, no one else would be running it either. Jacques' pen tapped against his leg, but the hieroglyphics weren't particularly frenetic, so I took that to mean his surprise and stress level weren't on the high end of the scale.

After Pete's benevolent words, he and A.J. did the obligatory, "Keep up the good work and see you tomorrow at the party," before scurrying out.

They had probably expected a less volatile meeting where they could give advice on handling customers, rather than a nervous crowd focused on profit sharing.

As soon as the meeting was over, I stopped by Becky's office. "Busy?"

"Like an ant," she said, staring at her fingernails. "Pete and A.J. took off for lunch."

"Ah, good." I came in and shut the door.

She sat up and her eyebrows wiggled in anticipation. "What?"

"No, nothing juicy. We just got out of a meeting with the elite. Pete said the reorganization was done. Did we actually get a new org chart?"

She waved her hand. "It looked like it was going to be a huge deal, but Pete gave me the info for the new chart yesterday afternoon. They didn't do the changes they were talking about." She turned to her mouse. "He hasn't told me to send it out yet, not that there is much to see, but promise not to tell, and I'll show you."

That was the reason the door was shut, but I didn't mention that. And Huntington didn't count as telling, did it?

She opened a power point slide. "Before A.J. and Pete showed up from the San Jose office to reorganize Denton, the sparks were flying. It was obvious that Jacques had a huge leg up on getting promoted to run the Denton office."

"Why was it obvious?"

"He had permission to hire--you know, he hired you. No one else had permission to hire, not even in San Jose. Jacques gloated up and down the hallways and started working on a new personal improvement survey." She rolled her eyes. "Then A.J. arrived, and he let Arnold take two of Jacques' people. They both originally worked with Ben, the contractor that was let go, but now he's back too." She pulled up another chart. "For whatever reason, after A.J. and Pete came this time, Arnold announced that A.J. was rearranging people so that he could be made director of the Denton office. A.J. even gave the go-ahead for Arnold to promote one of his guys to team lead."

"But what happened? Why didn't Arnold get promoted?"

She shrugged. "Who knows?"

"You're saying A.J. reneged on his promise?"

Becky sniffed. "I wouldn't say that. I think A.J. honestly intended to come here and figure out which of the managers to put in charge. That's what the whole reorganization was supposed to be about--get things cleaned up and make sure that business got handled better so that we didn't end up with layoffs again." She pointed to the chart. "But it turned out that Pete decided we needed a financial person here more than any other change, so they hired Ben back. Pete and A.J. never chose a manager to run the office. They leave on Thursday or Friday so as far as I know this is final. I have no idea what changed their minds."

I did. Huntington had been shot, and I was floating around the place stirring up all kinds of trouble. I looked over the chart carefully. Obviously there was no sign of Sandra Garcia or any of the other post office box employees.

"Interesting," I said. "I bet neither Jacques nor Arnold are very happy to find out the reorganization is done."

"I'm not sure Arnold wanted the job as badly as Jacques, but Arnold's girlfriend will probably be disappointed. He dates this really nice lady. She's a lawyer and just made, what do you call it, partner at her firm."

It was hard to fathom who Arnold might date since he seemed to have trouble looking anyone directly in the eyes. "Arnold seemed pretty disappointed. Do you know that he actually suggested we start splitting the profit sharing up so that groups with a higher case load would get fatter checks?"

Her eyes went wide. "*No! He totally wouldn't dare!*"

"Oh, yes he did. Apparently he didn't bother to run it by A.J. before mentioning it in the meeting."

"He asked about it in front of everyone? Oh, my!" The gleam in her eye disappeared as another thought occurred to her. "What did A.J. say about profit sharing?"

"It sounds like it will be a while before they award it again."

"Rats." Becky gave a forlorn sigh. "I was hoping that since the managers got retention bonuses, there would be something left over for us little guys."

"A.J. wouldn't even give a time frame for profit sharing or talk about how it might work." I raised my hands helplessly. "We're all in the same boat."

"Yeah and it's sinking. Dirtballs."

I didn't disagree. The problem was there was too much dirt covering everyone. The lack of ethics made it awfully hard to pinpoint who had crossed what line. As Huntington had pointed out, greed wasn't illegal. The trick was to find out who had decided to turn simple greed into unlawful profits. It was time for a pow-wow, and we needed more information than I could provide. The good news was that I knew who might be able to dig in and find the right details.

I followed Radar's example and slipped him a note under the server door.

The note said, "Meet in server room, seven tonight. Burn note." I hoped Mark caught him burning the note on camera. It would make Radar look nicely paranoid.

Chapter 31

Huntington and Mark met me at the outer door of Acetel. It was dark and lonely in the parking lot this time of night; my car was still there, but I saw no other vehicles. Since neither had a badge to enter the building, and I doubted Mark wanted to pick the lock, I was their ticket inside.

Huntington ducked in first and Mark followed. Both of them had black leather jackets; Huntington must have replaced his old one. The new one looked just as buttery soft and super-cool as the old one.

I was happy to see Mark, no matter the reason, but I was flustered. We weren't exactly dating. We weren't exactly not...interested either.

I let the door swing shut after Mark came in. He tilted his head, his eyes unreadable in the auxiliary hallway lighting. He didn't seem to know how to greet me either. A light kiss might work, but we hadn't moved to that comfortable stage. Our encounters were more...enthusiastic than that. Any other kiss would be rude or...some sort of display.

He settled for, "Hi," and grazed my cheek with his knuckles.

What did *that* mean??? I wasn't sure, but I blushed anyway.

Huntington didn't care or didn't notice the awkward moment. He moved to the side of the hallway, away from the door and unzipped his jacket. "Your buddy here? I'm glad you suggested we move in on him."

That got my attention. "You think he's guilty?"

Huntington said, "Don't know, but it will be nice to have him on the payroll. Even if he works both sides of the fence, it's always easier to catch the guilty if you have him on your payroll."

I wasn't sure that philosophy was true--or healthy. I wondered what that said about Huntington hiring me, but didn't want to think too hard about Huntington's multiple personalities.

I led the way down the hall into the lab. The lab had no lights on at this hour. I had turned them off after Vi left. I wasn't sure that Radar would be waiting because his only reply had been a cup of ashes left at my workstation sometime after five o'clock.

There were enough server lights flashing in the lab that I was comfortable moving through the equipment. Huntington must not have been quite so sanguine because he turned on a low beam LED flashlight.

At the back of the lab, I knocked on the server room door. If I knew Radar, he'd make me wait. Deliberately, I stepped back and off to the side a bit. That made both Mark and Huntington slide sideways too, following my caution, even if they didn't know why.

When nothing happened, I tried the knob. It wasn't locked. I started to move inside, but Mark put a hand on my arm and pulled me back gently. He went in first. Huntington followed.

When no shots rang out, I walked in and swung the door closed.

The room was slightly brighter than the lab, because Radar had left two monitors running. There was no sign of Radar, however. "Are there lights in here?" I asked.

Mark put his back up against the wall where a switch might be, blocking it. Both he and Huntington wore dark clothing. Guess it might be hard to identify them later given the low lighting--just in case someone else had added their own cameras.

"Okay, let's see what we have here," I said, taking a seat at the first monitor. Radar had left one directory open on the desktop. The first file in the list was named "Sedona." A glaring clue if there ever was one.

I moved the mouse over the file and clicked. The file contained a list of fourteen employees and three direct deposit account numbers. "Aha! I knew it!"

While I sorted and double-checked the names Radar had left, Mark sat down at the other monitor. "List of post office boxes. Matches what Steve and I found."

"What did you find?" I asked.

Huntington said, "The post office boxes are real, and they weren't opened all at once. No one is going to remember a face and even if they did, it could easily be the guys in the Lincoln or others like them following instructions via text messaging."

"So Beefy and Buns never came clean about who they were working for?"

Huntington shook his head. "Despite being delivered to the cops, neither have been much help. They claim they were hired strictly by text messaging. Their cell phone records back up a lot of calls coming from pay phones and public places--including a library. They were told where to pick up their pay, told who to follow and who to target."

"But in jail, they won't be shooting anyone else," Mark said.

Huntington ignored the comment. "Thanks to you--and your friend, Radar--we have a pretty good idea of how the money was siphoned away from Acetel. What we don't know is who took it. It will be interesting to see what we find if we're able to trace the owners of those three bank accounts."

"We have a lot of suspects," I said. "Jacques is definitely guilty of trying to prod his stock options. And Ben has been hired back."

Huntington said, "Getting hired here is not an automatic sign of wrongdoing. Ben said Pete called and asked if he would come back. At least this way we have all the players in one place."

"I guess so," I said. "Does Ben travel much? These post office boxes were opened in two different states. That means someone who traveled. I don't think whoever is behind this scheme hired Beefy and Buns to fly back and forth to do it. The two people who travel most are Pete and A.J." There, my idea was out in the open.

Mark said, "Most of the time Pete and A.J. come here, but a couple of times a year the Denton managers fly to San Jose for larger company meetings."

Twice a year wasn't often enough to open all those post office boxes. I would have preferred the bad news come from Huntington because it would be easier to argue with him. "And the lower-level engineers don't fly there at all?"

"Correct. Except for Radar, none of the other engineers or employees make regular trips back and forth."

I let that hint go and addressed Huntington. "Didn't you tell me that A.J. used to be an engineer?"

Huntington nodded. "Hardware."

"What about Pete?"

"Marketing background initially, but he was in finance at two companies before taking the CFO position here. Why?"

"Because either of them might have the know-how to hack into the system."

Huntington shook his head. "They wouldn't need to. If they were guilty, they could access any file they wanted, at any time."

I chewed my lip and disagreed. "It would be too obvious if A.J. or Pete changed the files outright," I said. "If they hack in...it may appear they weren't paying attention, but they wouldn't look guilty of embezzlement."

"They are no more likely a suspect than the other managers," Huntington said. "Or Radar for that matter."

He was right so I tried a more compelling attack. "Why didn't Pete or A.J. notice an extra fourteen salaries? At the annual salaries we're talking about, the price tag adds up to almost a million dollars a year. When you lay off fourteen people that don't exist, the severance packages had to be around a hundred thousand dollars for some of them."

Huntington said, "It would be possible for a clever accountant to hide a hundred thousand dollars here and there under layoff expenses." Before I could protest, he added, "But not so easy to account for a million dollars worth of salaries saved. Could all the paperwork have been changed after the layoffs were done?"

"Technically yes. A hacker can come in anytime he wants." I stared at the monitor wishing the answers would appear. "But if the goal was to save X million, you'd think the savings of fourteen non-existent employee salaries would stand out. Then too, no manager is willingly going to fire his employees. Final choices have to be done at a higher level. There's no office manager for Denton. That means Pete or A.J. had to look at a list of employees, figure out how to rank them and then choose which ones to layoff. Either of them are in a prime position to add fourteen non-existent names to that list."

"Anyone else could add them. Pete and A.J. don't know every single employee by name," Huntington said. "Neither do the managers. The setup with a San Jose office and a Denton office is perfect for this scheme. Everyone assumed the missing employees worked somewhere else."

I thought about it, but immediately found another flaw. "But once there is a final list, A.J. has to email the managers to inform them who is getting laid off. He doesn't know who to email for fourteen employees, because those people don't show up on the org chart." I threw up my hands. "There's no way A.J. can ignore the extra names."

"The names would have to be added after the real layoffs," Mark said.

I pulled up one of the old organization charts and pointed to Ben's name. "Since Pete wasn't in Denton full time, Ben probably put together a number of the reports on cost saving. He might have been in a prime position to know when it was safe to add fourteen extra names to the layoff list."

Mark slid his chair closer and looked at the list. "What about the other managers?"

"Jacques is the most likely candidate. He lies all the time, has no scruples, and he probably could use the money, but--" I stopped. I hated to admit it. "I don't think he has the brains to pull it off. He's too focused on inconsequential things like Kronology."

"Maybe the Kronology enthusiasm is a front to cover for his other activities," Mark said. "What about Arnold?"

"If anyone has the brains to pull it off, Arnold would be the person. He's pretty open about pushing for more money, but," I hesitated. "He mostly seems to do it to highlight himself and his team's accomplishments. Sort of an in-your-face directed at Jacques."

Huntington said, "Arnold isn't in debt. He lives with his girlfriend, and it's pretty clear she has plenty of money coming in from her law practice."

I threw up my hands. "There are also other engineers who could pull this off from a hacking standpoint. Bill, Vi and any engineer who has learned hacking as a second career. I don't think it's Bill though."

"Why not?" Huntington wanted to know.

"He has a bad dryer. It burns holes in his pants. He is not a man with an extra million to spend."

Huntington blinked. He opened his mouth and then shut it.

It's hard to counter burned pants--or explain them, really.

I typed Ben's name into the file Radar had left for me. With Huntington looking, I added Pete's name and also A.J. No one was above suspicion, but I doubted Radar would be able to start looking at every single account in the company.

So that Radar would know to look in the file, I changed the name of the file to "Radar." He would be smart enough to track down any computer activity by those listed, but I didn't think it was going to help. Our hacker was smart enough to cover his tracks.

Huntington smiled. "It's time for a plan, a nice little trap. Maybe we can hire your missing friend Radar to plant a nice electronic trap, a series of invitations to look at our suspect list? We need to lead the hacker in so deep we can get an ID."

"The last time you threw a party the bad guys didn't show," I said. "Only the innocent were harmed at that party."

Huntington didn't care for my reminder. "It's all a matter of timing."

"Maybe, but whoever did it knows we're looking. He can remain completely innocent just by sitting still alongside the other chickens. The money is gone. If the perp sits quietly, we have no evidence trail."

"Perhaps. How can I get in touch with Radar?"

I wasn't certain Radar wanted to be involved, but turned back to the file. I added Huntington's name and phone number. Then I typed in, "Make sure he pays you well."

I was pretty sure Huntington saw that part, but he ignored it.

"Can we check to see who created the layoff list?" Mark asked.

That was something I knew how to do. I pulled up the file properties. The date of the last change made to the file was the day of the layoff. Before my eyes scanned all the way through the data, I had already guessed who created the file: Silvanus.

Chapter 32

The entire Denton office went home at noon on Wednesday in order to get ready for the four o'clock holiday party. I had no idea what to wear, and I hated leaving the SUV behind because the party was out at Twin Lakes at Pete's personal "get-away." Unfortunately, people of my means did not generally own Mercedes, so in the Civic I went. Pete and company were going to have to accept me in my best pantsuit too, because I didn't feel like wearing a dress in the cold weather.

Once again, I didn't have a date, even though company rules said we could bring a spouse or significant other. The number one male interest in my life was disqualified, because it had to be bad form to invite a guy doing undercover work for the company to show up openly at the Christmas party.

Twin Lakes was a beautiful area and Pete could ski in his backyard if he wanted. The drive took just over an hour from Denton, but I noted that if Pete was in a hurry, he could fly in. There was a helicopter and pad off to the left of the house.

I was running late due to dithering over my clothes. The drive had also taken longer than expected. As I stepped out, I spotted Radar slinking over by the helicopter. Instead of going inside, I wandered over. "I thought you weren't coming."

"Can you believe this?" he asked, his eyes agog as two eggs in a frying pan.

"Nice."

"Nice?" He looked at me. "This is a McDonnell Douglas MD 900 Explorer--a NOTAR." He pointed to the back. "Look back there. No tail rotor. This baby can drop down on you, and make so little noise you'll think it's a lawnmower from next door. It's *awesome*."

"Oh."

He shook his head at my ignorance. "Unbelievable."

"I take it you've never flown one?"

Must have been another dumb question. "Are you kidding? Most people can't afford their own helicopter. They are incredibly expensive to maintain. I wonder if it's his or if the company paid for it."

His sudden disgust was probably the only reason I was able to pry him away and drag him inside. He was wearing a brand new pair of jeans in honor of the party. Although there wasn't a snagged hole anywhere on them, he was pulling at the seam as if his hands were used to picking at the old pair.

On the sidewalk leading in, we passed between two giant cat statues that guarded the entrance. "Wow, look at these things." The statues were both panther-black, watchful and half the size of the doors. "How does one get something like that delivered way out here, anyway?"

Radar rubbed two fingers together. "If he let me fly that helicopter, I'd walk them out here in a wagon from Wal-Mart if I had to."

The inside of Pete's vacation home was no less impressive than the outside. A little uniformed lady allowed us entrance and took our coats. At first I thought Pete had another cat statue standing atop the banister at the head of the stairs, but as I moved away, the little black feline yawned, leapt down and sauntered away.

Once our coats were properly stowed, the lady led us into the living room where sparkling, repeated French doors lined the outer wall of the room. The partially frozen lake gleamed back at us from the other side of the windows. Pete could bowl from the fireplace to the other end of the room, but if he missed, he would break some glass. The setting sun outside the windows was blocked by clouds that threatened snow. I should have brought the Mercedes.

Long tables covered with white linen cloths were strategically placed around the room for easy snacking. A magnificently adorned Christmas tree stood in front of a couple of the French doors off to one side.

I managed to help myself to a couple of crab cakes, veggies, and a sinfully delicious dip of some sort. Vi came over and introduced me to her husband. We chatted for a few minutes before finding ourselves running low on food samples. As we made our way to the dessert table to inspect its decadent treats, Becky waved at me rather more frantically than I thought necessary.

Before I could make my way over to her, she came running. She yanked on my arm. "Did you know that Jacques had a quadruple bypass?"

My eyes flew to hers. "No…when? Why?"

"He doesn't look so good, don't you think?" She pointed to one of the overstuffed leather chairs. Jacques wasn't sitting on the chair; he was standing behind it, leaning against it. He had a drink in one hand and some sort of fried cheese or something in the other.

Jacques did look kind of pasty and he was breathing hard, but in a stuttering way as if he had to work at it to get it right. "If he were having a heart attack don't you think he'd say something?" I asked.

Becky opened her mouth to answer just as Jacques rolled sideways against the chair and fell on the floor, spewing his glass of whatever and dropping the plate of stuffed cheese things. He landed on his back like a clumsy drunk.

A few people thought he was inebriated because I could hear laughter at first. I ignored the snickering and moved alongside Becky. When I knelt down, Jacques didn't do more than gurgle at me and gasp a few times.

"Do you have nitroglycerin?" I asked, thinking it might have been prescribed if he had heart problems.

He clutched his chest and groaned, trying to roll away. I don't know where he thought he was going to go.

I looked up and found Bill staring at us with a look of deep concentration. "Bill, can you find some aspirin? Not Tylenol, but aspirin?"

Like his gaming name, Wildebeest, Bill cleared the area with a roar. He wasn't a small man anyway and with him bearing down on people as he rushed out of the room, no one got in the way. Radar was suddenly in the space he emptied.

"We could take him to the hospital in the helicopter." His voice was a reverent whisper. He stared at the floor as though guilty of a crime for suggesting it.

"Well, don't just stand there," I shouted. "Find Pete and see if the thing has gas in it or whatever it needs!"

I looked around and spotted Becky still beside me. "Becky..."

Becky didn't need my orders. I heard Art before I saw him, but Becky planted her big Texas hair in front of him and yelled, "You stand right there. You don't *move* unless Sedona gives you an order. You don't *move! Do you hear me?"*

I should have sent her to the balcony to call for an ambulance instead of telling Radar to ready the helicopter. Crestwood Hospital could have heard her bellow all the way in Denton.

Bill clomped back and handed me a bottle of coated aspirin. Even though we were in the midst of an emergency, I noticed that Bill had also bought a new pair of pants for the party. They weren't ironed and had probably not been washed yet, but they weren't burned.

"Jacques, you've got to chew these," I instructed. "Now. You can't swallow them, chew them." I forced two between his lips and wondered if I should give him three. Jacques wasn't a skinny man, which was probably part of the reason for the heart condition in the first place.

He made weak chewing motions.

Bill, being Bill, grabbed the nearest tablecloth from the fancy feast. It became quickly evident that Bill was no magician. Food went everywhere, glasses broke, plates clattered, and he hadn't even managed to work it completely free.

"Stop," one of the little uniformed ladies yelled at him. "Clean linens!" She wove her way forward, flagging him with a stack of neatly folded tablecloths.

Pete touched my shoulder and knelt down. "The chopper is ready, but we need to move fast. It's almost dark, and it could snow at any moment."

"We can carry him in this," Bill said, as he unrolled a tablecloth.

Arnold grabbed another cloth from the uniformed lady and disagreed. "No, we should tie them together. Look," he started demonstrating. "Tied together they will be twice as strong. We could double them like this." He started to take the tablecloth from Bill.

Bill protested. "No! Then we'll have nothing in the middle, and he'll fall right out. That design won't work, I tell you!"

"Go, let's go!" I shouted.

Art leaned over and put his face next to mine. His mouth was working up and down, his hands fluttering in little circles. "Nitroglycerin is only for the pain. It doesn't actually do anything about a heart attack. I'm sure of it. I remember from my studies."

"Great, Art, thanks." I didn't point out that Jacques hadn't had any of the stuff anyway.

Vi grabbed a corner of another tablecloth, and she, Becky and I carefully rolled Jacques onto it. Bill and Arnold shouted about distributing mass and whether it was best to carry him with his head elevated or lowered.

Becky and I grabbed the ends near his head. Vi and the uniformed lady went for Jacques' feet. I don't know what Becky was thinking. Maybe it was because Jacques was so heavy or maybe it was the season, but like Santa Claus, she flung one end across her back to put her weight under it.

That would have worked except Becky was a good foot taller than me. I was still playing slip and slide with my corner. Before I knew it, Jacques tilted, and all the weight was on my end.

Bam!

Jacques rolled out with a big splat, hitting a slick of spilled vanilla pudding. His mass, that Bill and Arnold had been so worried about, forced that pudding right out from under his belly in large spatters. His face landed in the banana bread, and if he didn't die from the heart attack he was likely to expire from suffocation by banana bread. I didn't know how I was going to explain to the hospital that a bunch of engineers thought banana bread up the nose was part of CPR. Maybe I could introduce them to Art, and the mistake would become all too clear.

"We could use some help here!" Becky let lose with her request and everything in the room except the vibrating windows came to a halt. "Get him on the tablecloth. *This one*," she yelled before anyone could argue. "Now, y'all heft him up there!"

Suddenly twelve guys were holding up various parts of Jacques and the tablecloth. "Yeehaw! Now, we go!" Becky marched right on out in front. There wasn't a single murmur from the carriers either.

If it had been springtime, maybe Pete would have had a golf cart or some sort of riding lawnmower that we could have used to get Jacques to the helicopter. Instead, the group carried him until we got to the landing pad. Arms and legs were everywhere for a few moments while we tried to figure out how to stuff him inside.

Radar was already in the helicopter working the radio. I could hear him asking for clearance to land at Crestwood Hospital. He seemed to have worked it out by the time we shoved Jacques into the back area. There were two seats in back, but sitting Jacques upright wasn't a good idea so we laid him down and half secured him with a couple of wide luggage tie straps. Becky climbed right in with Jacques and sat herself in one of the seats. Jacques' head was near her feet so she put her hand smack on his neck artery to monitor his heartbeat, assuming we hadn't killed him.

I looked around for Pete since I assumed he was going to help fly, but he wasn't there anymore. He must have backed off with the others after loading Jacques. I hopped into the empty front seat and strapped myself in. "How long have you, uh, been flying?" I yelled at Radar. He didn't look more than maybe twenty-five years old.

Ooh, out came the engineering grin. I regretted the question. He ignored me and concentrated on the digital displays and got the helicopter airborne. He headed us straight over the lake before angling up. Even without the clouds, darkness was rapidly approaching. After we were well clear of trees and mountaintops, Radar pointed to headphones, and I put them on. He gave me a full grin and pressed a transmitter button so I could hear him. "My dad started me flying when I was sixteen. He did air service, tours, whatever he could to keep flying."

"You know how to fly in snow?" It looked impossibly bleak out.

"Gosh, I guess."

I didn't bother to look over. The "heh, heh, heh," laugh came out and then some nasty air hit. He either tilted the thing on purpose into a turn or we were rolling sideways and about to die. Either way I had to fight my stomach.

"I forgot he had that heart thing," Radar transmitted. "He told me about it when I first showed up."

I looked over my shoulder, but it was really impossible to tell how Becky and Jacques were doing.

It didn't take long before I could see the lights of Denton peeking in and around dark objects that were muffled in what I considered heavy snow. Because of the flurries, the buildings appeared to be moving, getting bigger, then smaller with odd angles. It didn't help that my stomach was lurching all over the place.

"Is he still breathing?" I screamed back at Becky. I don't know if she heard me, but she gave a thumbs up. She wasn't scrambling to get away from a dead body so I figured it was probably okay. At least it was as good as could be expected for a guy that had just had a heart attack and then had food plastered on him from his bald head all the way down his pants.

Closing in, the helicopter descended rapidly. I didn't like the way the hospital loomed out more suddenly than I expected. My stomach rolled again. I made the mistake of looking over at Radar. Uh-oh.

He had a funny look on his face and one hand was near his cell phone for a scant moment.

"It's the snow, isn't it?" The flakes were only drifting lightly, but our motion caused them to swirl like crazy, impeding our vision as we tried to land. The closer we got to the pad, the more snow the rotor pushed into the air around us. With the ground lights, it was blinding. There were colors and reflections in all directions. I was positive we were about to die.

"Can you do this?" The old adage about more people dying in the hospital than anywhere else chose that moment to pop into my worried brain.

Radar grunted. He didn't have time for questions. He put all his concentration into the task at hand. The front panel was an engineering dream; two six-inch screens presented everything digitally, but now that we were landing, Radar seemed to trust his eyes more than anything.

We touched down solidly without bouncing. He flicked buttons and spoke into the headphones again. Hospital personnel with a gurney made their way through the drifting snow, keeping their heads down against the slowing rotor wind. Radar finished shutting things down, and opened his door. Cold air swirled.

My legs shook, but I managed to get out and make my way around the chopper.

Radar snagged my arm. "When we were landing," he reached down and detached his cell phone from his waist. "I got paged." He showed me the panel, but the message meant nothing to me so he explained, "I had it set up to send a particular message if someone accessed those laid off employee files we're watching."

"You're saying…you just got paged now?" Jacques had been in the helicopter with us. He couldn't have been checking on those files. That would mean my pet theory, that Jacques was guilty, was wrong.

My shoulders slumped. In my heart I had known Jacques lacked the raw ability to be a hacker, but he had such other, obvious, criminal qualities. I sighed. "Why now? What were they accessing?"

But Radar trotted off to talk to a guy waving fluorescent batons.

Maybe Jacques had people that worked for him. Maybe someone had panicked when Jacques had his heart attack and...and...something.

Becky came out of the back and dusted off her hands. "Can we fly back?" she asked as we watched Jacques get rolled into the building.

I looked at her dubiously and wondered how much she had had to drink at the party.

She patted my shoulder. "It wasn't that bad, was it? He kept breathing the entire time and geez, I guess my hubby is going to have to drive back all by himself. Do you think he'll know to pick me up here?"

"If he remembers to get your purse, you could call your cell phone." Radar appeared to be taking care of details. I decided to get myself out of this mess and find some other way home.

On my way by, Radar flagged me down. "We'll need to leave the chopper here overnight. I'm not going to fly it back out tonight. You two want to join me in the morning?"

"No, I'm sure my husband will find me." Becky waved and scurried towards the building. "I'm gonna go call the cell phone. Can you guys believe this?"

I couldn't tell if she was yelling because the noise of the helicopter had damaged her eardrums or if she was just wound up from the events.

I shook my head at Radar's offer. "I'll find some way back over there tomorrow."

"Wasn't it *sweet*?" He didn't seem to need my confirmation, so I let the question go.

Shaking my head, I followed Becky into the warm air of the hospital. I had no idea where they had taken Jacques. Since he would be undergoing tests anyway, there was nothing more I could do. I checked my watch. It was quite early. I had managed to leave the party before it even got started. It was barely six o'clock.

Had the party been on Thursday, Brenda would have been getting off work and could have taken me home. Oh well. I didn't really want to be seen with a Mrs. Santa Claus. My reputation for oddness was bad enough without me adding fuel to the fire.

Sean would be getting home from work shortly. He was gonna be mad at having to leave right away to come and get me.

I called him anyway. That's what brothers were for.

Chapter 33

Apparently Radar had failed to notice my reluctance to fly again. He called at six-thirty in the morning, thinking I wanted to fly back in the helicopter.

"Are you crazed?" I had fully planned on using the excuse that I didn't have a car so that I could take the morning off.

"Be there in ten."

The fuzzy cotton robe that I had owned since I was fifteen was definitely not appropriate for answering the door. I hung up and stomped into the shower.

Radar showed up before I finished drying my hair. The marathon shower and rushed blow dry was the perfect recipe for a bad hair day. I settled for not looking too closely in the mirror.

Radar followed me through the living room into the kitchen. "The wind is supposed to pick up later this morning, but right now it's clear, cold and beautiful. It's an awesome day to fly."

"Hmph." I nuked some frozen kolaches. "I'm not flying on an empty stomach."

I handed him one. He eyed the other one in my hand as if he was going to take it. I had forgotten about his appetite. "Forget it bud. Nothing gets between me and my food." I grabbed my backpack and locked the place up.

He was driving a brown Ford. "The rental place gave me another car for the day when I explained I left the first one up in the mountains. I guess if Acetel can afford to pay for that little bird, it can pay for an extra car rental for a couple of days."

Radar was right about the morning. It was blindingly bright out with a dusting of white covering everything. The snow had been light enough that the roads were clear, albeit a bit wet.

The hospital landing pad had either been swept or never had much snow settle, because it was pristine. I was still glad Radar didn't need a runway to take off.

My stomach wasn't really all that nervous until we were strapped in. In the light of day and with the mountains of Colorado all around us, Radar was right, I could enjoy myself a lot more than the previous evening. After we were cleared and in the air, he said, "I checked the computer last night after that page. The layoff list has been deleted. Completely erased."

My nerves were suddenly back. "Oh no!"

He nodded. The evil grin was nowhere to be found. Now that I wanted it, he had to be serious.

"Even the people that really existed?"

"Gone. The legal agreements were also gone. Any record of the severance package, gone."

"For San Jose and Denton?" My heart sank to my toes, and it wasn't the flight this time.

"I have no idea if the guy has gotten to the backup tapes yet, but my guess is if he hasn't, he will. That guy, Patel, that I told you about--he and Art are supposed to run nightly partial backups and weekly full backups. It's hard to say if either of them are really on schedule. I don't pay that much attention. There are probably some tapes somewhere that have those lists, but it's a good thing your buddy Huntington had me make copies of some things."

My stomach came back online. "You did? Everything is okay then?"

He shrugged. "I don't know. How did you get hooked up with that guy anyway?"

"Huntington? Sheer accident."

"He hired me to protect a few areas, as he called it."

"He has a way with assignments."

Radar grinned. "He didn't think it was a bad idea for me to try some electronic tracking of whoever is nosing around, but unless we find the computer that was used to do the damage, and that computer happens to be accessible to only one person, it's going to be impossible to prove who did it. In addition to the administrator's account, I found two other accounts being used that don't belong to real employees. I should have found them faster; they stick out like a sore thumb. I assumed the guy would be more clever so I outsmarted myself trying to follow email messages instead of looking through the login names for anything unusual."

We circled the lake and came down over the water. "Are the fake accounts the ones that were collecting the emails when we were snooping?"

As the helicopter descended, it looked as though we were going to land in the water, but sure enough, Radar brought us through an opening in the trees. As we climbed out of the helicopter Radar gave me more details. "I traced the emails back to the accounts all right, but it isn't going to do us any good. The guy can pick up his email from any machine, anytime. Although from now on, I did make sure any unopened mail doesn't make it to him." He shrugged. "It's a little late though. Obviously if he started deleting evidence, he knows we were there."

"No clues in the fake login names?"

Radar gave the helicopter a last pat. "What a nice bird."

We walked toward our cars and he answered my question. "I tracked two accounts that obviously weren't real. You know anyone named Thoth?"

"Gosh, I'll have to look through my Rolodex."

"Two or three times just to be sure," he said sarcastically. "How about Silvanus? That was the other one."

I stopped walking. All I managed was a squeak. "Silvanus?"

Radar continued talking. "The names are from ancient gods, one is Egyptian and the other is…Roman I think. Anyway both names are common enough, so that doesn't mean much."

Roman! That's exactly what Ben had said! "Did you tell Huntington?" Ben hadn't mentioned Thoth, but whoever was accessing the accounts illegally was probably the same person who had created a lot of the accounting files that Ben requested. Not that the connection would do any good since we still had no idea who was using Thoth or Silvanus.

Radar finally noticed my expression. "No, I didn't mention it. Why? Do you think he knows them?"

It still seemed like a good idea to tell him. "Lemme borrow your cell." I knew without looking, I had forgotten mine.

He raised an eyebrow, but unclipped it and watched me dial. The condo phone rang and rang. I sent Huntington a page and then dug through my backpack until I found Mark's cell number.

He answered. "Yeah?"

"Hi Mark, it's me. Listen, uh, you know about Silvanus appearing on some of the file attributes as the author of certain accounting documents? And the one we saw in the lab?"

Radar looked at me in surprise.

"Of course. Why?" Mark asked.

"Radar tracked the name of the user account that was watching certain files. One of the user accounts was Silvanus. The other was Thoth. Did Thoth happen to be on any of the files that went to Ben?"

"Not a common name either, is it?" To my dismay he asked, "Are you absolutely sure it isn't Radar?"

I glanced nervously at my companion. "Yes, I'm sure." I wasn't sure. How could I be? But why would he tell me the names, one of which happened to match the one already known, if it were his own user name?

Mark didn't say anything for a while. "Look, we're meeting with A.J. this morning. I don't imagine he's going to know who is using those names, but maybe we can get some info out of him. Maybe he can pinpoint who in the company had responsibility for creating the files in question. That's when the files get assigned an author, right?"

"Yes. It can be changed after that, but I doubt that the guy changed it to Silvanus on purpose. It's more likely that he is the one who authored the originals, and he never noticed he was logged in as that user. If we can find out who the likeliest person is to have created them, we might get somewhere."

"It sounds a lot like a gamer name," Mark mentioned again.

"Yeah," I swallowed, "Radar said something about both names being common."

"It's a long shot that A.J. is going to know anyone on his staff that happens to be a gamer."

I could tell he still didn't like Radar's involvement or his obvious skill set. "Thanks. Tell Huntington, will you?" Huntington would be jealous if I only told Mark. He was picky that way.

"He'll be at the meeting. A.J. flies back to San Jose tonight."

"Okay. See you." I hung up and handed the phone back to Radar. "Thanks."

Radar looked at me in disgust. "You already knew the name that was being used?"

I didn't really want to meet his eyes. If Mark had known Radar was standing in front of me while I reported those names, he wouldn't have thought me very bright. Radar could easily be guilty. He certainly had the talent to pull the whole thing off. "No, I didn't know both names. Huntington mentioned a long time ago that some files he saw had an author of Silvanus. I didn't think much of it until you said the name again just now."

"But you didn't mention it to me." He added a couple of things up in his head and his smile brightened a notch. "Does Huntington think I'm guilty?"

His amusement annoyed me. "Well, you are a gamer."

Radar out-and-out laughed. "If I was pulling this scam, I'd be a hellava lot more careful, and I would have ditched the whole operation the minute I noticed someone on my tail."

I looked him eye to eye, but I still wasn't absolutely positive. There were no cameras way out here. He looked like he was having an awful lot of fun. "Did you tell Pete we were bringing it in?" I looked back at the helicopter. In the cold morning every sound was magnified. The lake had bits of ice frozen near the edges and funny snow ledges all the way around. There was no reason for me to feel uneasy unless I counted the fact that I had been chased twice in the last two weeks and was standing with a suspect that if guilty, was a diabolical lunatic.

"Pete said to make sure I got it here early because he needs it to get to the airport so he can catch his plane back to San Jose." He looked back at the helicopter longingly. "I would have been waiting outside until that thing was home. No, I'd have gone and gotten it myself."

His distraction seemed like a good time for me to get to my Civic, but as I turned, I spotted Pete waving from the porch. "Come on up," he called out. "Have a cup of coffee."

I really wasn't in the mood to deal with Pete--or even Radar any longer, but it would have been rude to yell no. At least with Pete now on the scene, it wasn't likely Radar would conk me over the head and drag my body into the lake.

I headed towards the house with Radar trailing slightly behind.

"Come in, come in." Pete pulled the door open wide. "Great that you got the bird back!" He ushered us into a small study, complete with racks of books lined up like a professional library. "I had tea and coffee made and baked goods delivered before I let the staff off. I only have a skeleton crew come in and take care of the place when I'm not here." Pete moved a tray of cakes and donuts from his desk onto a round table. He seemed a bit at a loss as far as serving went, so we helped ourselves.

"I called the hospital," he said.

"How is Jacques doing?" I asked.

"It doesn't look good. His heart hasn't been that healthy for a while, you know."

"Becky mentioned it."

"The last few months have been a God-awful nightmare. How is the investigation going?"

The point-blank question caught me completely off guard. I glanced at Radar, but he had taken a seat on the plush leather couch and was quite busy with his second donut.

"Uh, investigation?"

Pete waved a hand at my hesitation. "Don't be ridiculous. I'm the CFO and on the board. Since you showed up right after A.J. gave the go ahead to hire investigators, it's pretty obvious you're on the team. A.J. mentioned you're making good progress."

Apparently my being part of the team had been obvious to a lot of people. "Well, there are a lot of strange things going on at Acetel, but nothing completely concrete. It's hard to say who might be responsible for any real problems."

"Strange things such as what?"

I shrugged meekly.

He stared at me impatiently, his dark eyes drilling into me with that "coach" look--like he was about to tell me to run laps.

Even Radar noticed the tension. He chewed slower and slower. I heard him gulp when he tried to wash the third donut down with a sip of coffee. He coughed.

"I was hoping nothing *strange*, as you put it, would show up." Pete walked away from us and stared out a window. "We've given people a chance at something great. If someone is taking advantage of all the hard work we've put in let's either catch him at it or let's close this thing and move on." He might have been angry, but he sounded more inconvenienced than anything.

He strode back to the middle of the room and loomed over us with his arms folded. "How hard can it be to sort through this mess and find out if someone is siphoning off business or money?"

To my surprise, Radar said, "It's not that easy to figure out."

I threw in my support. "None of the managers are squeaky clean."

That didn't improve Pete's mood any. He kind of growled as he spun away from us and marched back to the window. "My managers have the right synergies. They're driven people. It's a matter of balancing the skills and having the vision to understand the future. You can replace engineers, but do you know how hard it is to replace a good manager?" He paced his way to the front of the desk. For the first time, I noticed a cat sprawled underneath the back edge. As Pete went by, little black paws swiped at the edge of his pants.

I wished I had some nice, lethal claws. Where did Pete get off trying to convince two engineers that technical help was a dime a dozen while talking up his questionable management? "Jacques may be driven, but he's wasting a lot of resources. I know for a fact that he's trying to help Kronology to line his own pockets. He owns a large number of Kronology shares. Surely, you could do better."

Pete didn't even have the grace to fake surprise. "I told Jacques a long time ago not to get too attached to the cases that came our way from those guys."

"You know about his stock and spending extra resources on the cases?"

He shrugged. "If anyone can get Kronology to shape up, it is Jacques. You told me yourself he took on challenges."

I had been backed into a corner by Arnold at the time. "If not illegal, wouldn't you say it was unethical? At *best?*"

Pete was nothing if not a politician; he held the umbrella, but pretended it wasn't raining. "That stock is not a big deal. Don't let little things like that side-track you--if you haven't found anything more concrete, move on." He waved his arm again. "Every one of us has to diversify holdings. It hardly makes Jacques a criminal. He is one of our best customer advocates."

Customer advocate? What about the customers left holding Kronology equipment? I looked at Radar. He was still eating and his mouth was so full, he couldn't have offered an opinion if he even had one. "Yeah, sure." Brenda was right. No point in telling your boss's boss what was going on. Pete was going to back Jacques even if Jacques sold the last donut right in front of him and walked off with the profits.

If I had had the evidence, I'd have happily dumped it on him, but Pete was right about Jacques not being the guilty party on the embezzlement. Jacques had been on the way to the hospital when Radar's pager went off indicating evidence was being destroyed. So long as I had Pete's ear, I asked, "Did the financial guy--Ben--handle the layoff analysis for Denton?"

Pete didn't look up from staring at the plate of goodies. For a minute I thought he was counting the pastries and standing stock-still in amazement. I know I was pretty shocked. Radar had eaten five of them already and had a sixth in his hand.

"Ben?" he echoed. "No. He's strictly expense reports and equipment for the Denton office. Arnold handles the project analysis and overhead for the Denton office. He's the brightest of the bunch, a real numbers man."

"Arnold?"

Pete looked at me. He smiled. "The guy is a genius. I wouldn't want to lose him, not for any reason. Don't let the fact that he's dating that lawyer who works for our biggest customer side-track you into worrying about his ethics."

Now there was a piece of information we didn't have. "Of...course not."

"He's good, but he's in too much of a hurry to move up. I've told him, it's all a matter of paying the dues. I walk a fine line, feeding ambition and yet not choosing one manager over another. Arnold is the best though. He handled the entire layoff for us, down to the last detail."

My mouth made a round little 'oh.' Before I could verify exactly what Pete meant by that, a voice from the hallway interrupted.

"It has finally occurred to you that she really is getting close to the truth, hasn't it?"

I almost jumped into Radar's lap. As I spun around, I forgot about the little round table. I fell over the thing and splatted onto the floor.

A lone donut bounced off the plate onto the carpet. It slowly toppled over, leaving a trail of flaked icing. The cat took umbrage with the disturbance and darted out from under the desk to a more secure location beneath the couch.

Arnold, not looking quite so smudged as previous occasions, stood in the doorway. Maybe he didn't often wash his hair, but with a gun in his hand, he still looked pretty impressive for a geek. "You had to throw my name in there, didn't you?" Arnold's eyes weren't unfocused, nor were they lost in numbers. "Little too concerned they are on your trail and not mine?"

Pete's face turned into a bag of flour with gray splotches over the white. "I have no idea what you're talking about. I demand an explanation. As a board member--"

"That's right, isn't it? A nobody engineer isn't allowed a seat on the board. No matter how many contracts he gets the company or how many problems he solves. Only the pretty boys make it to the top. They sit and play with numbers as if they understand them. Then, when the going gets tough, they throw the crap down to the engineer, just like you were about to do." Arnold advanced into the room. "I'm not taking the fall for this, Pete."

Pete held very still, but his eyes darted to the desk. Arnold noticed. "Move away from the drawers, Pete."

Pete just looked at him.

Arnold aimed the gun and fired.

Before the sound even reached my ears, Pete moved towards me.

I scrambled away. No way was he using me as a barrier. Scooting backwards and sideways put me right up against Radar's legs. It didn't put Radar in a very mobile position, but it was the only open space.

Radar solved his mobility problem by hopping over the side of the couch away from Pete. He made a strangled noise when he landed.

I was having trouble swallowing myself, and I wasn't trying to choke down the last of a donut.

"Stop!" Arnold shifted the weapon towards Radar and myself. We both froze. "You aren't going anywhere."

"Wouldn't...wouldn't think of it." My heart hurt from beating so fast.

"Tell me, Sedona. If you're such a good investigator, why did you have to involve Radar? Or is investigating just like engineering? You get the big bucks, while Radar does the real work?"

My mouth fell open. Gee, when you put it like that, it sounded as if I had been using Radar. "I'm not as good as Radar." And I had no idea what Huntington might be paying him, either.

"Just like Pete here. He couldn't complete the plan on his own. But it was his idea, wasn't it, Pete? You told me yourself the idea was eighty percent of the profits, right?" Arnold laughed, a high-pitched squeal.

"You get paid for what you do," Pete said.

"You bet I do, but not because you were generous. As you pointed out many, many times, you still sign the paychecks--whether they go to real people or not. All the prestige and board seats, those go to you. There isn't room for me, is there? And where is my retention bonus?" Arnold's hand was shaking, he was so angry.

"You got yours, just like the others did!" Pete snapped.

"Not half the size of yours!"

"You got the same as the other managers at your rank."

"And you control that rank, asshole!" He leveled the gun at Pete's chest.

"I didn't get one at all," I mentioned helpfully, hoping he wouldn't shoot Pete right in front of us.

Arnold didn't notice the interruption. "And now, when it falls apart, you were more than willing to nudge them to look at me. What made you think I wouldn't tell anyone it was your idea to start with? Are you that stupid?"

Apparently Pete was that stupid. "Who would believe you, fool? I have no reason to pull such stunts." He waved his arms. "You need to impress your girlfriend or she'll dump you for someone that matters."

"You voted yourself a bigger salary, but that wasn't enough, was it? No, you needed more bogus employees. Then Ben started asking questions. You decide on the brilliant plan of a layoff to clean up all the evidence. Even that wasn't enough. You voted yourself a retention bonus. Great stuff, these ideas." He waved the gun in my direction and for the first time in my life, I longed for a nice harmless laser pointer. "What in the hell was I thinking?"

"I don't know, man. What were you thinking?" Radar, now that he had managed to swallow the bite that had been stuck in his throat, was relatively calm. "You're a good hacker. Why'd you bother with him anyway?"

"I wasn't involved, I tell you!" Pete shrieked. "I was only trying to lure him in! I wouldn't stoop so low."

Arnold trained the gun on Pete again, and I thought he was going to shoot. He held the gun there for several seconds before he changed his mind. "Basement, Pete. Now."

Pete strode forward as though he were walking away from an unpleasant meal at a restaurant. Even now, when he wasn't in the obvious position of power, he seemed to think the whole problem a minor detail that would go away if he ordered it so.

Arnold moved in a wide circle until Pete was past him. Then, before Radar or I could move, he got behind him, the gun in Pete's back. "You two-- move into the hallway. If you don't, I shoot him first and then turn to get you."

I probably could have let Pete get shot without too much heartburn, but I had no guarantee that Radar wouldn't get killed if I ran, so I dutifully trudged into the hallway. Arnold positioned himself near the doorway, keeping all of us in sight. As soon as we were lined up, he said, "Pete knows where the basement is. If I were you, I'd make sure my aim is clear to shoot him. Don't think he cares either. He's been trying to kill you for almost three weeks."

It seemed to me that we probably weren't going into the basement for tea, but I didn't think it was a good idea to suggest he go ahead and shoot us in the hallway.

Arnold followed closely behind us, muttering about his own stupidity. "I should have run my own paycheck collection scheme. He would never have known. But no, I take up with mister idea man. He had a five-minute stinking idea, and what did he do with it?" Arnold snarled, "No, Pete, not the stairs. Take the elevator."

Stairs might have allowed us to go single file. At least one of us could have run. Of course if there wasn't another way out of the basement, what difference would it make?

The elevator wasn't terribly fancy, and once we got to the basement, I understood why. The area was little more than a large storage room. A summer grill and propane tank had been shoved into a corner by the stairs; rakes, gardening equipment and rolled up hoses were neatly stacked on shelves. Up another set of stairs across the room, there was a heavy door that looked like it led directly outside.

In the center of the room, two workbenches were filled with state-of-the-art computer equipment, and I wasn't talking Kronology junk either.

Radar was very interested in the equipment. Arnold noticed his fascination. "Nice isn't it? Probably the only real perk of this mess." He didn't seem to mind Radar moving around as long as Radar was focused on the equipment. Acting just as smitten, I followed Radar to the workbenches. Unfortunately the benches didn't run all the way across the room near the outside stairwell.

"Pete, for all his pointing the finger at me, doesn't seem to know that once these machines are traced, it will be quite clear that this equipment was used. The idiot used his own equipment from San Jose too. You see," he explained to Pete, "it won't matter if you try to lay all the blame on me. You left an evidence trail."

"You broke in here!" Pete said wildly. "I'm hardly ever here. You knew about this retreat and the equipment. You used it!"

"Of course you're not here often. But I never added employees without the big boss running the show," Arnold said with a tight smile.

"You waited until he was here in town," I guessed, remembering the strange pattern of fake hiring.

The cat meandered down the stairs into the basement. It waved its tail slowly, and then sauntered to its litter box. It must be used to fits and yelling because it completely ignored Pete and Arnold and went about its business.

Arnold positioned himself close to Radar, but he had to turn slightly in order to see Pete, because Pete was still near the elevator. "Pete could barely remember the simplest name and password combinations that I set up specifically for him to use. Fool."

Radar must have been thinking about the stairs behind us. He edged back at the same time I did. One of us had our aim off. "Oof." When we bumped shoulders, I accidentally stepped on his foot. He yanked away. I over-corrected, bouncing into the computer workbench. The keyboard skidded into a flat screen monitor, ricocheted off the side and crashed to the floor.

"Smooth," Radar grunted.

I gave him a look usually reserved for Huntington, which is why I didn't notice Arnold until after he took the shot.

Bam! The twenty-some-inch expensive monitor shattered like so much cheap plastic.

"Aaaah!" I dove for the side of the workbench furthest from the enemy. Radar went in the opposite direction, throwing himself under the stairs that led outside. He scooted quickly behind the water heater.

Arnold stared at the gun as if he hadn't meant for it to go off.

Leave it to our esteemed executive to keep his cool and do something incredibly stupid. Pete grabbed the propane tank and opened the nozzle. He held up a lighter, the type used when the grill sparker no longer worked. "Put the gun down, Arnold."

Radar didn't wait to see who won the game of chicken. He shot out from under the stairs and jumped them halfway up. I was right there with him. I'd rather have Arnold take pot shots at me than wait around to see what Pete would do with anything ignitable.

"You let me handle this, Arnold, and it will all work out," Pete said. "This is all a mistake. When I explain it, everyone will understand."

Arnold was no dummy. He had seen Pete in action more than we had. He shoved me from behind and despite my desperation, he pushed me under the stair railing, back onto the basement floor. "Oof."

Radar must have gotten to the door, but the door opened into the basement. He was forced back down a step or two in order to open the door. Arnold clubbed Radar over the head with the butt of the pistol. Like a cannon, it went off again.

Radar crashed down the stairs like so much discarded luggage.

"Turn it off, Pete," I yelled.

But the man was entranced, either with the tableau or his own sudden power or...maybe gas fumes.

Propane leaked steadily into the room. If he hit that little trigger button on the lighter, we were going to blow sky high. I leaned over to help Radar up, but he was woozy from the hit on the head or the subsequent ones he took on his tumble down the stairs. Unfortunately he had also fallen victim to the Donut and Cake Diet Law. All women know that a donut weighing scant ounces converts instantly to ten thigh and butt pounds after consumption. Radar had eaten six of the suckers, and carting him back up the steps was almost impossible. "Pete, you gotta turn that off and..." I swallowed at the fanatic gleam on his face.

"I'm not guilty, you know."

"Of course not." I didn't stop trying to crawl under Radar and get him in a fireman's hold. It was unnerving to watch Pete anyway. If he flicked that switch, I was pretty sure I didn't want to see it.

"You heard what Arnold claimed. But you're the only ones. If you go away, then I can still convince them it's all a mistake. Just an accounting snafu. Arnold got carried away. A temporary problem."

"I'm going away, right now, no problem." I finally got a shoulder placed under Radar's prone form. Standing was a problem. "Unngh--" I settled for a half crawl. Wasn't a fireman's carry supposed to be possible even for a lightweight?

There was no noise of warning. I was almost out, crawling up one painful step at a time when fire shot across my leg, a burning from hell. Had I been standing I would have dropped Radar. I shrieked as the shooting pain moved up part of my back and onto my shoulders.

Intense burning shot across the top of my head, wrapping its tiny black paws around my hair. I couldn't see Pete now if I tried. The cat added his scream to my own, although I was fairly certain no one had run up *his* back with claws out.

I grabbed the next step and kept right on moving. "Pete! If you blow us up, you'll go too, you idiot!" I stumbled out into the bright light of day, staggering. I was still unable to see. The cat had one paw across my eyes and its lower two legs around my neck.

"What the hell is that?" Mark's deep baritone yelped.

"Help," I screeched.

"It's Silvanus!" Huntington shouted. "And...Sedona? Get down!"

Silvanus? Did they mean Arnold? Or had Pete come out behind me?

The cat didn't like my stumbling. Out came the claws. As the little weapons raked across my nose, I crashed to the ground only a few yards from the house, but around the corner from the basement door. Arnold, or for all I knew maybe it was Pete--took a shot from somewhere, but I was already down. Radar took another bad bump, but I would blame it on the stairs if I lived to talk about it.

Of course, I wasn't counting on Huntington. "Into the trees," he yelled and there were more shots.

Once on the relative safety of the ground, the cat shot away like his tail was on fire.

I blinked blearily. Mark peered at me from behind a garden statue.

I resumed dragging myself away from the door making it to Mark, but it was too late. I knew Arnold hadn't been shooting at me. He was going for something in the basement, anything that would make it ignite. It's hard to say if he got lucky or if the water heater pilot finally got enough propane.

There was a funny whooshing sound, almost like the backwards sucking of a vacuum. The door to the basement slammed shut, forced closed by the explosion and then burst back open, shattering outward.

Mark grabbed Radar's free arm. We dragged him to safety further around the corner of the house to the closest car. I could hear sirens. "Backup on the way," Mark shouted.

"It better be fire engines!"

He looked me up and down carefully. Gently, he touched my bleeding cheek. He stared at me hard as if he wanted to say something, but instead, he gave my shoulder a last squeeze, put his gun at his back and went for his bike. The lightning decorated sword on the motorcycle flashed by as he took off into the trees after Arnold.

I propped my bleeding self up against the car. My eyes were closed, so I missed Huntington sneaking up on me.

"Here," he said.

My eyes flew opened, but it was too late to avoid the cat he dropped in my lap. "Me? I don't want it. It doesn't like me." That should have been obvious from the injuries I had suffered. My cheek felt like it was missing completely, blood continued to ooze down my back, and I was pretty sure I was missing a significant chunk of hair.

"He's evidence. We need to take him with us."

"Evidence?"

He grinned down at me and pointed at my lap. "Silvanus," he said.

My mouth fell open. "The *cat*?"

He nodded. "When we asked A.J. about the names this morning, A.J. happened to know the names of Pete's cats. He informed us that Silvanus here has a brother that looks just like him in San Jose in Pete's other house."

"And his name is Thoth," I finished for him, holding tight to the still upset feline.

Chapter 34

My last plea for sanity had made its way through Pete's brain and struck a cord. The guy had barely enough sense to turn the propane off and take the inside set of stairs out of the basement. He made good on his escape by less than a whisker. It helped that the basement was mostly concrete. The fire, with limited oxygen and combustibles, was contained to the basement and one upper room right over the water heater. Not that Pete was going to be around to repair the place; once Huntington and Mark were on the right trail, they pulled out all the stops.

After getting me out of the spider's web, Huntington and Mark got busy subpoenaing records. Pete had enough debt to actually need the side income he had been generating. From what Ben pieced together once he knew what to look for, it appeared that Pete had been running his scheme for quite some time. Huntington was smug as he told us the details.

"During the first layoff before the IPO, twenty people were let go," Huntington revealed. "At least five employees never existed. Pete actually set up several bank accounts for the false employees--most of them were opened in a variation of his name. For two of the accounts he used his middle name. For the other three, he used variations of his initials. The scam wasn't very clever because every account had some version of his name on it somewhere."

"But that made it easy for him to access the money," I guessed.

Huntington nodded. "He had the money transferred to his regular account whenever he needed it. Now and again, he made sure the pay stubs got picked up from the post office boxes, even going so far as to have forwarding addresses on them so that he could pick them up at one location."

"Not a very good way to collect the loot," Radar said.

Huntington ignored Radar's disapproval of the low-tech scheme. "It worked though. Pete went through with the first set of layoffs, destroyed the evidence and no one was the wiser. He told himself it had been a temporary need for cash. Then, as he got himself further into debt, he needed one or two extra salaries. He hired imaginary people and kept adding new employees as he needed more money."

I set down the appetizer plate I was carrying. With both Huntingtons, Sean, Brenda, Radar and Turbo at my house, I was going to have to cook faster. "When did Arnold get involved?" I asked. "He didn't seem very satisfied with his cut."

Huntington helped himself to a celery stick smothered in peanut butter. "Arnold probably wasn't getting much. My guess is that at some point in the last five years, Arnold discovered the discrepancies somehow--maybe in the org charts or maybe he hacked into the system and started looking around. Naturally, he was never supposed to know about the extra people. Pete added the expenses for them after Arnold and the other managers turned in their budgets. For whatever reason, by whatever method, Arnold must have figured out what Pete was up to."

I nodded. "At Pete's house, Arnold blamed Pete for the idea. He never said when he got involved or described his part in the scheme."

Huntington added, "The incredible part is that there isn't a trace of anything illegal done by Arnold in the system. We've got his bank records, credit card history and other records. Based on some recent purchases, it's possible he was collecting one extra salary other than his own, but there's no trace of illegal gains."

I thought about it. "He seemed to think that Pete should be throwing him legitimate perks," I said. "A board seat or a promotion. Maybe he kept his hands off the money."

"Or," Radar chortled, "Maybe he's such a good hacker, he eliminated any evidence against him." He chomped down happily on a cheese cracker while we stared at him. "What?"

"You don't have to sound like you admire the guy," Sean complained. "He was a thief."

Radar disagreed. "Wrong." He held up a finger like a professor happily informing his students of a clever twist to a problem. "Innocent until proven guilty. He was certainly helping a thief, but there isn't any gold tied to him. I looked."

"Splitting straws," I argued. "Why did he bother to get involved if he wasn't getting money?"

"If he was, it doesn't show up anywhere obvious," Radar said. "My guess is that Arnold became involved after Pete erased signs of evidence during the first layoff scheme. It was only during the second scheme that Pete started using the more sophisticated way of getting fake employees' paychecks deposited. HR needed separate post office boxes and unique names so that everything looked legitimate, but," he held up the professor finger again, "the auto-deposit software doesn't care where it deposits money. It's all account numbers, not names, as Sedona figured out. No one noticed that bundles of salary checks all happened to be funneled into one account." Around another cracker he continued, "It's all done electronically these days. No one has to verify anything other than the routing number of the bank and the account number. Those numbers are so long, even if the same payroll person saw the numbers one right after the other, that person wasn't likely to notice a duplicate."

Mark finally added the results of his own detective work. "One of the bank accounts they were using had Pete's wife's name on it. It's listed as a business account with a "consultant" title. The large influx of cash on a monthly basis, if noticed at all, would be assumed to be a legitimate expense, much like paying Ben or another contractor."

I was stunned. "But if it was all going into accounts that Pete had access to, Arnold would have to trust Pete to pay him his share! No wonder Arnold was angry."

Radar chuckled. "I'm betting Arnold made Pete deliver his share of the loot in cash under the table so his name wasn't attached to anything."

Mark raised his eyebrows, but was more amused than disgusted at Radar's admiration. "From the looks of things, though, Arnold was probably getting drawn in pretty deep, especially lately. Ben was asking for more and more company records every quarter because the expenses were climbing. Good management would have tamped down on expenses and hiring. Pete panicked and decided he'd better get rid of Ben and the extra employees."

Huntington gave a grunt of disapproval. "Unfortunately, Pete wasn't willing to let the severance go. When it was five or so nonexistent employees no one noticed anything. But this time around he had a lot more fakes and a much larger charge." He looked at Radar. Radar was still eating as fast as his hands could move to his mouth. "It's possible that Arnold only recently changed things to make sure the money and the evidence were all funneled in Pete's direction."

Radar shrugged and agreed. "Easily."

I nabbed the last cookie out from under Sean's questing fingers. "Arnold was careful from the very start. There's a pattern of hiring fake people right after earnings announcements, and I checked back with Becky's calendar. The employee additions coincide with when Pete was in town. Even though Arnold was helping, he knew how easily things could be traced. He was very careful to make sure evidence always pointed to Pete."

The food was fast disappearing, and it wasn't even all Radar's fault. At this rate, I was going to have to serve every item in the house. I pulled out all available cookie dough from the freezer and started mixing a new batch of peanut butter cookies from scratch.

Radar asked me, "Remember when I got paged in the helicopter?"

I nodded.

"Whoever logged in was doing so from the equipment that was in one of Pete's houses. Since it was his equipment, he would believe himself the supreme commander no matter who was really running the show. The IP address was funneled through false locations all over the country, much like happens with spam machines."

"Why couldn't Ben figure any of this out when he was looking at the company records?" I complained. "I would never have gone back to Pete's house if I believed he was guilty. I would have told Radar to keep the helicopter for a while."

At that suggestion, Radar's eyes lit up and he smiled big.

Mark said, "Turns out you saved your own bacon. Since you had called me that morning asking about Silvanus, when A.J. tied the names to Pete's cats, Steve and I headed straight over there."

"And now you've gathered the rest of the proof necessary?" I asked.

"We're still subpoenaing records." He half nodded in Radar's direction. "When you do things the legal way, it takes more time."

"I can't believe Pete was stupid enough to use his own cat's names on the accounts." It certainly put the cross hairs directly on his back.

Radar held up his finger again. "Ah, but how else was he going to remember the false accounts? The guy was already trying to juggle his legit job and cooking the books. He had to have a way onto the system that he could use reliably and remember. I bet Arnold suggested it." He laughed his engineer laugh. "Heh, heh, heh. That's what I would have done."

Great. My hacker buddy had a new hero. If he followed in Arnold's footsteps, I hoped he was learning from Arnold's mistakes.

"Are you planning on staying at Acetel?" Turbo wanted to know. "You might not want to keep working for Jacques."

Turbo knew about Jacques' not playing entirely fair with my career, even if it turned out Jacques wasn't the one skimming. "What choice do I have?"

Turbo grinned. "It seems that management at Strandfrost has reconsidered."

"What?" I couldn't believe my ears.

Turbo nodded happily. "Once Ross found out you were pregnant, he took it straight to John, the V.P. The way they figure it, you're bound to sue over the way you were treated. Ross was really worried. He figures that since he pressured you on the schedule, he would be named in the lawsuit. Based on the wording of your resignation, he was positive you knew about their plan to get rid of you."

I stared at Turbo while everyone else stared at me. Sean's mouth opened and closed, but I couldn't tell if he was in shock or salivating at the word "lawsuit." I managed a small squeak and nothing else. Mark cocked an eyebrow in my direction before another thought occurred to him, and he turned to stare at Huntington. Huntington glared accusingly at Mark.

Another weak peep passed my frozen lips, and then everyone started talking at once.

"They are going to beg you to come back and pretend they never wanted you to leave." This from Turbo.

"You're *what*?" Sean now looked murderously at every man in the room including Turbo, which was ridiculous. Turbo was not likely to have publicly announced such a transgression were he guilty---the man was married after all.

"Interesting," from Mark and Steve at the same time.

"Heh, heh, heh," was all Radar had to contribute.

I waved my hands wildly. "*I am not pregnant!* Where in the world did Ross get such an idea?" I looked down at my stomach. It was hard to tell if I had put on weight given that I had just eaten four or five appetizers and at least three cookies.

Turbo looked innocent. "I'm not certain, but I did chat with Ross. Seems he saw you in the mall." He paused and took a bite out of a cookie. We all leaned in closer as he did his usual careful consideration of wording. He finally noticed my snarl and hurriedly continued, "With a bunch of packages and coming out of the maternity store."

When my anger didn't immediately dissipate, he put his palms out in an innocent gesture. "What was he supposed to think?"

"I will quietly kill him," I promised.

"What's this about Strandfrost trying to force you out?" Sean narrowed in on the next point he found pertinent. "Did they try to force you out because they thought you were pregnant? Completely illegal."

Mark still watched me carefully.

"Brenda, remember?" I pointed at my sister-in-law. "I was helping her shop."

Huntington took the opportunity to eye me up and down rather too intently. "Uh-huh. Of course."

"You people are insane." I sat down before I could fall and refused to answer any more questions. Turbo was more than happy to fill in his opinion on lawsuit details. I lost track of the speculation.

By the time everyone left, I was exhausted. Sleep had a hypnotic appeal. I headed for the bedroom and found that someone had been there before me. A giant wrapped box sat on the center of my bed with shiny red paper and a big gold ribbon beckoning. The card on top was one of those pre-printed ones that said, "Merry Christmas."

I'd never been one to take time with presents. I ripped the paper off and flung it behind me. The white box gave me no better clue, but it wasn't taped so it didn't take long to open. Nestled inside in delicate white tissue paper was a beautiful, supple black leather jacket. "Ooooh," I squealed and clapped my hands.

A big smile broke across my face, and I raced to the mirror. It fit perfectly. Lovely! Even with dark circles under my eyes and three scratches across my face, I looked sophisticated.

My smile faded, as curiosity struck. I went back to the box. Despite very careful searching through the paper and the box, no card appeared. I sighed. Yet another mystery to be solved.

Which Huntington had left the gift?

More Books by Maria E. Schneider

Most of my other works are also mysteries. **Catch an Honest Thief** is a stand-alone mystery set in the New Mexico desert. Alexia goes undercover, but will she be mistaken for the real thief?

One Good Eclair is the first book in another cozy mystery series set in New Mexico.

Under Witch Moon is the first in an urban fantasy series: When dead bodies start turning up Adriel has no choice but to talk to White Feather, an undercover cop. Unfortunately, Adriel is a witch, and White Feather isn't convinced she's innocent of wrongdoing. She's going to have to talk fast-- and set spells even faster to get herself out of trouble. **Under Witch Aura, Under Witch Curse** and **Ghost Shadow** are the other books in the series.

Dragons of Wendal is a fantasy adventure: Learning new magic isn't as easy as Zoe expected, especially when the mages at Gorgon University seem dead set against teaching. Add in some necessary late-night sneaking about, and Zoe is almost certain to be kicked out. As for exploring the intriguing mysteries across the border in Wendal, well, it has more teeth than she ever imagined. **DragonKin** is book two in the series.

Soul of the Desert is about a boy on the run from the mafia. Which is worse, the guns of New York or the dangerous desert of New Mexico?

Magical Mayhem (A Compilation) is a collection of short stories compiled from **Tracking Magic**, **Sage**, and some individual tales that were not part of an anthology.

Please visit me at my blog: www.BearMountainBooks.com and say hello!

www.ingramcontent.com/pod-product-compliance
Lightning Source LLC
Chambersburg PA
CBHW021033130626
46552CB00005B/1828